I0645793

SWAN
OUT OF
WATER

SWAN
OUT OF
WATER

Irmgarde Brown

Also by Irmgarde Brown
Sister Jane
Sister Jane's Lenten Journal
Children in the City of the Czars

Co-authored with Benedict & Kathleen Schwartz
Evidence Now Seen:
How God Used One Couple to Touch the Lives of
Orphaned and Vulnerable Children in Zambia

Copyright © 2025 Irmgarde Brown
All rights reserved. No part of this book may be reproduced in any form or by electronic or mechanical means, including information storage and retrieval systems, without permission in writing from the publisher, except by a reviewer who may quote brief passages in a review.

The events and conversations in this book have been set down to the best of the author's ability, although some names and details have been changed or omitted to protect the privacy of individuals.

Published in the United States by
Serey/Jones Publishers, Inc.
www.sereyjones.com

ISBN: 9781881276371 (paperback)

DEDICATION

To my beloved brother

Zig Berzins

Sibling, Mentor, Friend

FOREWORD

Special thanks to all the people who have supported me throughout my writing journey, particularly Lorie Conway, my spiritual director and friend, Kathy Reno, who has shared my joys and sorrows and angst for over fifty years (I still wish you lived closer), and Christine O'Neal for her ongoing encouragement. Thanks also to my Beta readers, Katherine McGuire who plowed through the first draft and fixed a million things, Thom Hawkins who agreed to give a male perspective, Deborah Stathes and Pat Dickinson from my book group, Joy Brown from my spiritual group, and my amazing teen focus group (Audry, Morgan, and Naomi) whose insights validated my understanding of the teen brain. I also appreciate and thank my editor, Michele Krueger, and my publishers, David & Jody Serey.

CONTENTS

CHAPTER 1
Towson, Maryland

On a Saturday night in early January 2010, four girls were about to change their lives forever. Fortified with shots of sour apple schnapps, they glammed up in the ladies' room of the Round One Towson Bowling Alley for a night on the town and lots of dancing. River, Shelly, and LaShonda regarded these outings as quite routine and a chance to earn easy money, but for Annie, it was monumental. Tonight was her first time. For the other three, it would be their last.

"This is how it works," River said. "Lincoln texts me at eight fifty-five and we have five minutes to get outside. A driver pulls up in a black SUV or limo, we climb in, and off we go to a party somewhere in the city. Once, they dropped us off at a party bus and it drove around all night. Epic!"

All four girls whooped, and River gave Annie an enormous hug and whispered in her ear, "I'm so glad you're here."

In the last four months, River had become Annie's best friend. Her first friend, really. They met during a detention on Annie's second day of public high school back in September. It all started when Annie failed to get her locker open. When she finally got the combination right, her stuff spilled out onto the hall floor. She grabbed the lot and made a mad dash for her class as the bell rang. She didn't know the young woman who yelled at her was a teacher, so without thinking, Annie flipped her off. Stupid. And what did Annie get? Three days of after-school detention. Her mother screamed for twenty minutes. All her life, Annie had collected screw-ups like little boys collected marbles. She got nothing right.

At detention, River was the only other person there and talked nonstop about getting caught smoking in the girls' restroom. When Annie told her own story, River laughed so hard she fell off her chair.

"You could use a friend," River said, and effortlessly enfolded Annie into her circle of girlfriends the following week.

Annie marveled at how these girls, most of them two or three years older, included her. Where Annie was blonde and petite, River was a busty, exotic-looking Filipino/Black girl mix. LaShonda was chocolate-brown with a belly laugh and a potty mouth. Shelly was a white girl like Annie, but tall and chunky around the middle with bright red hair. LaShonda dyed it for her. In fact, LaShonda did everyone's hair that night, including Annie's, by spiking it with lots of product. LaShonda dreamed of being a hairstylist for the stars.

"I want to graduate without getting pregnant," Shelly said. "If I make it to June, I'll be the first one in my family to wear the cap and gown."

River never spoke about her secret dreams; she said it was bad luck. When the girls asked Annie what she wanted to do with her life, Annie shrank into herself. She didn't want to say. Her future had felt bleak until meeting River. So much so, she had already tried to off herself. What a big pain that turned out to be. She got nothing out of the attempt except a fast track into a shrink's office. Annie teared up at the memory. River came up and hugged her from behind and spoke into the restroom mirror.

"Girl, you need to lighten up. Have some fun. Don't take life so serious-like."

"I'm not very good around people," Annie said.

"Sometimes, you gotta jump into the water with both feet."

"And drown?"

"Nah. You find out it's only three foot deep." River cackled.

Shelly and LaShonda giggled. "River, you gotta fix that laugh," LaShonda said. "You sound like the witch from the *Wizard of Oz*."

"No way! I don't care. It's my signature."

Indeed, Annie thought. River laughed at the whole world. She wasn't afraid of anything. She was the big sister Annie had never had. And when she was with River, her body wasn't so twitchy all the time.

Of course, Annie's mother would never approve of these girls if she knew the truth about them. Things got dicey right before Halloween when Susan, her mother, caught her playing hooky from class with the posse at the mall. The look on Susan's face was priceless. She put Annie on lockdown for five days and peppered her with questions about "those" girls, where they lived, and so on.

In frustration, Annie pulled out the Jesus card and said, "I'm practicing what we learned in youth group: friendship evangelism."

"How does that work?"

"Well, you get to know people, make friends, and eventually, you tell them about your faith," Annie said.

"And how long does it take?" Susan asked.

"I don't know. Ask Jake. He's your *friend*," Annie added air quotes.

"Please call him Pastor Jake, Annie. He's your youth group leader."

"Fine." Annie said.

After that, Annie had to give Susan weekly updates on her evangelism progress. Jake's warnings at youth group about teens getting sucked into the world escalated as well. Susan must have told Jake about her new friends at school. By late November, her mother wanted concrete proof of Annie's progress in her friendship evangelism project. So, Annie begged River to come to a Sunday night youth group meeting, just to get her mother off her back. Annie's plan worked out until River snuck out the back door to smoke a joint and make out with Joshua Matthews. Luckily, Jake didn't blame Annie for their screw-up, but Joshua's parents grounded him for a month. Her youth group branded her a black sheep after that episode.

After Christmas, River told Annie, "You owe me. Come with us to the next mobile party."

"What's a mobile party?"

"They're all different. Sometimes, it's a party on a bus that travels around, or a bash in a semi-truck filled with arcade games. But our parties usually take place in a row house. It's a blowout with lots of good-looking guys, sexy foreign accents, and dancing. Lots of dancing. In fact, there's a dance contest where you can earn real money. I made three hundred bucks last time."

"Wow."

"We'll tell your mother it's a sleepover. I'll get my friend Shangri-LA to call her and pretend to be LaShonda's grandmother."

"She's willing to do that?"

"He, well, sometimes he and sometimes she."

"What?"

"Never mind."

They were all together at the coffee shop after school when Shangri-LA called Annie's mother. Annie finally understood this person was somewhere in the middle of being a man and a woman. In any case, he/she did a great job and Susan fell for it. And so, here they were, the posse of four getting ready at the bowling alley for the mobile party.

LaShonda's playlist blazed in the bathroom as they changed their clothes and grooved to the music.

"Don't you love our animal prints?" LaShonda asked River and Annie.

"Very hot," River said. "You and Shelly match."

"We're doing a duo routine at the party," Shelly said.

Lucky for Annie, the girls made contributions to her outfit: lots of black and silver.

After LaShonda did Annie's hair and the other two did her makeup, Annie looked in the mirror, yelped, laughed, and gave high fives all around. Annie looked red hot. She could pass for sixteen for sure, and maybe even eighteen.

Once dressed, the girls had fifteen minutes to kill, so they grabbed a soda from River's cousin Lacy who worked the snack counter and then tested their looks on the local boys. As they walked around in their stilettos and boots, Annie could feel eyes on her, and for once, she enjoyed the attention. She felt pretty for the first time ever. While they sauntered around, River coached Annie on the dance contest.

"You don't have to worry a bit; I'll be there with you. Just try to relax and remember, it's all a show. Every dance is worth money, so make it good," River said.

"I'm not really much of a dancer."

"You'll be fine. You can even close your eyes. Feel the music and go for it. It's the same moves we were doing in the john. But one thing you need to avoid is the word 'No.'"

"What? Why?"

"It's part of the game. Remember, this is all about the money. And another thing, Lincoln told me this is a different crowd. And guess what? Some of them speak Russian. Didn't you tell me you speak it? That is so awesome. You're the only person I know who speaks Russian."

"Well, a little. I mean, yeah, I'm pretty good. I take classes. My mother makes me," Annie said, and looked away. She didn't remember telling River she was adopted from Russia. River acted like Annie was cool because of it. But to everyone else, it might be one more weird thing about her. Then she remembered her other weird secret, the one her mother had kept from her for years, the one Annie found out about right before eighth grade graduation. Whenever she thought about it, she fumed.

CHAPTER 2
Towson, Maryland
Eight Months Earlier, May 2009

Sunday afternoon was another "go to your room" moment for talking back. This time, Annie's confinement was to the guest room, decorated in a trendy blend of coral and turquoise. Pastor Jake had convinced Susan that Annie enjoyed her own room too much, so it wasn't much of a punishment to send her there. *True that*, Annie thought. Little did her mother know how Annie's curiosity would send her into the farthest reaches of the guest closet. Annie found two boxes of Russian mementos Susan had collected when she went to St. Petersburg to complete Annie's adoption ten years earlier.

Annie opened the bigger of the two boxes first. Some things were more interesting than others. She found typical items like airfare stubs, programs, and little tickets with holes stamped through them from traveling by tram. She found a shot glass with "The Idiot" inscribed on it, which made no sense. Who would call a restaurant "The Idiot?" She kept it anyway and slipped it into the end table drawer. At the bottom of the box, she found binders full of paperwork labeled "Home Study," "Follow-up Meetings," and "Financial Reports."

She also found an album with pictures of their house and, best of all, pictures of Susan with her husband, Tom. Annie grew sad every time she thought about what she had missed: a father. In all the album pictures, he looked quite healthy. Obviously, before he got sick. It wouldn't have served to send pictures of the emaciated Tom to the Russian authorities.

Annie kept looking. Tucked inside the binders were lots of maps, most of them in Russian. She could make out most of the words—things like 'streets,' 'theaters,' and 'shopping.' One of the maps had circles drawn around what she figured were the orphanage and the hotel. She slipped this map into the end table drawer with the shot glass.

The second box was much smaller but held the biggest find of all: more pictures of Annie as a toddler in Russia, and several black-and-white composition books her mother must have used as travel diaries. Annie picked out a favorite picture of herself standing in what appeared to be the front hall of the orphanage and added it to her stash of goodies.

Susan was over-the-top organized and had numbered the notebooks in order by date. Annie started with the first one. By the time she reached notebook four, her anger and anxiety hit her stomach. She fled into the bathroom and vomited. A roiling stomach accompanied most of her stressed-out moments.

As she staggered back into the bedroom, she understood one thing for sure: her adoption was illegal, and worse still, she was the consolation prize. The girl they had intended to adopt had died. Her name was Anya, while the other girl, Irina, became the substitute.

I am the replacement child. Susan gave me a dead girl's name and a dead girl's identity. I was Irina by birth, but Irina has been erased.

She collapsed on the bed and sobbed into a pillow.

Annie lay on the bed and stared out the window, seeing nothing. Her thoughts bounced around until she remembered the little dolls she had carried all the way from St. Petersburg. She got up, peeked out the guest room door to make sure her mother wasn't nearby, and slipped into her own bedroom.

There they were, sitting on top of her bookcase. Fedya and Elena. She climbed onto a chair to pull them down and clutched them to her chest like she used to do as a little girl. Tears streamed down her face again as she carried them back to her guest room prison.

"Hello, Fedya. Hello, Elena," she said aloud.

Wait. I must speak to them in Russian. That was part of the magic.

"*Privet!* Hi. I'm sorry I haven't talked to you in a long time. I've grown up. You are my brother and sister, aren't you?" Neither said a word. "I'm Irina, and I didn't die in the orphanage. But you'll never find me because I have a different name."

Yes. You'll never find me. They must have stopped looking for me a long time ago. And why did they think their baby sister was dead?

Because of Susan. It was all Susan's fault. The only way to change things would be for me, the real Irina, to find them. To find Fedya and Elena, and show them I'm alive. This must be my quest.

An hour later, at dinner, Annie, still furious with her mother's deception, moved the roasted brussels sprouts around her plate while Susan drilled her with stupid questions.

"How was your day at school Friday? I've barely seen you since then."

If she said, "Fine," then her mother would have several follow-up questions. Annie stuck with silence.

"What did you have for lunch?"

Annie shook her head.

"You can't keep skipping lunch, Annie." Pause. "Did you turn in the form I filled out for your cap and gown?"

Annie nodded.

"Did you have any more trouble with those mean girls?"

Annie shrugged.

Susan sighed the "I'm trying" sigh, but Annie didn't have the energy to help her through it. Not after the revelations she found upstairs.

Besides, her mother couldn't change anything. All of Annie's days at the Academy were crappy. She couldn't wait to graduate. On Friday, after homeroom, two of the cheerleaders pushed her into the boy's bathroom. Humiliating. In gym, she was the last one picked for the volleyball game, as usual. At lunch, she didn't eat because she was already feeling nauseated. Then, in math, Mr. Slaykis mocked her in front of the entire class for turning in the wrong homework. When she bolted out of class without permission because she was about to be sick, the kids laughed, and he gave her a demerit.

Susan tried again. "How did you do on your math test? And please try to use words to answer."

"Okay." Annie took a bite of food so she wouldn't have to say anything else.

"You have homework this weekend?"

Annie nodded.

Susan sighed. "I saw Pamela at the store yesterday. She asked about you."

Not a question, so Annie would wait her mother out.

"Could you at least acknowledge I'm talking to you?" Susan said.

Annie put down her fork, folded her hands in her lap, and stared at her mother.

Susan said, "When I was in eighth grade, we still respected grown-ups. Apparently, those days are over."

"Apparently."

"Don't do that, Annie. It's hurtful. I'm not your enemy."

"May I be excused from the table?" Annie asked.

"Not yet. Pamela asked if you and I would like to come over to their house tomorrow after church. They are opening their pool early since the weather has been so nice. Her daughter, Leslie, is in sixth grade and her son, Ian, is your age. They both go to Dumbarton Middle. Last fall, I invited them to the harvest festival at our church. Remember? They are a nice family. It could be a lovely day playing together in the pool."

OMG. Humiliate me. Go ahead. That's great. Ian Richards is super cute and super popular. He plays travel soccer with boys from my school. He wouldn't be caught dead hanging around me, and second, I wouldn't wear a bathing suit in front of an eighth-grade boy even if my life depended on it. I'd look like Flat Stanley.

"No thanks," Annie said instead. "I think I'm going to be sick. May I please leave the table?"

Annie left the table without waiting for an answer and ran into the half bath in the front hall. To make sure her mother got the point, she stuck a finger down her throat to vomit. The food coming back up burned her mouth.

She heard her mother's footsteps and a tap on the door.

"Honey, I've brought you a glass of water. May I come in?"

"No."

"I'll leave it on the credenza."

Annie thought her mother had stepped away. Instead, Susan said through the door, "I love you, Annie. I will always love you. Nothing you do or say, or don't do, will stop me from loving you."

But Annie knew what would come next. Her mother would call the shrink, Dr. Madelyn. And then Annie would have to go over this whole thing again.

*

"What do you think caused you to be sick on Saturday?" Madelyn Rescate asked.

"I don't know. I'm sick all the time. I don't keep track."

"Annie, we agreed that anxiety can cause vomiting. If we can address the anxiety-producing situations, you will grow stronger and be less likely to become nauseated to the point of throwing up."

I can't tell her about the travel journals, about finding out I am not the chosen adopted daughter at all, but a stand-in. I have to say something, or she'll keep probing.

"Susan wanted us to visit a family with a boy my age. I would have been humiliated. He would have told his friends, and the name-calling would have gone through the roof."

"What are some labels you are called at school?" Madelyn asked.

"Loser, or pancake chest or Awkward Annie. And if they remember my adoption from Russia, they might call me a 'commie' or tell me I was a mistake, and to go back to where I came from. But most of the time, just weird. Always weird or weirdo."

"That must be difficult. But tell me, Annie, what does it mean to be weird?"

Annie threw her head back on the soft cushion of the doctor's sofa and grabbed a pillow to hug. "You're kidding, right? Look it up."

"I know Webster's definition, but what do you think?"

"Okay, strange or odd. That's me."

"It also means fantastic and remarkable. Look, there is a defense to name-calling, particularly when those words can make you feel like you don't fit in."

"I don't fit in. I have never fit in. I never will."

Annie's unbidden tears flowed. Madelyn calmly sat and waited.

CHAPTER 3
TOWSON, MARYLAND
Same Day in January

"Listen," River said as she grabbed Annie by the elbow, "say some of those Russian words, like in a sexy voice, you know? They'll eat it up. You look amazing. Black and silver are your colors."

The text came and River rounded up the girls. They fell out of the front door giggling, with the sound of bowling pins trailing behind them. Outside, Lincoln grabbed River and kissed her neck. River laughed. He led them to a big black car. When they piled in, three other girls, definitely older, like Shelly, were already in the back. Most of them wore lots of shiny and colorful outfits. Annie ended up next to a window with LaShonda beside her. She watched as the driver powered down the front passenger window and handed Lincoln an envelope. *Ah,* she thought, *it's all about the money. It's always about the money.* She caught the driver's eye in the rearview mirror, and he winked. He looked familiar, but she couldn't place him.

Within minutes, they were out of any neighborhoods she recognized. The girls passed around a joint, but Annie shook her head. It was already hot and close. She gulped down a few times, something like bile. She might get seriously car sick if they didn't arrive soon. The last thing she needed was to get high or throw up.

The driver got a phone call, and of all things, he spoke in Russian. Annie understood his words, but the overall meaning remained fuzzy. He said the products were on the way and told them how many he was dropping off. Was she a product? When he hung up, Annie tapped his shoulder and spoke in Russian to ask his name. His eyes met hers in the rearview mirror.

He laughed, and answered in Russian, "Maksim, but everyone calls me Maks. What's your name, *malenkaya kukla*, little doll?"

"Anya. I was born in St. Petersburg. But everyone calls me Annie now."

"Really? Little Orphan Annie?"

"Very funny. Like you think you're the first person to make that stupid joke?"

"No. But you were, yes? An orphan? And now you live here. Your Russian sounds American."

"Hey," River interrupted. "What are you guys talking about? Here Annie, take a sip. It's really tasty and burns good all the way down."

"No thanks. I don't like to share spit."

"What did I tell you about 'No'?" All the girls cackled.

LaShonda topped the laughter and said, "Wait, wait. I've got a question. How do you say no in Russian?"

Several of the girls said, "Nyet, nyet Soviet," and they laughed again. Annie looked at Maks in the mirror and they both rolled their eyes.

Maks pulled up to a curb, and the girls climbed out. Annie could tell the neighborhood was a little rough because most of the row houses looked empty or boarded up. This one, in the middle of the block, had lights flashing to the rhythm of the bass they could hear from the street. The girls started calling out, "Let's parteeee!" Annie couldn't see an address or anything else to distinguish this house from any of the other Baltimore row houses.

When the girls reached the stoop, the door opened like magic. A woman met them and offered to take their coats. She had an accent. Annie was about to speak to her in Russian, but then thought better of it. Somehow, she didn't like the way the woman looked at each girl from head to toe.

Annie kept her jean jacket and backpack, and lied to the woman, "Sorry, I carry medicine in my bag, just in case I have an asthma attack."

What a liar she had become. Hilarious, the way the woman had stepped away from her as though asthma was contagious. As the woman closed the door, Annie heard the big car drive away. How would they get back to LaShonda's apartment?

At least a dozen guys and half as many women of varying ages milled around the nearly furniture-less front and middle rooms. As soon as the girls from the car stepped in, several of the men grabbed a girl to dance. She saw River, quite tall in her heels, dance with a guy who was a head shorter than she was, while LaShonda and another girl danced with a man who acted drunk already. Annie's stomach took a minor blip, and for the first time, she felt a tiny bit afraid. She heard someone say there was food down the hall in the kitchen, so Annie inched her way through the crowd, just for something to do.

Before she reached the kitchen, an overweight man with a comb-over and jowls pulled her toward the dancing couples. She resisted and said, "No, thank you," but then remembered what River had told her. She relented, and he led her to an open spot on the floor. The music slowed, and he yanked off her backpack and tossed it into a corner. He pulled her close, ran his hands up and down her back under her jacket, and whispered filthy sex words into her ear in Russian. At least, she assumed that's what they were. Her face suddenly dripped with sweat, and it was hard to breathe.

She stepped away and told him in clear Russian, "I'm going to throw up." He let her go.

On her way, she repeated, *"tualet, tualet."* The bodies parted, and she found a tiny half bath off the kitchen.

Once inside, she collapsed against the door, and prayed, *"Oh God, I'm so sorry. Please God. Please Jesus. I've made a terrible mistake."* She repeated the words over and over again until someone knocked on the door.

"In a minute," she said to the door and then perched on the toilet. She had to collect herself.

What a laugh. Here I am praying and I'm the one who claims I don't believe in God anymore. I've got to pull myself together. Breathe.

She only had one option. If she embarrassed her friends or ruined it for them, she would be dissed forever. Somehow, she had to make it through the night. She crept out of the bathroom, found her backpack, and stood close to the windows of the middle room. The fat man had disappeared, so she hoped it was a safe place to stand and watch. She couldn't see Shelly anywhere either, but both River and LaShonda seemed fine on the dance floor. Annie needed to breathe and relax. She had a bad first impression, that's all. In fact, when she looked around a little more, some guys were pretty good-looking. River waved her over. But Annie shook her head and mimed throwing up. River gave her an "I'm sorry" grimace and returned to her dance partner, who nuzzled her neck.

Before Annie considered dancing or anything else, she needed an escape plan, just in case. She did this wherever she was, ever since the Columbine anniversary program last spring. But even before that, as a kid while her mother slept, she visualized what she would do if a burglar came into the house. One scenario might be to mound the covers to look like no one was in the bed. Or she would slip into the back of the walk-in closet and cover herself in clothes. In case of fire, she saw herself slip out her bedroom window, inch along the roof, and then slide down the water pipe. Tonight, maybe because of the tremor in her gut, she needed one of those plans.

Returning to the kitchen, Annie headed to the back door. Once outside, she found three people on the small porch smoking. She slipped past them to get a better look at the yard, which turned out to be a dumping ground for broken furniture, black garbage bags filled with who knew what, a tilting shed with its door hanging by a single hinge, and an old car jacked up on cement blocks along the left side. A tall fence encircled the mess, except for a shorter gate in the back corner. She headed toward it.

One guy called out. "Hey, where are you going?" Everyone's head turned in her direction like a herd of animals who scented danger.

"Nowhere. I feel a little sick and someone's in the john." Once again, the word "sick" had the push-away polarity of a magnet.

One girl tossed her cigarette into the yard and opened the storm door to go back inside. When Annie reached the other side of the old car, she made gagging sounds, and the other two followed their friend. As soon as the coast was clear, she moved toward the back gate but tripped over car parts in the dark and nearly fell flat on her face. She cursed her mother again for not letting her have a phone, if for nothing else, a flashlight. All the high school kids had phones. When she reached the double-wide gate, a light came on from a garage on the other side of the alley. She jerked back and crouched down.

When she stood up, she screeched. A man on the other side had pulled out a gun.

"Holy shit," he said. "You trying to get yourself killed? What are you doing out here?" It was Maks, their driver. He jammed the gun back into the waistband of his jeans and under his black leather jacket.

"Sorry. I felt sick. Where did you go? I heard you drive away." She had learned from a YouTube video to respond to a question with a question. *What was it called? Deflecting, or something like that.*

"I had to find a place to park away from the house."

"Why?"

"You ask too many questions." He switched to Russian. He used a key to unlock the padlocked gate, stepped through it, and pulled it shut. "You must be cold. Come on, you're supposed to be inside bringing sexy back."

He put his muscled arm around her, and as they walked inside, he said, "You know, you're a very pretty girl."

My God, he thinks I'm pretty. It's working. The hair, the make-up, the clothes.

"Listen, you call me if you need help. Here's my card. We have a connection, right?"

She put it in the side pocket of her backpack. His closeness thrilled and comforted at the same time as he pulled her even closer. The smoke in the car had masked his woodsy cologne. She didn't know what it was, but she liked it. High school boys were immature. But Maks was a man, and a hunk. She loved his look, in a black leather jacket, jeans, and combat boots. Inside, River saw them right away and dragged her away from Maks and into a corner of the dining room.

"Where have you been? They're about to start the competition. This is why we're here, and this is where you can make at least a hundred bucks in ten minutes."

"I don't think so."

"See what I mean? You've got all that 'nyet' going on. Watch us first. You'll get the idea. Play right into the camera."

"Camera?"

"Yeah, they videotape us. It helps you get into the mood. It's like being a movie star. I play right to the camera."

A man in a ponytail got everyone's attention and explained how each girl would dance to same song and the men would judge and vote. He spoke in heavily accented English, "And don't forget gentlemen, your votes mean tips for the girls." In Russian, he said to the camera, "Anatole is adding up your votes. Please use the numbers pinned to the girls to make your selections for future activity."

And sure enough, someone handed Annie a plastic number bib and a safety pin. The song started, and she understood Maks's comment about bringing sexy back; it was Justin Timberlake's old song filling the house. Apparently, she and her friends, along with the other three girls from the car, were the only ones with numbers. She was number seven, the last one. Her mind jumped to her mother's voice, calling out "lucky seven" whenever they played board games. Was it lucky tonight?

She felt claustrophobic again, like she often did in crowds. Everyone was so close and crammed into those two rooms like a crowded subway car with a small space at the front. She wasn't so sure this was worth the money.

With the first girl, the one who brought the vodka, everyone (men and girls alike) whooped and sang along. The girl wasn't really dancing so much as pretending to be a pole dancer without a pole. Next up were the other two girls, who acted like they were having sex. It was gross. Annie turned to leave, but behind her was the first man, the fat man, smiling at her. She turned her back on him. He grabbed her butt and squeezed.

"Hey!" she said.

"I pay very good for your dancing, you will see," he said into her ear and then wormed through the group to the ponytail man.

Annie's breathing got shallow. She felt a kind of panic rising, but then River got up to dance. Just watching her liquid moves and her face light up with laughter helped Annie relax a bit. *It will be over soon.* Besides, River's body was amazing. She could go pro. When they made eye contact, Annie gave her two thumbs up. Men threw money at River and called out her number repeatedly. When the bell finally rang, the floor was littered with twenties and tens. River swept up the bills quickly.

LaShonda and Shelly were next and danced as a duo, but theirs was a real routine and again, they raked in the bucks.

When the announcer called Annie's number, she froze. The fat man shoved her into the little dance circle. She heard him shout *"Snimi eto, deta."* Take it off, baby.

So far, none of the girls had stripped. Not really. Most of their outfits were already skimpy, but Annie had on several layers, which gave her an idea. What the hell. She told them to turn off the music. She heard murmuring, but then she asked them to play a Russian song, *"Zakroy Za Mnoy Dver."* In English, it would be "Close the Door I'm Taking Off." Annie asked for the song again, first in English and again in Russian. The place went wild. Once the music started, she pretended she was the female version of Magic Mike. She became someone else. It was a kind of magic. And since she had a sports bra underneath everything, she felt pretty safe. It was like stripping to a bathing suit. To finish the dance, she stomped and clapped her hands to the rhythm of the music, and they all joined in. When the bell rang, the floor around her was littered with money, and not only twenties and tens, but a hundred-dollar bill. She gloated. She grabbed everything off the floor and exulted in her success. This was a new Annie, a different Annie, a wild Annie. While dancing and moving, she had put on a second skin. Maybe that was all there was to it. Maybe she could put on a different skin at school, too.

But then things moved fast, and she didn't understand what was happening. The big man, the fat one, fanned out several bills and waved them in front of her face and started pulling her up the stairs.

"Hey, wait a minute. Wait a minute," Annie said. She tried to look back over the room to find her friends, but she couldn't see any of them. The girls had vanished. "Where are my friends?"

The man kept saying in broken English, "Your friends are busy. I pay good money, you'll see," he said.

When they got to the top of the stairs, he thrust her into the first open door, a bedroom. One lamp stood in the corner and there was nothing else but a huge king-sized bed.

"Stop, stop it," Annie cried as he grabbed the clothes and backpack from her arms. *My God*, she thought, *I'm about to be raped. Oh my God.*

He shoved her onto the bed, and she scampered to the head of it. She started crying and whimpering. She couldn't stop.

"Shut up," he said as he pulled down his pants and underpants.

When she saw his thing, she screamed. She looked around for a weapon, anything that might save her. Nothing. She threw the pillows at him, and he laughed as he started crawling across the bed toward her. She rolled away from him, as he grabbed for her foot and missed. She leaped off the bed and scrambled for her pack and pile of clothes and yanked at the door, thankfully unlocked.

"Come back here. There's no place to run."

He tried to stand on the bed, but then he fell off, hard. She didn't wait to see if he would get up. Still in her underwear, she could hear the party going downstairs. She ran to the end of the hall, thinking there had to be a bathroom. *Yes!* Annie closed the door behind her. The lock looked flimsy, a hook kind of thing she hoped would hold for now.

She stood in the middle of the little bathroom and cried until someone pounded on the door.

"In a minute, I'm sick." Her time was up. She tried the little window. At first, it seemed to be painted shut, but then it budged.

"Come on, you piece of crap. Open!"

The window would be a tight fit and she might fall off the roof and kill herself anyway, but no way was she going to let some big, fat, hairy old man put his hands on her. When she finally maneuvered half of her body out the window, she realized there was no ledge or roof below her. A wire ran from the house to a pole in the alley. Maybe it was a telephone wire. It was the only thing she could see to grab.

Annie turned her body around so her butt was on the windowsill. Her legs dangled inside the bathroom while her upper body dangled outside. She pulled on the wire. It seemed strong enough, but she wasn't sure what would happen if it had her full body weight.

"The hell with it." She pulled her body back into the bathroom as someone pounded on the door again. She flushed the toilet.

"Almost done," she called out.

She stuffed her clothes into the backpack and tossed it out the window. She slithered back out the tiny window and with two hands grabbed the wire right where it went into the house and pulled herself out the rest of the way. For several seconds, she dangled there, her feet groping for purchase against the wooden house. Nothing. She let herself slide down the wire and away from the house. The wire was slack and, for lack of momentum, her body stalled over the middle of the yard. She looked down. *God help me*, she screamed in her head. If she dropped to the ground, maybe eight or ten feet, she could break a leg or something. A crash came from the bathroom above. She let go.

CHAPTER 4
TOWSON, MARYLAND
Same Night

Susan stood by the fireplace as she listened to the telephone ring at the other end. Jake sat on the couch and appeared to be praying. Finally, someone answered.

"Hello, is this Mrs. West?… Hi. This is Susan Spencer. I'm Annie Spencer's mother. May I speak to Annie? She and her friends are spending the night over there, right?… I beg your pardon?… No, uh, no… she might have said something about going bowling… Isn't it rather late for bowling now?… Hello? Mrs. West?" Susan stared at her phone's screen.

"She hung up on me."

Jake rose from the couch and went to comfort Susan. He put his arms around her waist and rested his chin on the top of her head. She usually loved that. A tall man made her feel more secure.

"She hung up on me," Susan said again. "I thought I was being polite. I didn't accuse her of anything. Wasn't I polite?"

"Did the woman sound sober?"

"What?" She pulled out of his arms. "That's a terrible thing to say." Chilled, she pulled her favorite gray cardigan around her.

"Well," he said, "I mean, most people don't hang up on someone unless they're angry or not in their right mind."

Susan moved back to the couch. Jake followed and sat beside her. She tried to remember how they had reached the decision for Susan to call the Wests in the first place. Jake looked at the world as a glass half empty. Ever since Mrs. Matthews told Jake about Annie's friend smoking a joint behind the church, he believed Annie needed more supervision,

20

particularly if the River girl was any sign of her new friends. Susan had let it go and refused to punish her since Annie wasn't directly involved.

All the same, Susan had tried to institute more rules, but there was a limit. How many times could she ground the girl, or remove screen time, or send her to the guest room where there was nothing to do? And then Susan's mother had come for a weeklong visit. They needed the guest room, so Annie went back to her own room for timeouts, which was nearly every day because Annie and her grandmother never got along. Susan tried to forget the chaos of her mother's last visit. Like Jake, her mother believed in total obedience and lots of ground rules. None of which worked well with Annie. Susan had to wonder if Jake's children were as perfect as he made them out to be. No behavior issues, straight A students, keepers of all the memory verses—she secretly harbored jealous feelings.

No. I have the most difficult child ever! And every time something like this happens, I end up replaying the warnings from the orphanage director.

"This one is very difficult. She has many emotional problems already. She will cause you much pain," the director had said.

And it was true. Annie had caused Susan many sleepless nights and tearful visits to a therapist. But Susan didn't love Annie any less. If only Tom were still alive. He would have known what to do, how to love a little troubled girl and bring her out of her shell.

When Tom got sick, he insisted Susan go forward with the adoption after he died. She had been so sure she could handle everything: the paperwork, the trips to St. Petersburg, the court hearings—everything. She had held her grief at bay over Tom's death. But when little Anya died, the day before they were to head back to the States, she collapsed. And yet, impossibly, in her worst moment, God moved. That's how it seemed. Not even an hour later, another little girl walked into the waiting room, chattering away. Sweet, charming, funny, a little towhead with deep blue eyes, and a grin to melt any heart. Susan knew in an instant, here stood God's answer to her prayers, her miracle. Better still, the two little girls, this one and her dead Anya, were nearly identical.

But her Anya wasn't the only child who had contracted a whooping cough that month. And if it hadn't been for Susan's quick assessment, the waiting room girl, Irina, could have died as well, having been quite

21

feverish. But Irina didn't die, and Susan wanted the girl for herself, a second Anya.

Then the complications piled up. Susan had to convince the director to switch the girls' paperwork: the living Irina for the dead Anya. Only after quarreling and with many reservations and warnings, the director swore Susan to secrecy and made the switch. No one could know, because what they did was illegal. Once home, Susan couldn't keep such a secret, and she finally told her mother—a mistake, and her best friend, Kate—a Godsend, who gave her a journal to record everything. More recently, she confessed to Jake in the name of transparency. One day, Susan wanted Annie to know, too. One day.

Oh, how the orphanage staff had warned her about the girl seeing things and talking into the air and sitting alone instead of playing with other children. But Susan knew about invisible friends. Kate's daughter had had one. Susan also knew about grief. She knew how grief could feel like an igloo. Every behavior little Irina exhibited was understandable. Susan could handle it. Even when the child went silent after arriving in Maryland, Susan believed the little girl needed time. But days grew into weeks and even months. When the acting out began in earnest with tantrums, biting, bedwetting, and refusing to eat, Susan questioned her choices. Had she done the right thing after all? She had pleaded with God to intervene. Begged everyone at church for prayer. Argued with her mother, who wanted the girl committed to an institution. My God, it was awful.

Finally, around the time Annie entered second grade, things got better. She still had many anxieties and fears, but at least she started talking. She amazed everyone when she seamlessly leaped from Russian to silence to English. Kate's brother-in-law, Lukyan, a Russian-American, suggested they enroll Annie in a Saturday Russian language school so she wouldn't lose her Russian altogether. Susan agreed to the plan. And when she finally returned to full-time work, once again, Lukyan came to the rescue with a Russian-speaking childcare provider.

Now, his name triggered shame as she remembered their affair while he was still married. Lukyan was in law enforcement, one reason he and his wife divorced. She couldn't handle the stress and fear. At first, Susan found it exciting, but it didn't take long for her to understand his ex-wife's point of view. Lukyan lived his job. He didn't really have space for a healthy relationship. And now, here she was again, dating a married man.

What is wrong with me?

"Susan?" Jake said. "You're a million miles away."

"Sorry, just reminiscing."

"I think we should call the police," he said.

"Oh, dear Lord, I don't want to do that. She's been doing so much better. Surely, she hasn't run away again. It's these rough girls, I know it."

Jake took her hand in his and stroked her back. She stood up again and went to the window. Susan knew he meant well, but right now, his touch felt patronizing. Had Annie guessed they were dating? Well, not quite dating, but seeing each other and being intimate. They didn't exactly go out. But they spent time together whenever they could. What a mess if Annie knew. She had made several wisecracks already about him and did a lot of eye-rolling every time Susan mentioned youth group or Pastor Jake.

This could all be pushback against Susan for shacking up with the youth group leader. Granted, he was nearly divorced, but what message were they sending? Just because no one knew about it didn't make it right. Maybe they should break it off for a while until Annie was—what? Out of youth group? *I'm a fool.*

Her grandmother's cuckoo clock chimed midnight. She had to call the police.

CHAPTER 5
BALTIMORE, MARYLAND
Same Night

The landing wasn't as bad as Annie thought it would be. Apparently, the black bags were full of old clothes or something similar. All the same, her left arm hurt like she had scratched it, but there wasn't enough light to check. The music started blaring again and urgency bubbled up. She groped for her backpack and finally found it in some kind of squishy mess. She couldn't think about that, nor could she decide whether to dress here in the dark or jump the fence in her underwear and dress somewhere else. When she heard voices, she ran.

Annie would never know if Maks had his own reasons for leaving the gate unlocked, or if someone else had come in late, when she pushed through it half naked. She didn't bother to latch it either but ran down the alley, hunching down as she heard people step out onto the porch again, probably to smoke.

The neighborhood creeped her out with so few street lights, open and stinking garbage cans along the sidewalks, and very little traffic. She looked for a place where she could safely stop and dress. When she hit the first major cross street, she saw headlights coming her way, so she dropped behind a parked car. This would have to do. She pulled out her wadded up clothes from the bag. Of course, with typical Annie luck, she only had one shoe. She imagined her fat prince going from house to house and instead of trying on a glass slipper, the girls would try on one of her Doc Martens. She shivered. If she had a phone, she would know what time it was. *Thanks, Mom.*

If she could find a familiar street nearby, she could get a cab. That is, if a cab would stop for a kid. Or another scumbag might offer to give her a ride. *No, thank you—forget the rides.* She rifled through the backpack again, looking for the money she had made from dancing. Nothing. How was it possible? She thought she put it in the side pocket. It must have fallen out. *Great. I am such a loser, loser, loser.*

After snapping up her jean jacket all the way, she wrapped her hoodie around her neck and pulled her jeans up over her leggings for warmth. She had to get moving. She looked ridiculous, with only one shoe and no coat or gloves in the middle of the night.

How am I going to explain this one to my mother?

As she walked, the night replayed in her head, over and over. While she was in escape mode, the scene had stayed in the back of her brain. Now, everything was in vivid color and surround sound. Unwelcome tears flowed. At one point, she bent over while sobs wracked her body. *Holy crap, he was ready to hurt me. And where are my friends?*

Maybe fifteen minutes passed, maybe longer, when Annie looked up and saw a busier street to the right. She headed toward it and made out the name Reisterstown Road. Great. Her Russian school was near here, but Annie had never paid attention when her mother or Aunt Kate drove her. She was obviously miles from home and on a street where most of the businesses closed at night. She stood on the corner for a good long while, trying to decide which way might be the beltway and which way downtown. There had to be a convenience store somewhere. A couple of cars slowed, and guys whistled at her. She gave them the finger.

In the end, she walked to the right and hoped for the best. But, as always, her luck sucked. A cop car pulled over and the partner's window rolled down.

"Hey there, miss. Need some help?" the woman cop said.

"Uh, I don't know. Maybe." She sounded stupid, but she didn't want to cry and blubber about the nightmare she had been through. "I was looking for my shoe."

"Oh, yeah. I see that. It's pretty cold out here. Maybe you should hop in and warm up first."

"Am I under arrest?"

The woman looked at her partner, then said, "Don't think so. Should you be?"

"No. I mean, it's kind of awkward sitting behind the fencing in the back seat."

"Got it. We kinda have to have it when we pick up bad guys. But it is warmer in the car. What do you say?"

"Okay. Yeah, but only for a bit. I'm meeting some friends later."

Once she closed the car door, it locked. *What the hell was I thinking?*

"Hey!" Annie said. "I can't get out."

"Sorry, miss," the driver said. "It's automatic. You'll be okay. We open it up from here. But we just want to talk, right?"

Of course, now the woman cop is picking up her radio and reporting they have found a girl on the street with one shoe. Great.

"Would you like something to drink, maybe a hot chocolate? There's a convenience store nearby," the driver said while his partner spoke into the radio.

"I'm not a kid. Do I look like a kid who drinks hot chocolate?"

"Right," he said. "Sorry, what would you like?"

"I'll take coffee, lots of sugar and cream."

They pulled into a 7-Eleven. While they waited in the parking lot, the woman handed Annie some wet wipes through the wires.

"What's that for?"

"I thought you might like to clean up some of your makeup."

"What?" Annie scooted over to look in the rearview mirror. "Oh my God."

"Looks like you've been crying, hon. Really, are you okay? Did someone hurt you or try to hurt you?"

Tears sprang unbidden, but before Annie could come up with an answer, the radio crackled to life. The cop lady answered. "Moore. 4578. Go ahead."

Even with code talk, Annie could tell she'd been caught out. *Her mother must have called the police.* Annie had hoped to get them to drop her off at the bowling alley—it was open till two. She assumed her friends would show up there eventually, then they could head back to LaShonda's together. As bad as her night had been so far, it was going to get worse. She could see it now: her mother screaming, then trying to hug her, then more screaming, then sighing, then dispensing the punishment, then reminding her of church the next day. *God help me.* And with that, she laughed.

"What's so funny?" the woman cop said.

"My mother will murder me." The cop looked at her oddly. "No, I mean, not murder-murder, just teenager murder for getting into trouble again."

"What's your name? I'm Officer Moore, Jaqui Moore, spelled with a 'q,' short for Jacqueline," she said.

"Annie," she said and sighed. "Annie Spencer. My full name is Anya Irina Spencer, but that's not my real name. I'm adopted." *Shut up, Annie. She doesn't care about that.* But there was no point in lying about her name. "I wasn't running away, if that's what you think. Just having some fun. A party with my friends. It kinda went bad."

"How did it go bad?"

"I don't know. I just had to get out of there. I have lots of phobias."

The partner came back with coffee and donuts. Jacqui rolled down the back window, and he gave Annie her drink and snack.

"You know you're perpetuating a cliché," Annie said to him.

"Nothin' wrong with that," he said. "You try riding around all night with Moore."

"Hilarious, Lancaster, very funny," Jaqui said.

With that, Annie told Jaqui her address and Lancaster drove her home. At the house, Jaqui walked her to the door. No flashing lights, but already, her mother stood at the front, arms crossed over her chest, holding back for now. Annie didn't like hugs either. Dr. Madelyn, the woo-woo therapist, said it was because Annie had a distinct personal space, particularly in social situations. This little escapade would guarantee the first available appointment next week.

"Mrs. Spencer? I'm Officer Moore."

"Yes, thank you. Please come in. Annie, what happened to your face? Are you hurt?"

Annie rolled her eyes and walked past her mother into the foyer. She heard Jaqui tell her mother where they found her.

"Either Lancaster and I or another set of officers will contact you on Monday for a more complete account. Since you filed a report, we will need to follow up," Jaqui said.

Great, thought Annie, *more questions.*

Hoping to escape while her mother talked with the officer, Annie started up the stairs, glanced through the French doors, and saw a man. When he turned, Annie couldn't believe it. Pastor Jake Peterson stood in her living room. He waved. *What the hell?!*

"Annie?" Jaqui said, "Take care of yourself. It's a little rough on that side of town."

Annie nodded but said nothing until the door closed behind the officer. She went on the offensive.

"What is Pastor Jake doing here?"

Her mother looked over and saw him as well.

"Pastor Jake is here for support. But let's not get off the real subject which is where have you been? And your face, my God. Annie, honey, I've been so worried."

"I don't appreciate my personal stuff being discussed with some guy from the church."

"He's not just some guy, he's the youth pastor and, like the story about the shepherd going after the one lost sheep, he's here to help."

"That's bull pucky."

"That's enough! Sit down and listen to me."

Annie sat on the third step.

"Where is your other shoe?"

Annie shrugged. "Might be in the police car."

"For heaven's sake." Susan stopped and took a breath. "Darling, I was so worried. Something has to change. Tell me the truth. Were you with those girls, those new friends of yours?" She paused again. "Your silence will not help your cause. As far as I'm concerned, this experiment with public school is finished—."

Annie jumped up. "Noooo! That's not fair."

"Fair? Everything you promised you would change upon leaving the Christian academy has not happened."

Annie snarled and turned to run up the stairs.

"Come back here. Now. You can't run away from this. You just turned fourteen, for God's sake. You look like a tramp. You think I don't know you change clothes when you go to school? You think I don't know you put on heavy makeup there? You think I don't know you lie to me all the time? I'm trying my best—"

"Poor you. Well, I'm sorry I'm not the other one. The little girl you really wanted. You should have given me back while you still could. You never loved me, the real me. I was the consolation prize."

"What are you talking about?"

"I found the journals, Mother. All those punishment hours in the boring guest room gave me plenty of time to rummage through the closet."

"Oh, dear Lord." Her mother's hand covered her mouth and Annie felt vindicated.

Jake opened the French doors and said, "Susan? Uh, maybe we should all sit down a minute."

Annie watched, incredulously, as her mother ran into Jake's arms, crying.

CHAPTER 6
RĪGA, LATVIA
Saturday, Ironically the Same Saturday
as the Mobile Party

Elena sat alone in the hallway outside the dance studio, exchanging her jazz shoes for the warm snow boots she would need to walk to the tram and her job at the museum. She rarely minded working Saturdays, but Hugo should have given her this one day off. Her birthday. All he cared about was his precious schedule. But then she thought, *I should be grateful to have a job.*

Almost every day, Uncle would lecture whoever would listen: "So many dreams of a free society, a free market, and what did it get us? More poverty and joblessness. People are getting more and more desperate. It's a powder keg."

Ausma would pet him like a little puppy. "It will get better, Uldis. You'll see. You'll see."

It had to get better. Elena thought. *She hoped Ausma was right.* More than likely, Ausma's connections and money had kept them going and re-started Uldis's career. They were an odd couple. Despite their age difference, Ausma kept herself looking younger, with impeccably styled hair, makeup, nice clothes, and, like most Northern Europeans, she kept fit by walking. Uncle Uldis, on the other hand, had grown paunchy over the past ten years and quite gray. But his piano playing had soared. Sometimes they played together, but rarely, since harp and piano were not as common. But, according to Ausma, on their next tour to the United States, the orchestra would premiere the duet Uncle wrote for the two of them. *And somehow, I must be with them in New York.*

30

Elena shrugged on her coat. She had to get moving. *I need to keep things in perspective. One step at a time.* And yet, today was a milestone birthday. *My God, I am finally out of my teens.* Ausma promised to make Elena's favorite Russian dinner of *ryzhik* and cabbage salad tonight, while Uncle Uldis promised to buy a torte. Over coffee, they would discuss everyone's three favorite subjects: music, dance, and politics. She doubted her brother would even show up: Mr. Busy with his conservatory classes, his band, his motorcycle, and his new girlfriend, Daina. Elena couldn't decide which of those Fedya liked better, or which was most important. Once upon a time, she knew it was piano, like their uncle, but lately he seemed preoccupied. One thing was certain, Elena wasn't even on the list. Not anymore.

As Elena stepped into the cold winter air, she shivered. Already, it had been a snowy winter and barely January. People hunched into layers of coats and scarves and sweaters. She heard a church bell ring. She was running late. When she saw the tram slowing at her stop, she raced to catch it. Leaping in through the back door before it closed, she scanned for a seat, but of course, there weren't any. She grabbed on to a strap as the tram lurched along. Everyone looked so dour today. Even though their little country had finally taken a step in the right direction with elections, the recession was heavy on people's hearts and lives. Since her family wrapped itself in the arts, their lives were better than average. Yes, the arts and sports flourished, and thank God for it. And finally, tourists had found Rīga. Things were looking up, as Ausma had said.

Here she was, turning twenty, and she had very little to show for those years. She had had a few appearances in the corps de ballet at the Opera House, but only one solo last season in the Nutcracker. Oh bother, the Nutcracker. Little girls could do better than she had. And this past December, she was back in the flower corps. She had wanted the Arabian dance, but apparently, she was not exotic enough. *No, I must face it. I am no prima ballerina; I am barely above average.*

"But Elena," Ausma had asked. "Do you love it? Do you love the ballet? That's what matters."

But it wasn't the only thing that mattered, not at all. Elena wanted to excel. She needed a change of plans. She had told no one yet, and perhaps tonight would be the night. She had moved her studies to theater jazz. It felt good in her body, and her ballet base was perfect. Ballet

Master Alise had agreed to it and even offered Elena an assistant job with the little ones and a discount on her new classes. But two things had to happen: Elena needed to drop out of university and Uncle Uldis and Ausma needed to take her with them to America on the symphony tour. Theater jazz meant Broadway, and that's where she needed to be. New York, New York.

"Pardon me, love, would you like my seat?" a man's voice said in heavily accented English.

Elena looked around and found an attractive, tall, muscular man in his early twenties with sandy hair and intense hazel eyes offering her his seat. Very attractive. And very tall. He pointed to the seat in case she didn't understand his English. But she did. She had studied English since she was twelve. And she was good with languages, Uncle Uldis had said so. Ausma, too, had encouraged her from the beginning to continue with her Russian while she learned Latvian, and then English.

"Yes, sure," she replied in English. "Very polite of you, but I don't believe you are from England."

"No. Australia." He kept staring at her and she couldn't decide what to do next.

"I'm visiting," he said. "My ice hockey team is here for a few months of training. We're the opposite, you know. Our season starts in April."

"Oh," she said. "That's nice." Tongue-tied, she pulled out her mobile.

"Listen, love, could we have a coffee? Or tea? Do you drink tea here? It's a bit lonely."

"You have an entire team with you."

"Right you are, but me and my mates are pretty sick of each other already. Maybe you could show me around?"

"I didn't know Australians were so bold?"

Elena looked around and realized everyone in the car listened and watched them. Most Latvians barely spoke on a tram, much less with foreigners.

"Look," she said, "I'm on my way to work. In fact, this is my stop."

She got off, but then he got off too.

"I'm not stalking you, mate. I think you're pretty and I'm tired of going places with the team, so I skipped out early from practice this morning for an adventure. Would you like to have an adventure with me? What's your name, by the way? I'm Aidan, but my friends call me Danny."

Elena kept walking, but Aidan, or Danny, kept pace.

"Honestly. I don't know you. Maybe they do this in your country, but not so much here."

"Where do you work? Here? Right here? You work in a museum? That's champion. Ah, I see the hours here. You probably work until the end, right? Eighteen hundred hours? So, I'll meet you right here. If you want to, mind. If you want to take a chance with me, I'll meet you right here on the steps. But you never told me your name. Did you?" He handed her a piece of paper with his mobile number on it. "So, see, in case we miss each other, or it gets crowded here on the steps, right?"

She blushed. He talked so much and so fast. And the faster he talked, the harder it was to understand him. She finally whispered, "Elena. My name is Elena." And with that, she buzzed herself into the museum staff door. When she turned back, she could see him through the glass. He waved.

*

Sparks flew as Uncle Uldis and Fedya argued. After ten years, Fedya was nearly fluent in Latvian, but his native Russian would creep in when he was tired or became angry, like now.

"You're not listening to me, Uncle."

"You only have one more year before you graduate. Why would you jeopardize everything we have worked for by missing classes and skipping your studio time?"

Fedya wearied of the same old argument. His uncle's voice droned on and on about what Fedya should do or wasn't doing or could be doing. Blah, blah, blah. He laid his head on the back of the couch and scrolled through his messages.

"Fyodor, please look at me when I'm speaking to you. You're almost there. You love the music."

"I have more than a year to go—"

"And speak in Latvian, for God's sake," Uldis said.

"Fine. I have a full year and a half, and it feels like forever. No, I should be auditioning. Plus, I have the band. We are good. We are making money. I need no more training right now."

"You are speaking like a braggart. How many hours did you put in today?"

This argument was going downhill fast. Fedya could hear Uldis's voice getting louder and louder. He lied, "Four hours this morning. I still have studio time this afternoon. All right?" His phone buzzed, and he saw Daina's name appear. *Oh shit,* he thought. *I was supposed to meet her for lunch.*

"I've got to go," Fedya said, as he grabbed his backpack off the floor.

"Dinner is at Ausma's place, nineteen hundred hours. She is cooking Russian tonight. Don't be late."

"I have a gig tonight. I'll eat with the band."

"It's your sister's birthday, Fedya. Or, perhaps being around for Elena means nothing to you anymore. I can remember a time when you risked your life for her."

Fedya, almost out the door, turned. "Don't manipulate me, Uncle. I'm no child and I can make my own choices."

He slammed the door on his way out and thundered down the stairs. But his uncle's words hit hard. After their mother died, when he and Elena had tried to survive on their own, they were close then. His love for Elena and Irina and his promises to his dying mother had driven him. But it was never enough. He had failed, despite all his "trying" to save them. After he turned them in to the orphanage, he thought everything would be better on his own. But it wasn't. He pushed those painful memories away once again—the rape and humiliation, the beatings from the madman Yegor, and all the running, endless running.

And then there was Irina, his little sister. He didn't think about her much anymore. No point. Once all their leads went dead and Putin's government jailed their former benefactor, Stepanoff, they lost hope. It was easier to let Irina die along with his mother. The little girl would be a teenager by now, and if an American adopted her, as they assumed or hoped, then she would be living the big life. Besides, she was so young when they were together, she wouldn't even remember him, or the hunger, or the cold. No, he had to let go of her. If only Elena would do the same and stop bringing her up.

He pulled his knit hat over his head and shoved his hands into his pockets. He loved the music. But it was different now. He couldn't explain it to his uncle. From the first time he had touched his uncle's grand piano, Fedya had wanted to make music more than anything else. And so, Uncle Uldis taught him and pushed him, and Fedya made it into the conservatory. But for the past year, the school drained the joy out of him. Uncle had insisted Fedya be classically trained and said the modern stuff would develop later. Everything was always "later." Fedya didn't want to wait any longer.

Fedya had composed two songs he thought were good enough to sell. He needed the right voice to sing them, which is where Daina came in. Today, he planned to take her out for lunch, ask her to record the songs, and then meet at Edgar's to make a rough cut. He wanted to tell Uncle his plans for the recordings, but he dreaded his uncle's negativity. He texted Daina and told her to meet him at the café and apologized for being late. She sent back a kissy emoji.

Maybe he could bring Daina to Ausma's for the birthday dinner. Ausma always cooked more than enough food. Elena's birthday. Crap! He forgot. Maybe Daina could help him pick out something. He texted Ausma and asked if Daina could come to the dinner, explained they had to leave by 20:30 to get to the club in time for his first set at 21:30. Ausma could smooth anything over. He never understood why Ausma hadn't married his uncle. Despite their ten-year difference, she looked younger than Uncle and more vibrant. She had a few more lines, but they were lines of love. Ausma had become the mother he lost over ten years ago.

A tram pulled to a stop and Fedya grabbed it to ride the next three stops, even though he usually walked. The cold slithered into his jacket. As the tram approached the last stop before the Vansu Bridge, Fedya hopped off, walked across the bridge, and into the old city.

One thing Fedya knew for sure, he was dropping out of the conservatory. But it wouldn't do to tell his uncle tonight, not on Elena's birthday. When she found out, she would give him another earful. Either way, he knew one thing for sure: he didn't want to be a classical pianist. Not anymore. He had the right to choose. Yes, Uncle saved their lives. Yes,

Fedya owed him so much, but how long did he have to be grateful? He wanted to move on with his life. He could still become famous. But, unlike Uldis, who knew fame within the circle of the symphony and classical music enthusiasts, Fedya wanted household fame. He wanted to be a star. Why not?

*

Ausma surveyed the table and pronounced it less than perfect but serviceable. When Fedya had texted with the request to bring his new friend along, she worried there might not be enough food and sent Uldis out to get some carrots she could roast and then toss together a few tomatoes and cucumbers for a second salad. Uldis had teased her, saying the Latvian girl Fedya dated was quite skinny, and he doubted she would eat much. But Ausma preferred to be over-prepared. She was the same with her instrument. In fact, she looked at her harp lovingly and wished she could review her solo a few more times before bedtime. But with the younger people there, she doubted she would have the opportunity.

Her mobile chirped. Elena was calling. When she checked the time, nearly eighteen hundred hours, Ausma assumed Elena should be on her way. *Surely, she isn't canceling.*

"Ausma? I need your advice," Elena jumped right in.

"All right. But only if you remember you don't have to take it. So, what can I do for you?"

"I met someone today for five minutes on the tram, an Australian, and well, he seems nice, and he asked me out for coffee after work, and I'm sure it would include food, but I'm thinking it wouldn't be smart to go somewhere with someone I hardly know, so I thought it might be safer to bring him to the dinner tonight. What do you think?"

Stunned into silence, Ausma didn't know what to say. Elena rarely went out on dates and was usually tentative with men. For her to take such a leap was astounding. Ausma guessed this kind of spontaneity happened because of her birthday, getting older, and her brother always having a beautiful girl on his arm. Uldis might be uneasy with a stranger, but honestly, in some ways, Elena was right. Safety in numbers.

"All right. Why not? I'll set another plate. Your brother's coming and he's bringing a date. Oh dear, I've forgotten her name, maybe Dace or Dagnija—"

"Daina, it's Daina, the singer. He must be up to something if he's hanging out with her. She's a reset after Urzula. If worse comes to worse, we can throw Danny and Daina together."

Ausma laughed and once they hung up, she scurried around, making more room at the table.

"Who was that?" Uldis asked as he came into the front room, buttoning his shirt.

"Lenushka called. Believe it or not, we now have a proper party and both of your children, well, they're not children anymore. Both of your protégés are bringing dates, one nearly a blind one."

"I don't understand. Elena is bringing a blind man?"

"No, no. Uldis, you are so literal. Let's say he's like a mystery date. Now, finish getting dressed. You forgot to put on your trousers."

He looked down, and when he looked back at Ausma, they exchanged a smile. He was becoming quite an absent-minded professor. As he shambled out, she wondered if he would tell his news to the children. She would always see them as the same children they were when they came to live in Rīga. But would he tell them he had accepted a teaching position at the conservatory where Fedya was going? Uldis wouldn't leave the symphony, no, neither of them would unless forced to retire, but the added income would be a godsend. Living in the city had become more and more expensive. She pondered again if they should combine households.

The pros and cons were many. His flat was a little bigger, with two bedrooms and an extra-large living area that accommodated his piano, a kitchenette and table, plus a full bath. Hers only had one bedroom, but a full-sized kitchen and bathroom. While her living area was sizeable, it was not as spacious as his. Often, they had to use the pop-up coffee table for dining when guests came. Uldis lived on the third floor, which worked fine for him, but if they put her harp in there, she'd hate to move it up and down those stairs. Best of all, her flat was in the old city, which she loved. He didn't care about the location one bit. *What to do, what to do?*

Elena and her new friend arrived first since it was less than a ten-minute walk from the museum. Only when the young man walked in did

Ausma remember how rusty her English had become. Uldis's would not be much better.

"How do you do?" Ausma said as she held out her hand.

"Charmed, I'm sure," he said, and a smile blossomed on his face. He appeared so disarming despite his size. No wonder Elena liked him.

"This is Aidan, but his familiar name is Danny," Elena said, as Uldis walked in. "This is my Uncle Uldis. He is like a father to me."

Elena put an arm around her uncle's waist, which he accepted readily, and Ausma surmised this was a way Elena established who held her affection. The two men shook hands, and Uldis directed him to an armchair.

Elena said, "Danny only speaks English, so I'll ask him to slow down."

"Righto. I suppose I do speak a little Koori which some tribes speak, but that's not very useful up north here," he laughed. Uldis looked perplexed.

"Let me take your outer coat," Ausma said.

"Here in Latvia, we take off our shoes and put on these little *tapochki*. It's a custom," Elena said.

"Oh, all right, love, but I'll be surprised if you have a pair that fit my big hoofers."

Once everyone settled, a small silence descended.

"Danny is an ice hockey player," Elena said. But then she realized no one in their family did sports except to watch them occasionally.

"Oh," Uncle Uldis said. "You are a professional?"

"Yes, more or less. There aren't many teams, you see? I mean, it never gets as cold at home as it is here already. So, we come up to the Northern Hemisphere to train."

In this way, the conversation stumbled along, but Danny had many social graces and never seemed embarrassed or uncomfortable. All the same, she was grateful when Fedya arrived, even if he brought Daina.

"What's this? A stranger in our midst?" Fedya said in Latvian.

"English, English," Ausma said. "We will all respect our guest and include him in our talking."

"Hello. My name is Daina."

"Wow, you have great English," Danny said.

"Yes, I'm hoping to become an English interpreter, and I also sing mostly in English."

And in no time at all, Daina had taken Danny under her wing. Elena watched Fedya and, as she had suspected, theirs was not a love match, but one of convenience. Ausma passed out drinks and soon they were sitting around the coffee table—raised now to accommodate dining—and enjoying Ausma's wonderful cooking. Danny complimented everything, and Daina helped translate when he spoke too fast or used words most of them couldn't catch.

Finally, when Ausma brought out the coffee and torte, only then did Danny realize the occasion was Elena's birthday. He proposed a toast and said, "Here's to celebrating you today! May the koalas and kangaroos bring extra joy to your birthday." Everyone laughed and cheered, and a certain familial warmth spread through the group. Danny didn't even blink twice when he noticed Uncle Uldis only drank sparkling water in his wine glass. Elena was having a lovely birthday dinner and then Uncle stood to make his announcements.

He clanked his glass with a fork, and everyone gave him attention. "We are having such a fine evening; it's a wonderful time to tell you my news. Number one: I have bought us a car!" They all applauded. Elena couldn't believe it. She had always wanted to learn how to drive one and Fedya, too. "We have depended on Ausma's car so much, I thought it was time to give her little car a vacation. Plus, I felt I might afford it more readily because," and he took a breath here, "The conservatory director has asked me to join the faculty. What do you think, Fedya? We'll be walking the same halls together, and I can even drive you occasionally when our classes coincide."

"That's wonderful, Uncle Uldis," Elena said, but when she turned to Fedya, she saw a darkness come over his face. She also saw Daina grab his hand under the table. She felt trouble before she heard another word spoken.

Fedya said, "Uncle Uldis, this is not the time to have a discussion, but you will find out sooner than later. I have taken a leave of absence from the conservatory."

Elena knew her uncle would not take this news well, and the smoldering anger could explode any moment. *I can't believe he's ruining my birthday again. He could have waited.*

Uncle's tirade started with calling Fedya an idiot and it went down from there. And not for a mere minute, but for nearly five minutes, he roared and exclaimed and tortured all of them with his yelling and gesticulating. When Elena looked at Danny, she realized everyone had given up on English. He held his hands lightly together and looked at his feet. So embarrassing.

Finally, Fedya stood up and calmly signaled for Daina to get her coat. When he spoke, it was in a cruel kind of coldness. "Ausma, thank you for the lovely dinner. Uncle Uldis, thank you for everything you have done for me. I will only come back to the flat to retrieve my clothes and a few of my things. I am not a child, and I will take responsibility for my choices. From now on, I refuse to feel guilty for playing and writing the kind of music I want to create."

"Fedya," Elena stood up. "Please don't do this."

Uncle Uldis grabbed the wine bottle and poured himself a drink, something he had not done for the last nine or ten years.

"Uldis," Ausma stood up too.

"Oh, that's fine," Fedya said. "I knew you were always a weak man, but this is unparalleled. Now you can blame me for your slide. I won't stop you this time. Drink yourself to death for all I care."

Fedya grabbed his jacket and left, Daina trailing as she mouthed an "I'm sorry."

Instead of drinking the wine, Uncle threw it at the door, shattering the fine crystal into hundreds of pieces. Ausma collapsed and wept while Danny stooped down to pick up the shards.

CHAPTER 7
BALTIMORE, MARYLAND
Monday Afternoon

"Thanks for fitting us into your schedule, Madelyn," Susan said and smiled at Madelyn Rescate who had been Susan's therapist for nearly fifteen years and Annie's for the past seven.

"No problem. Annie's in the waiting room?"

"Yes, I wanted to talk to you first. I believe we are at a crisis point, but I need to confess something."

"All right."

"I've withheld some vital information from you about Annie, and me, and her adoption. You remember the little picture I had of Anya before Tom died? She was my talisman. She was a gift from God. But the little girl in the picture," Susan paused, "she died during my second trip, right after the court hearing where they signed her over to me. And then there was this other little girl who could have been Anya's twin, and so I convinced them, and paid them, to let me take her instead. Totally illegal. Anyway, the orphanage staff had all kinds of concerns about this substitute child, but I refused to hear any of it."

Susan stopped speaking as tears and memories flooded over her. She looked at Madelyn for a reaction. Nothing. Madelyn was the ultimate professional. She had been a psychotherapist for over thirty years, mostly in private practice. Everything she said was simple, but measured.

"Go on," Madelyn said.

"For this reason, whenever Annie struggled, I often heard a little voice in my head remind me of the orphanage director's warnings. I am grateful for everything you have done to help me and to help her as we navigated through her emotional turmoil. I had been so sure our beautiful

41

house and neighborhood, the perfect dog, my vibrant church family, and all the prayers and prophecies, would work out. Tom was watching over us. God was watching over us. We had all the comforts and yet, Annie wandered around in a cocoon of silence, carrying around those boy and girl dolls for years, not to mention the little blue stuffed cat. Anyway, thanks to you and Kate, we got her through it, and things stabilized, until they didn't."

Susan continued. "You said adoptees often go through seven- year cycles. Well, that's where we are. And now, apparently, Annie found my 'tell-all' journals from my time in St. Petersburg. She's so upset. So angry. To her, it's a monumental betrayal. I've failed her. But I swore to keep our arrangement secret. I don't know if it matters anymore. Legally, I mean. But it matters to her."

Madelyn sat quietly in her blue armchair as Susan wept, wiped her tears, and then wept again.

Susan added, "Annie wants to go back to Russia. She thinks she has siblings. She wants to find them. But we can't. We can't do that."

"I understand. Do you need another minute? I'd like to bring Annie in to join us."

Madelyn paused.

"You must remember, Susan, every child, whether by birth or by adoption, brings challenges. For some families, it's physical health issues and for others, its mental instabilities. We cannot know what is happening inside her head. Your Annie has always had an uncanny set of images or memories, if you will, despite being adopted at a young age. It's like a little movie inside her head. She has spoken to me before about these supposed siblings, and honestly, it may be true. But she is not the first child to have left a family back in the home country by being adopted. Now she is older, she must integrate yet another truth, more loss and grief if she can never find her siblings."

"All right. I'm as ready as I'll ever be."

When Annie came into the office, she slumped onto the opposite end of the couch. Annie liked Dr. Madelyn well enough. She had learned early on she couldn't shock Dr. Madelyn with her words, so eventually, they had come to a meeting of the minds, a kind of plateau that excluded her mother.

"Is she staying?" Annie asked as she pointed at her mother.

"She doesn't have to, but I thought talking to each other with my third ear might help you both listen better. I believe you're upset because your mother held back a big secret about how you were adopted. Perhaps a sense of betrayal?"

"No kidding."

"But tell me, Annie, what is it you want today?" Madelyn asked.

"I want to find my sister and brother."

"But why now? According to your mother, you found out months ago. You never mentioned it."

"I don't know. I've always thought I had to be ashamed of being Russian. But now, maybe it's the only cool thing about me. And my brother and sister, they're my real family—"

"But honey, we don't even know if they exist," Susan interrupted.

"Hold on, Susan. Annie, what makes you so sure you have a brother and sister? According to Susan, the orphanage never indicated there were siblings."

Annie sulked. *Awesome, that's just great*, she thought. *Nobody's on my side*. As much as she had liked Dr. Madelyn in the past, neither of them understood what Annie felt in her heart. She remembered the mantra she had said before bed every night: *"Fedya and Elena. Elena and Fedya Lebedev."* For some of those years, she had forgotten what the words even meant. But then, in sixth grade, she looked them up. Names, they were Russian names and the word Lebedev meant "swan." She was a Swan, not a Spencer at all.

The session went on like that, Dr. Madelyn asking questions, while her mother interrupted and cried a lot. Annie didn't cry. One good thing, the Saturday night disaster had moved to the back seat. Susan had already grounded her for six weeks, anyway. Luckily, Susan hadn't moved on the threat of pulling her out of the public high school…yet.

Unbeknownst to her mother, Annie had a bigger concern: she couldn't find her friends. When they didn't show up at school today, she borrowed a girl's cell phone in homeroom to call River, the only phone number she knew by heart, but no answer. After school, and before the appointment, she walked over to the Towers to ring their doorbells, but two police cars stood outside the front doors, so Annie changed her mind, and walked home. She couldn't help but wonder if something had gone wrong for them at the mobile party, too. Or worse, Annie's getaway had caused a problem for River.

On the way home after Dr. Madelyn's session, neither one of them said much. Annie knew, no matter what she might say, her mother would either defend herself or cry again. Silence was better for now. Snow began to fall, and Annie wondered if Tuesday might turn into a snow day, which might make it even harder to reach out to the girls. What she needed was computer time to send out messages to River, LaShonda, and Shelly. No chance of that with the "no screen" rule still in force.

When her mother suggested they order pizza, Annie was fine with that.

They sat at the long white quartz counter with a large pepperoni pizza between them and watched the local news on the little kitchen TV. So often, if there was a bad report or tragedy, and in Baltimore, violence occurred every day, her mother would say a heartfelt prayer out loud. *So cheesy.*

But the newscast jerked Annie out of her thoughts about her friends when an on-the-scene reporter stood in front of the Towers and recounted how the police had found a teenager who lived there, dead, in a dumpster early that morning. They showed a school picture with her name underneath: Shelly Everett, aged seventeen, senior at Towson High School.

"Oh my God," Annie said.

Her mother turned to her. "You know her?"

"Of course I know her. She went to my school," Annie said. "I'm going to be sick."

Thirty minutes later, the front doorbell rang. When Annie went to answer it, her mother on her heels, they found Officers Moore, Lancaster, and, of all people, Lukyan Buzinsky.

Once they sat down and Susan went through the niceties of offering coffee or water, which they all declined, Lancaster started the interview.

"Annie, Mrs. Spencer? This is Detective Buzinsky. I believe you know each other. I only found out today his grandparents were Russian, and he still speaks the language."

"Yes, we've met," Susan said. "But it's been a while. Nice to see you again, Luke. Congratulations on your promotion."

Luke grinned. "Yes. Thanks. Maybe it's been five years?" he said as he shook hands with Susan, holding her hand a little longer than necessary. To Annie, he said in Russian, "*Zdravstvuyte*," Hello.

She whispered, "*Privet*," back to him. She blushed.

Although Luke was much older than Maks, probably as old as her mother, maybe even in his forties, he was still handsome. Annie had been too young to appreciate his good looks back in the day when he took her, Aunt Kate, and Susan to the Russian Festivals in Baltimore and D.C. He probably worked out in a gym or something. He was certainly dark and mysterious, like Maks, with black hair and brown eyes. He hadn't shaved recently either, so he was a little scruffy. Like detectives on TV, he didn't wear a uniform, just an anorak over a sweater and jeans. Annie noticed all of this in seconds, but her attention swiveled to Officer Jaqui who started the questioning in earnest.

"We're here to follow up on last Saturday night and to talk to you about Shelly Everett," Jaqui said. "She's a friend of yours, right?"

They know. They know I was Shelly's friend. How? I'm not ready to talk about her. I only found out an hour ago. How did they find out I was her friend?

Susan watched her daughter's body shrink away from the officers, then jumped into the conversation.

"Is she one of the girls you went out with over the weekend?" Susan asked. Annie gave her a glare. "Don't look at me like that. You gave me a terrible scare and now, here are the police, and that girl's picture is on the news, and you said nothing to me—as though it didn't matter how all of this might have happened. Annie, you must tell the police everything you know."

"Mrs. Spencer," Jaqui said, "please, we are grateful, and of course, we want you to be part of this interview, but we need to hear from Annie herself. It's important. If you could simply listen for now, we will have questions for you too."

"Me? All right. Of course. Sorry, I'm sorry."

Annie got up from the chair without a word and rushed off to the bathroom. Jaqui looked befuddled.

"She's going to be sick. It's a reaction to stress. It's like her body can't hold it all in and it must come out somehow. Let me check on her," Susan said.

She went to the powder room and knocked softly. "Annie, honey, can I get you something?"

"Go away. Give me a minute, can you?"

Susan returned to the living room and sat on a straight-backed chair.

Jaqui said, "Mrs. Spencer, we need to continue. Perhaps we'll start with you. Had you met Shelly Everett?"

"No, not really. I only met one girl, River Smyth. Annie ran with a little clique of four. Another girl's name is LaShonda West. I'm pretty sure all three girls live at the Towers. Oh, God, this is so terrible."

"Yes, ma'am. Has Annie seen the girls after Saturday night?" Lancaster asked.

"No, I grounded her. Unless she saw them at school today."

Jaqui and Lancaster looked at each other, somehow knowingly, then Lancaster said, "No ma'am, the girls haven't been at school either. We think they bolted because of Shelly. They probably know something, but don't want to get involved. We're hoping they contacted your daughter, maybe by text?"

"Annie doesn't have a cell phone and part of being grounded is no screens, except at school or for school. I can't control all of it. How was this girl killed?"

"We can't discuss that, sorry."

Luke, who had been silent but watchful, sat up. "Susan, I'm here with a slightly different angle. But related. You see, my department has reason to believe these girls were caught up in trafficking. In recent months, we've had several girls snatched from neighborhoods, many of them Russian, but not all. Mostly, the girls come from the poorer areas of the city where they might be influenced by the prospect of making a quick buck or a gaining a sympathetic ear."

"Oh my God. That's dreadful."

"Yes. It's difficult to catch them in the act, as they say, to have actual evidence to pick up the men who groom these girls. If we pick up a girl, she won't talk. They protect the guys who are grooming them, good-looking young men who make the girls feel beautiful or smart."

"Yes, I've heard of these things at my church. Our women's group supports an agency that helps rescue such girls. But that's in Florida or California, not here."

"Anyway," Luke continued, "since Annie apparently attended one of these parties and survived, we believe she could be in some danger down the road. We'd like to keep an eye on her, but at her age, it's more difficult, plus we don't have enough detectives—"

Susan interrupted him. "You're scaring me."

"Mrs. Spencer, I'm sorry to upset you. We're trying to be proactive here. That's why we brought Detective Buzinsky along," Jaqui said.

"There is probably nothing to worry about. I'd like a little extra protection for your family. How would you feel about a retired K-9?" Luke asked.

"But those dogs are aggressive," Susan said, wrapping her arms around her shoulders.

"Only when they're working. They usually live with families the rest of the time and are wonderful pets. I'd be willing to help orient her to you both."

"Luke, you know some of Annie's story. I'm not sure it's a good idea. She's not like other girls, she's troubled—"

Susan saw the detective look over her shoulder and realized Annie had come back into the living room.

"Gee thanks, Mother. Maybe you should give them the name of my shrink next."

"Honey—"

Susan knew she had put up another wall between them. Each day, the wall got higher and thicker. Whatever gains they had made over the past seven years with Madelyn were being eroded away.

Maybe a new dog isn't a bad idea. Sebastian helped to bring Annie out of her shell as a child. But a police dog?

She watched Annie sit rigidly on the edge of the stuffed chair. Annie closed her eyes to prepare for the first question. At least, that's what Susan thought she was doing. But honestly, did she know her own daughter?

Annie never behaved or reacted the way other girls would. Even when she came out of her silent period, she never jabbered or danced around the living room like other little girls. Annie seemed like a coiled snake, ready to strike, always on the defensive. She hated crowds and often vomited on the street if she couldn't get away soon enough. She lived with anxiety every day. The girl never played with Barbie dolls like other little girls, just the Russian ones she received back in St. Petersburg. And yet, she loved to be outside. She was always a bit of a tomboy, which Susan didn't mind, but it never developed into anything athletic. The few times she tried to put Annie in a team sport, she stood around looking bewildered. Making friends was nearly impossible. Susan assumed Annie said or did the wrong things around kids her own age all the time, and as a result, they labeled her as weird. Annie's natural expressions ranged from somewhere between neutral to a frown. Right now, her expression, on the frown side, had frozen in place.

Jaqui said, "I'm truly sorry about your friend Annie. I know this has been a real shock. But I must tell you, Shelly didn't die by accident. This is a murder investigation."

Annie's hands flew up to her mouth, almost forcing it to remain closed. Her head shook slowly at first, but then more quickly, like she was trying to shake something out of her mind.

"Did you see what happened?" Jaqui asked, then left a space for Annie to answer. "You're not in trouble, you know. But hey, when we found you, you were pretty upset. You looked like something bad had happened to you. Can you tell us today what happened?"

Annie shook her hand in front of Jaqui to stop the woman from talking. Susan knew what the frenetic hand shaking meant. It was the "I can't talk" gesture.

"Did someone hurt you, honey? Please tell us. Did—did a man hurt you?" Jaqui said.

Susan stood. She wanted to scream. Her mouth went dry. But Annie shook one hand again and then the other one. Susan feared Annie might have an acute stress reaction and shut down any minute. Frozen. Annie was signaling them to stop asking, stop talking, just stop. But they were doing their jobs. Susan imagined the worst. Rape came to mind. My God, she should have taken Annie to the hospital.

Susan turned to Officer Jaqui. "Did you take her to the hospital? Did anyone think to do that? Did... did... did someone—?"

"Mrs. Spencer, please," Lancaster said again.

"Susan, it's better they ask these questions here than down at the station," Luke said.

Jaqui continued speaking, but to Annie. "We want to find the girls who were with you, Annie, that's all. We know you didn't see them at school today, because we checked. Do you have any idea where they might have gone?"

Annie shook her head.

"Did they try to contact you in any way?"

Another shake.

Luke asked, "Excuse me, Jaqui. I'd like to step in here. Susan, may I speak to Annie in Russian?"

"Why?" Susan asked. She noticed Jaqui's eye roll at her partner.

"It might make it easier to talk," Luke said as he turned to Annie. In Russian, he asked, "You understand me, right?"

She nodded.

"Did you hear any Russian that night? Did anyone speak Russian?"

Annie shrugged her shoulders, then whispered, "*Da.*"

"Do you think you could recognize any of the people you saw that night? I have some pictures I'd like to show you," Luke said, still in Russian. He pulled a folder out and handed it to her. She took it from him and flipped through the pictures quickly. She hesitated twice, then pulled out only one picture.

"Maybe this one," she answered. It was the guy with the long ponytail who had given her the number seven.

"What about this one?" Luke asked, still in Russian.

It's Maks, she thought. But that can't be right. He was nice to me. He said we had a connection.

She started hiccupping. She hated this reaction, and it rarely came upon her, but when it did, she suffered for several hours. Once it happened at the Academy and they sent her home from school. For days after that, kids would pretend to hiccup when they saw her in the halls.

"Can you tell us where you were Saturday night? Where the party was, I mean?" Luke asked. He had switched to English.

She mumbled back in English, in between hiccups. "Look, I don't know, Okay?" Hiccup. "Not really. I get claustrophobic, you see. You can ask my mother." Hiccup. "I had to get out of there and I ran until I found a street I recognized." Hiccup. "I'm sorry. I'm very sorry. I don't know anything." She cried then and covered her face with a throw pillow, muffling her hiccups.

"Can you please give her a break? This will go on for a while. It's stress," Susan said.

"All right, Mrs. Spencer," Lancaster said, "that's enough for now. We're on separate tracks, anyway. Officer Moore and I are looking into the murder and Detective Buzinsky is on a task force to follow leads on a human trafficking operation. We'll need to talk to you again separately. We'll be in touch." The two officers stood to go, and Luke followed reluctantly.

"Susan, what do you say about that idea of getting a guard dog?" Luke said.

Annie swiveled to Luke. "What dog?"

Susan gave Luke a withering look, but he plowed on, taking advantage of what he remembered was Annie's affection for their first dog.

"This dog I'm talking about isn't like Sebastian," Luke said. "She's a retired K-9, so she's super smart and knows all kinds of tricks."

Annie turned to Susan, her eyes saying everything.

"Oh God, I hope I don't regret this," Susan said, and stood

"When?" Annie said. Hiccup. "When can you bring her over?"

"Maybe Saturday?"

Annie nodded. Susan noted that the other two officers looked on with what appeared to be disapproval.

Lancaster said, "We'd better head out. We'll be in touch. Thanks, Annie. Mrs. Spencer."

Susan followed them to the door while Annie waited at the foot of the stairs, still hiccupping.

Jaqui stopped and turned before leaving. "One more question, Annie. How'd you get to the party?"

"What?"

"How'd you get there? The girls. The four of you. All together? Separately?"

"A friend of a friend." Hiccup. "He picked all of us up at the bowling alley."

"The Round One, in Towson? What time?" Lancaster asked.

"Yeah. At nine. Right at nine."

"Okay," Jaqui said. "Good job. Thanks. Hope you feel better, honey."

Luke shook Susan's hand and spoke quietly to her in the doorway, but Annie couldn't catch his words. He might have said coffee. She wasn't sure.

She heard Lancaster say to his partner as they waited for the detective, "I'll check for security footage." And all Annie could think was she might have given away Maks all the same.

He had been so nice to me. And he was so good looking. He wouldn't have hurt anyone. But what happened after I left? Did some other man corner Shelly the way the fat man grabbed me? Did she fight back and say no? And what about River and LaShonda? They were older, bigger. They could fight. If they wanted to.

Annie couldn't get her head around anything as she headed up the stairs to her room, still hiccupping. She hadn't thought about her friends while she was running away. Whatever happened to them might have been her fault, like everything else.

She stood at the top of the stairs where her mother had hung family pictures. Sebastian, that goofy fluffy white mutt, was in most of the pictures with Annie. She took down the last picture they had of him, wearing bunny ears at the church's egg hunt, and carried it into her room. Everyone loved Sebastian, but not as much as she did. Sebastian never cared how many mistakes she made. Hiccup.

She wasn't sure she could love another dog as much as she loved Sebastian. But right now, she was willing to try.

CHAPTER 8
RĪGA, LATVIA
Same Night as Elena's Birthday Dinner

Fedya sat on his bed in Uncle's flat. Daina had wanted to help him pack since he would stay with her for a while, but he told her he needed to be alone. Daina huffed about that. Somehow, it didn't matter what he said; it was always the wrong thing. By the time he had taken the tram from Ausma's and walked the last six or seven blocks, his anger had abated. He wasn't even sure why he got so angry. *No, not true.* He knew. Anger was a placeholder for not pleasing his uncle, for not sticking with classical piano, for not appreciating everything others had done for him. He didn't like those feelings. Anger was easier.

He looked around the room and remembered the first time he saw it ten years ago, floor to ceiling publicity pictures of Uncle Uldis's piano playing from all over the world. Uncle stood with dignitaries and other famous musicians that, as a child, Fedya couldn't have imagined their importance. But now, he knew his uncle had been on the brink of international stardom when his wife and children were killed by a Chechen bomb in Moscow. Uncle's world collapsed. But Fedya's world had collapsed as well when his mother died. Where Uncle climbed down into the hole of his flat and nearly drank himself to death, Fedya had to keep going and try to take care of his sisters. Neither one of them, not Uncle nor Fedya, had done a very good job.

Fedya lay back on his bed and stared at the plaster ceiling and its many cracks. The ceiling had become a metaphor for his life. No matter how many times his uncle repaired it, the cracks returned. Nothing worked. No true healing was possible. Supposedly, he was an adult now, but inside, he still felt like the kid who rang Uncle's doorbell looking for a savior. Who would save him now?

53

Originally, he thought the music might save him the way it ultimately rescued his uncle. When Uncle Uldis finally returned to the piano, his recovery began in earnest. But Fedya could not explain how differently the music spoke to him. Yes, the classics were beautiful. He even respected the masters. But the joy had disappeared. Over the years, he had watched his uncle play, day in and day out, and often, he saw ecstasy on the man's face. Fedya had felt it, too. But when had the intoxication stopped?

Maybe three years earlier. The night he and Elena had talked into the night over shots of vodka when their uncle was out of town on tour. It was his twentieth birthday. Elena, already tipsy, began confessing, as many drunks do.

"I have a secret, Fedya. Do you want to know a secret?"

"You don't have to tell me your secrets, Elena. As soon as you tell me, it's not a secret anymore."

Elena put her finger to her lips and leaned close to her brother where they sat on the floor, their backs up against his bed. As she whispered to him, Fedya's mind wandered back to another time he sat on a floor drinking teacups of vodka with Zoya. He had hated Zoya and loved her all at the same time. She had pulled him out of the worst of it in the end, but she had also ruined him. Those dreadful movies. And then she died at the hand of a madman, the same one who almost killed him and Elena.

"Fedya, you're not listening to me."

"Yes, yes, I am. You are telling me secrets."

"Well, this one is the biggest of all: I still write to Irishka. I bet you didn't know that, did you?"

"What do you mean?"

"Just that. I write letters to her as though I know where she is and describe our lives and how lucky we are to live in a nice flat with plenty of food and clothes, and music. I tell her how beautifully you play the piano and how I have been living my dream too, to dance in the ballet."

He grunted. "What's the point? She'll never see them."

"But someday. I still believe."

"You are in the clouds. I knew we would never see her again when the old man, Vasiliy, died."

"He wasn't so old. He drank too much and ate too much. Did I ever tell you he loved our mother?"

"Too little, too late." He shook his head. Fedya didn't like to ponder "what ifs," they only caused heartache.

"I thought Stepanov would still help us, even after Vasiliy died. But then they arrested him like all the rest of Putin's old cronies who were no longer useful," Elena said.

Fedya used to think fondly of their homeland, of Mother Russia, but as Putin gained power and the oligarchs divided up the spoils, Fedya lost hope. And poor Stepanov, even he was too small to fight the Moscow machine. Despite everything, Stepanov had had a conscience, even a heart.

"Do you believe Stepanov is still alive? I mean, in prison?" Elena asked her brother.

"I don't know, and I don't care. Nothing ever works out the way we want it to. Listen, Elena, yes, we have a better life, but it's been a bit of a fake."

"Why do you say that?"

"I don't know. The music is not real anymore. It's Uncle's music, but it's not mine."

"You're being ridiculous. You are very good."

"Yes, but Elena, don't you see? It's not reaching my heart. There is no color. Oh, never mind, you're too young to understand."

"That's bull. You don't want to work hard."

"Shut up! What do you know?"

His temper had broken up their little party back then, like it did to-night. When the door to his bedroom opened, it startled him. He must have fallen asleep. Elena stood there, staring at him.

"Don't be angry with me, Elena."

She said nothing.

"I was thinking of Irishka," he said. "She's dead to us, you know. She has a life. It's time we moved on to live our lives."

"I don't believe you. Irina is not in your thoughts. You only think about yourself. Our lost sister is not some dream, like being a prima ballerina or a concert pianist. Finding our sister is part of who I am. I send out my energy to her. I pray to God. I do it because I believe. And every time you say these negative things, you put holes in the net I'm sending out. So, stop it. These other dreams, the ones about our future, may have to die or change. I understand that. I mean, I know I won't reach my ballerina dream, but I will never let go of Irishka."

"Wait, what?" He sat up to look at her. "You're giving up dance?"

"You believe you are the only one who considers the future, the only one who may have to reshape a dream. You can't see past yourself, Fedya. You were cruel tonight, big brother. And you ruined my birthday, again." She left the room and closed his door with a quiet finality.

Elena was shutting him out, and he couldn't blame her. He deserved it. He got up and finished packing his bag. As he stepped into the main room, Uncle's grand piano called to him. He tried to ignore her siren call but couldn't. So, he sat, and once more, played the music that calmed his soul, his own music. After a long while, he finished, stood, and headed toward the front door of the flat. Elena's bedroom door opened. He turned, and she said, "I love you." He nodded, raised his hand in farewell, and she watched him go.

CHAPTER 9
TOWSON, MARYLAND
Wednesday, Same Week
as Police Visit to the House

The day shone brightly, and Susan appreciated living in balmy Maryland. She sat in her pastor's office, the winter sun filling the room with late afternoon light.

Pastor Charles sat in his wingback while she and Jake, who had insisted they attend the meeting together, sat apart on the office couch. In truth, Susan found Pastor's office tacky with a dense array of framed scripture verses on the walls along with his diplomas. Several large potted plants dotted the floor; she resisted touching them to determine if they were real. They were all so perfect, just like Pastor Charles seemed to be. She guessed his wife had done the decorating.

After Pastor Charles prayed at length, Jake took it upon himself to recount Annie's latest escapades.

"Can I jump in here?" Susan said. "I think the important thing is to help Annie navigate this situation. As you know, throughout the last ten years, she has struggled with a variety of post-traumatic behaviors. Now, with the death of one of her friends, I'm afraid she might do something drastic."

"Friends," Jake said, "those girls are out of control. No wonder one of them surrendered to the pressures of evil—"

Susan spoke over him, "I know the girls weren't the best choice in friends, but they were the first set of buddies Annie has ever had. My daughter has never made connections easily, which was one reason I didn't close her off from them altogether. Maybe I should have been stricter. It's so hard to know."

Pastor broke in. "You surprised me when you took Annie out of our school last August. High school is not an easy time, and public schools are particularly immoral."

"I'm sorry, but she had difficulties with several students at the academy."

Jake scooted closer and patted her knee as he spoke to her. "High school is different." Then to Pastor, he said, "I tried to counsel Susan against pulling Annie out of our school."

"Yes, indeedy," Pastor said. "Jake and I both agree that Annie needs more safeguards, which our small high school could provide. This may be a good time to reconsider your decision."

"All right, please, I had my reasons. Other students bullied her, for God's sake, and in a Christian school? Explain that if you can."

The pastor raised his hands to her in surrender.

"Fine. Look," Susan said, "can we move on? I made a choice, and I stand by it. But I have two other pressing concerns that could benefit from true discernment. Isn't that what you do here?"

Pastor leaned forward over the coffee table and placed his hand on the Bible. "Yes, yes, of course. We're listening and God is listening," Pastor Charles said.

"Amen," Jake added.

Susan couldn't understand why everything these men said today irritated her. She had always loved Pastor's sermons, so full of certainty and direction and confidence. But today, his attitude came across as arrogant. *God forgive me*, she thought.

She took a breath. "First, the detective who came to the house with the police—"

"He's Russian American and still speaks Russian," Jake said.

"Jake, give me a chance." Susan glared at him. "The detective wanted me to know that Annie was nearly caught up in a trafficking operation. He believes she could be in some danger if they reach out to her again. I wonder if he's blowing things out of proportion."

"I disagree," Jake said. "The police are professionals. They know what they are doing. They can protect Annie. I think they could put a wire on her and track her right to the gang."

"A wire? Track her? Good grief, Jake, this isn't television. She's fourteen. What if the traffickers caught her with a wire? What happens then?"

"Hold on a minute," Pastor Charles said. "I believe Susan has good reason to be cautious. But I wouldn't rule anything out. Perhaps your next meeting with the detective could be here in my office, Susan. Then we could discuss it as a team. The church could be at the forefront of stamping out this horrible gang."

"But—" Susan said, and then the men continued discussing the situation as though she wasn't in the room. She stood and pulled on her coat.

"What are you doing?" Jake asked.

"Oh, Susan. My apologies. You had something else to ask me. Please sit down. Sit down. I apologize for my rudeness," Pastor said.

She sat reluctantly, then said, "This is confidential information, Pastor. I ask you to keep everything I tell you between us."

"Naturally," Pastor Charles said.

"Ten years ago, when I went to Russia for the final hearing and to bring Anya home—"

"I remember your trip vividly," Pastor Charles said. "We were all here at home praying for you."

"I counted on that. But what you don't know is the worst possible thing happened on the day before we were scheduled to leave St. Petersburg."

Jake squirmed in his chair, and when Susan looked at him, he looked away. Then she saw the Pastor check his watch, which aggravated the hell out of her.

Pastor Charles stood and walked over to his desk. "I know where this is going. Jake updated me."

"I beg your pardon?"

Susan turned to see Jake shake his head as though to stop Pastor Charles from speaking, but Pastor was rifling through paperwork on his desk. Then he held up his planner.

"Yes, Jake told me Annie had confessed to him how she had found your journals and read the true story. It's so very poignant and such a testimony of God's provision. Please don't worry. This situation happened a long time ago and is over five thousand miles away. On this side of the ocean, you are safe and so is Annie. There are no legal ramifications to affect you here. Let's set our next appointment."

Susan turned to Jake. "Excuse me, but when did these confessions of Annie's take place? How long have you known this confidential information?"

"Last summer. Annie begged me not to tell you," Jake said.

"And where exactly did these confessions take place? Were you alone with Annie?"

Jake looked at Pastor and then at Susan.

"Come on, Susan. What are you implying? I wanted to help. She came to me very upset."

"And I suppose you comforted her. How sensitive of you." Susan scowled. Her thoughts swirled.

Maybe I made a mistake adopting Annie—I don't know. And yes, she is an emotionally challenged child, but I love her. Damn it, I am Annie's mother. And I will do everything in my power to help her heal. Thank God I didn't tell Jake the real reason for attending this meeting.

"I have more to say regarding Pastor Jake, but before we go there, I have my own confession. You see, I have already decided what the next steps should be to help Annie find closure. What she wants, more than anything else, is to return to St. Petersburg to find her sister and brother, if they even exist. Unfortunately, we cannot travel there. But I can do the next best thing. I'm going to hire a detective in St. Petersburg to look for Annie's siblings."

"But, Susan, I don't think that's wise." Jake said and then looked at Pastor Charles.

"An expensive proposition," Pastor said.

"I know. Which is why this meeting is so important. I need the church to help me financially."

Pastor Charles hadn't expected that. But he didn't say an outright "no" either.

She plowed on. "If my house burned down, I know the church would support me. Well, my house is burning down all around me, and I need your help."

"How much are you talking about?"

"I have no idea. Possibly several thousand."

"Let me pray on it, Susan. This is a unique situation. I appreciate your candor, but I'd have to run it by the board. They meet the first Monday of the month." He walked back around his desk and toward the door.

Susan stood, grabbed her bag, and followed him.

"All right," she said, her tone cool. "While you're busy praying on that, you might want to pray about another situation too—just to avoid any appearance of evil."

Pastor Charles turned to her; eyebrows raised.

She paused, then added with a faint smile, "You know how things can get blown out of proportion."

Jake leaped up. "Jesus, Susan. Where are you going with this?"

She stared him down and said, "As Pastor Charles is my witness, Jake, I don't know what, if anything, happened between you and Annie. But I'll find out. I do know what has been happening between you and me. And I'm guessing, we have had a little secret to which Pastor is oblivious. So, Pastor Charles, whether your youth leader has been inappropriate with my child, I don't know. But he has certainly been inappropriate with me. We kept our intimacy a secret and I am thoroughly ashamed. And I'm sure his wife and children would be equally astounded as you are right now. Not to mention the board."

Pastor turned to Jake and pointed to the couch. Jake sat.

"We're done here," Susan said as she walked out the door. "I'll let you know when I've found a detective, Pastor. And I'll be at that board meeting."

CHAPTER 10
TOWSON, MARYLAND
Saturday, One Week After the
Fateful Mobile Party

L ying seemed to be the only way to get what she wanted. Annie told her mother she had a huge paper due by the end of the semester and she had to go to the Towson library to do the research on Mesopotamia and Ancient Egypt. Not a *total* lie. She had the assignment, but the history teacher said everything they needed for the paper was available in their textbook, in the school library, or online. She could work on that anytime. Besides, schoolwork in the face of what was happening to her now seemed mundane. It was Saturday, only one week since the fateful mobile party.

Her mother dropped her off at the front door of the public library and said she would pick her up in a couple of hours. Annie told her to make it three and mentioned again how a cell phone might help their communication. Her mother gave her *the look*. Annie watched her drive away and then hurried through the library, out the parking lot door at the back of the building, and on to the next block to the mall and the bowling alley. She remembered River had a cousin who worked at the bowling alley snack bar, and maybe Annie could find out something from her. Plus, she might find Lincoln there.

Annie found the bowling alley busy and loud, even in the middle of the day. She tried to remember the cousin's name. Maybe Laila or Lucy? No, Lacey, that was it. The snack bar had a line, so Annie joined it as though to buy something. But before she got very far, she saw Lincoln. He lounged in the smoking area drinking a beer. Annie didn't realize people drank in bowling alleys. Obviously, she had a lot to learn.

She left the line and walked toward him. He saw her and moved toward her quickly.

"What the hell are you doing here?"

"I'm worried about my friends. Where's River, Lincoln?"

"Did you snitch?"

"What are you saying? Snitch to who?"

"Maks saw you run down the alley last Saturday. He drove around looking for you and saw you jump into a cop car. Your little stunt nearly broke down the operation for the night."

He stepped on his cigarette and pulled her by the elbow over to a darker corner near the men's room.

"Why are you being so mean? Where's River? Where's Maks?"

"Don't you worry 'bout River. She's livin' large in Florida."

"Florida? But what about school?"

"You are somethin'. Stupider and stupider. I don't know why she picked you out. She called you her pet project, a fixer-upper. What a waste of time. Look, keep your trap shut. Everybody's fine. Everything's gonna be fine."

Annie was momentarily stunned by this revelation, this new label. But then she snapped back, "It's not fine for Shelly."

"That was her fault. How many times we gotta tell you girls that 'no' is not an option?"

"She got killed for saying 'no'?"

Lincoln looked around and then slapped Annie hard across the face. She nearly crumpled to the ground. It hurt so much. He pulled her up to standing.

"Shut up! You don't know shit. So, go home to mommy and mind your own business."

"Give me River's phone number so I can talk to her. She's my—" Annie started to say more, but then Lincoln pressed her body against the wall.

"I should do you now," and he kissed her hard on the lips and then kissed her neck and ears.

"Stop it. Please stop it."

Lincoln snickered as he pulled away. He jerked up his pants and walked back into the bar area. Annie's head swam. She wanted to cry. Her whole body shook with fear. She still needed to talk to Lacey. But when she walked over to the snack bar, Lacey shook her head "no."

"What do you mean?" Annie mouthed.

Lacey turned away. A few seconds later, she slipped Annie a Coke and a piece of paper.

Go home. You cannot help River now. Go home before someone comes and takes you, too.

Annie wadded up the paper and put it in her jeans pocket. She felt the same fear she had felt Saturday night. As she looked around the bowling alley, all she saw were lots of men and today, they all seemed frightening. She left and walked back to the library. It would be dark in an hour, and all she wanted to do was go home. Her face burned where Lincoln had hit her. She went into the ladies' room and saw the mark was quite red.

Annie spent the next hour waiting for her ride, rereading the note, and thinking through her options. She needed to talk to someone nice, who would answer her questions. Despite what happened with Lincoln, she needed to know what happened to River, and why Shelly had to die. She needed to find Maks.

His name turned her thoughts to Russia. Her mother kept saying they couldn't return to St. Petersburg. She acted like Annie could just turn off her feelings. Susan expected her to get over it and back off.

"Travel to Russia is impossible for me," her mother had said. "I don't know how to say this any differently. I broke the law there. If I show up again, they will arrest me. Do you want that?"

But Annie didn't understand, not really. In fact, it was Susan who didn't understand how important it was to Annie to find her brother and sister. Ten years ago, someone gave her those two dolls as a token of remembrance along with the blue stuffed cat. Annie was supposed to remember. That was the point.

Sometimes, at night, half asleep and half awake, Annie saw what appeared to be a beautiful light blue cat sitting on her dresser. Not the stuffy either, but an actual cat. She knew, logically, it couldn't be real, and yet, if she didn't move and didn't look directly at it, the cat would lick his fur and purr. And, if she was very quiet, the cat seemed to speak to her, but always in Russian, and always the word "remember." But if she sat up or opened her eyes to get a better look, the cat would disappear and leave nothing behind, not even a grin. Annie had tried to tell Dr. Madelyn about the *Alice in Wonderland* cat, but Madelyn called it projecting.

Now, sitting by the front door of the library, she felt a stiff wind as people trudged in and out. Cold, like Russia. *Yes, I must get to Russia.* If her mother wouldn't take her there, then she had to find her own way. In her mind's eye, she could see herself standing amid the beautiful cathedrals and Hermitage Museum in St. Petersburg. She needed to know more, so she walked over to the information desk and asked the librarian for travel books to Russia.

Armed with two books on St. Petersburg, she scanned the pictures as her dream became more and more real, almost tangible. Next week, when she went to her Russian lesson, she would ask Galina Romanovna what she would need to travel to Russia with her mother. Annie often told Galina she wanted the inside story from a true Russian. Galina always chuckled about this, saying Annie's mother would never make it as a Russian. Too soft.

When Susan finally picked her up, Annie tried her best to hide her injury, but it didn't work out. The side of her face had puffed up, and a bruise was forming near her cheekbone.

"Annie, what happened?"

"I know. I'm so klutzy. You know how they have those pillars in the library? I walked right into one. The staff was all concerned and everything. They even gave me an ice pack, but I guess it didn't work."

"Tylenol will help."

When they got home, her mother let the car idle and stopped Annie from getting out of the car. "Listen, I need to tell you something."

Annie waited and watched her mother's face.

"First, I'd like you to take a break from youth group for a while."

"Really? Why?"

"Two reasons. One reason may be embarrassing for you to tell me, and the second reason is embarrassing for me to tell you."

Annie laughed despite herself. "You're kidding, right?"

"No, I'm serious. Please answer truthfully. Did Pastor Jake ever touch you inappropriately?"

"What?! No. Not me."

"Okay. That's good." She paused. "Not you, but other girls?"

"Maybe. He's very huggy. I don't know. They're not my friends."

"All right. But for now, we skip youth group as long as Jake is in charge."

"Wow. Okay. I never wanted to go, anyway, you know."

"Second, I owe you an apology. I got myself entangled with Jake, too. And, well, I was wrong."

"Because he's married?"

"Among other things. Anyway, I want to apologize to you. I didn't consider what my choice might be like for you. I'm sorry. I made a mistake."

"Okay," Annie said. They looked at each other steadily for a moment, and Annie patted Susan's hand. Of course, her mother's confession didn't change anything, not really. Annie was still determined to go to Russia. However, she had to admit, her mother had her good moments.

As they stepped out of the car, another one pulled up in front of their house.

"Who do we know drives a Ford Explorer?" Annie asked over the roof of the car.

"Oh Lord, it's Luke. I forgot he was coming by," Susan said. Annie saw her mother dip down and check herself in the side mirror. Annie rolled her eyes.

Luke got out and opened the car's back door; a large, beautiful dog hopped out. Annie raced over to greet them.

"A shepherd, she's amazing."

"Actually, she's a Belgian Malinois. She retired from the police force last year," Luke said. "Her name is Zelenka. She's from the Czech Republic. She's not a young dog. I hope that's all right. She needs to be loved. Like most of us." He glanced Susan's way, but she didn't notice.

"She's perfect!" Annie said. "But what's all this in your back seat?"

"Regular stuff like a dog bowl, dog food, and treats. And this is her crate. Here. You take the dog, and I'll bring the rest. We crate these dogs. They're used to it. It's her little home, especially when you are both gone from the house."

"I want her to sleep with me. Sebastian always slept with me."

"Let's give her a chance to get to know us. Plus, she's a lot bigger than Sebastian," Susan said.

"Does she do any tricks?" Annie asked.

"You mean besides taking down bad guys?" Luke said.

Susan made a gasping sound. Annie laughed.

"Just kidding. Kidding. Sure, she's well trained to sit and stay, and all those good things. She'll even roll over if there's a treat involved."

Annie immediately accepted the treat bag Luke offered, took Zelenka around the side of the house, and into the backyard.

"Are you sure about this? It's a lot of dog," Susan said as they walked to the front door.

"Look, I'm not trying to scare you, but these traffickers are rough characters who are deceiving young women. If they find out where Annie lives or track her somehow—" He stopped speaking when he saw Susan's face. "We'll be vigilant together. All right?"

CHAPTER 11
TOWSON, MARYLAND
Saturday, Three Weeks After
the Fateful Mobile Party

An entire week went by before Annie could figure out how to find Maks. She considered going back to the bowling alley, but the thought of running into Lincoln again scared her too much. River never mentioned Lincoln was a hitter, but after the slap he gave her, Annie guessed he used force to get his way with her, too. Why did River let him do that? Now, Annie would never know. River was gone. And LaShonda. And of course, worst of all, Shelly.

At school that week, a couple of girls asked her what happened to her friends. She didn't know a thing except what Lincoln told her, that River moved to Florida. *Well, he didn't say she moved to Florida, he said she went to Florida.* Mrs. Sanchez, the school principal, called for a moment of silence for Shelly at an assembly, and another teacher, Mrs. Cuapio, read her obituary. Mrs. Sanchez had asked Annie to read the tribute, but Annie didn't think she'd be able to get through it without crying. While Mrs. Cuapio read, a boy called out from the back, "Shelly was a slut." Some kids laughed, but a teacher stopped them.

Afterwards, Annie thought about the word "slut" and wondered how Shelly had earned such a label. She knew the girl liked guys, but it had never occurred to her that Shelly might have sex with them, and apparently, a lot of them. Shelly's fear of getting pregnant made more sense. But if Shelly was active in bed, the other girls must have been, too.

Annie had never even had a date, much less a boyfriend. Now, when she thought about sex, all she could picture was the fat man's pulled-down pants and his thing sticking out. *No, change that: his penis (I have to practice using the proper word).* Annie figured her friends must have been comfortable seeing a man's penis and even allowing a man to stick it into their privates *(another practice word needed here: vagina)* or into their mouths. *Why were the words for these body parts so nasty sounding?* The whole procedure still seemed gross to her, especially the mouth thing. She'd heard some girls did it for boys on the school bus, but she hadn't believed it. Now, she wasn't so sure.

Annie figured she was clueless about sex because she had gone to a private Christian school for eight years. But knowledgeable or not, Annie wasn't sure she would ever like it. She didn't even like girl hugs. Dr. Madelyn said it had to do with her sense of "personal space." Besides, the posse never talked about sex, not really. They must have known Annie was a virgin. Then Annie remembered what Lincoln had said about her being a fixer-upper. She cringed inside.

Her mother called up the stairs. Annie went to the door and yelled the typical answer, "What?"

"It's time for lunch."

"I'm not hungry."

"You are now. Your grounding includes attendance at meals."

"Damn it!" Annie said.

"I beg your pardon?"

"Nothing. I'll be right down," she said, and shut the door.

Annie closed her journal and slipped it under her pillow. Besides her plans for Russia, the book also had her game plan for finding Maks. When the girls had gone to the mall back in November, she now recalled how River had pointed out Lincoln hanging out with two other guys. That was why Maks had seemed familiar to her in the SUV. He was at the mall with Lincoln. He might still hang out there. She had to find out; he was her only hope. Zelenka jumped off the bed and followed Annie downstairs.

Despite being grounded, Annie got her mother's approval for another three hours at the library to work on her paper after lunch. The bad thing was, she'd better get serious and start her history paper at school because eventually her mother would ask to see it. But right now, she would focus on finding Maks.

Like last Saturday, her mother dropped her at the front door of the library. Zelenka barked when Annie got out of the car.

"Don't worry, girl, I'll be back before you know it."

"Annie," her mother said, "make good choices."

Susan said the same thing to Annie almost every morning when she left for school. Today, it felt like a warning. *Did she suspect something?*

Whatever, Annie thought. And before her mother could turn the corner and head home, Annie had stepped out the back door of the library and headed to the mall, an eight-minute walk.

The mall was packed. Mostly, she saw Valentine's Day decorations and if she had planned ahead, she could have done some shopping. *But honestly, who would I buy for?* Her mother, maybe, but no little trinkets for friends. *What friends?* Shelly's smile came to mind, then River's cackle, and LaShonda's giggle. Tears sprang into her eyes. She turned away from the crowd and looked at a window display.

On a small plaque, she read, "To my favorite grandma. Be my Valentine." *What a laugh.* Annie would never spend her allowance on her mother's parents. She liked her grandfather well enough. But she considered the grandmother totally obnoxious. *The woman hated me from the moment she met me. No exaggeration. Okay, maybe not at age four.* Annie's first visit to Atlanta was a nightmare. Every day there was a lecture on the rules: don't touch the windows, don't scuff the floors, don't talk with food in your mouth, don't mumble, don't, don't, don't. The truly pathetic part was how Grandma gave Susan, her own grown daughter, similar rants. Maybe that explained some of her mother's hang-ups.

Annie wandered around for nearly an hour. By the time she walked the mall three times, she had to accept her plan wasn't working. She saw a few kids from school, but no one spoke to her. Two girls from her Christian academy were passing out tracts, but Annie pulled her hoodie down over her eyes so they wouldn't recognize her.

When she was ready to give it up, she scrounged in her purse for enough change to buy a diet soda and sat at a table where she could watch people going up and down the stairs and escalators. She must have been there another hour when someone tapped her on the shoulder.

"My God, Maks, I've been looking everywhere for you."

He smiled and sat down at the table.

"You look very pretty today. But why are you searching for me?" Maks said.

"Don't act like that. You know something dreadful happened—"

"*Russki*, my pet, *Russki*. The walls have ears," he said in Russian.

She bent closer to him and spoke in Russian. "At the party house. The horrible fat man, he hurt me, Maks. Didn't you see him?"

"I am very sorry, princess. Truly, very sorry. There were many new guests there. They did not follow the protocols."

"But my friends, River and LaShonda?"

He lifted his hands and shoulders in an "I don't know" gesture.

She switched back to English without thinking. "Really, you don't know? But you know Shelly died?"

"*Russki*, my Anya."

"Anya? How did you know?"

"Isn't that your Russian name? I don't understand why you gave up such a beautiful name to be called 'Little Orphan Annie.'"

She reddened in embarrassment. "You make it sound distasteful," Annie said.

"I'm sorry. You are a beautiful girl, and I have seen too many American parents brainwash their Russian adoptees."

"By the way," she said. "Lincoln told me you looked for me after I ran away from the party. Thanks for caring enough to do that. But I never told the cops anything. I swear."

"You're a smart girl. I knew that from the minute I saw you."

His phone buzzed. While he read the message, she pondered his question about her name. She couldn't remember when that switch happened. It must have been Susan who did that. Susan was the one who started calling her Annie.

Again, in Russian, he said, "Listen, Anya, I must go. We should be friends, don't you think? I know you've had a hard time at home. Can you meet me here again? I must go out of town for a while. How about the day before Valentine's Day, same time? I'll have a surprise for you."

"Yes. But wait, you haven't told me anything."

"I will, but not today. May I kiss you on the cheeks, the way we do at home?" And before she could say yes or no, he stood her up and gave her a kiss on each cheek and gently pushed her hair out of her eyes. He checked his phone one more time and ran down the stairs.

She stood there a moment longer and took in the lingering scent of his cologne. She grabbed her backpack and walked toward the exit. *No. From now on, I am Anya. Or, maybe, I should take back my birth name: Irina.*

CHAPTER 12
ST. PETERSBURG, RUSSIA
Sunday - Wednesday, Late March

Rurik Popov had been a good private detective. Back in the day, his captain had commended him for his work as a criminal investigator in the Militsiya. That was before Gorbachev, before Glasnost, before the chaos of the nineties. But when the reforms came, he knew nothing would be the same, and he faltered.

Unfortunately, and not unlike many of his friends, the cheapest way to forget the good old days was to drink them away. He lost everything: his job, his wife, and even his beloved sons, both called into service, and one killed thanks to the Russian government's whims in Chechnya. So, Popov fled Moscow altogether and ended up in St. Petersburg where he worked for the city police for a while, but he chafed at all the reforms. Finally, he went into business for himself. His methods weren't always legal, but they were effective, and a few times, a client extolled him as a hero. It all depended on the circumstances and the importance of the clients.

The last thing he expected was a phone call from the son of his cousin Lev in the United States.

"How did you get my number?" he asked Fillip.

"I'm a detective, Cousin Rurik, like you. My father told me many stories about your time together in the old days, in Moscow."

"Yes, well, those were days, and then there were days. How is your father?"

"He is well, but forgetful. Lev is ten years your senior, you remember. He is living with other older people. They call it assisted living."

"So, you have wedged him into a nursing home. He was so much trouble for you?"

"It's not like that, cousin. I live in a difficult city where there is much crime and I have long hours. It is better for him to be with other people. Besides, he has a girlfriend there," Fillip said.

"Now, that's the Lev I knew. Such a ladies' man."

Popov laughed and thought of the many nights they had shared good times.

"All right, all right. What is on your mind, Fillip, my cousin's detective son? You are an American now?"

"Yes, I became a citizen here."

"The motherland weeps."

A silence fell between them. Perhaps Popov had gone too far.

"I have a job for you," Fillip said. "A detective friend of mine knows a woman, a nice woman, who adopted a Russian child ten years ago. There were some improper adjustments to records, and they switched her dead child for a living one."

"Interesting way to land in prison, no?"

"Yes, but no one did. She's looking for a detective there in St. Petersburg. I can email you with the details. The mother's daughter, the switched one, has discovered the deception, and believes she has a brother and sister who were left behind. Mrs. Spencer wants to verify the truth of existing siblings or refute the story once and for all. The case would require finesse. Prior to leaving St. Petersburg, the mother promised she would never divulge this secret, and she does not want anyone to suffer as you uncover information. Are you interested, cousin? I believe she will pay well."

"I would say 'no,' but then you added the magic words: American dollars."

"All right. I will send you the details, and you can send me a contract for her to sign. Do you have a contract? Or do I need to draw one up here for you?"

"Stop insulting me, son of Lev. Send me your information."

74

Of course, Popov hadn't used a contract in years. But his gut told him this would be a very lucrative job and probably not difficult.

Two days later, Popov sat at his kitchen table and spread out the information he had received and printed at his old girlfriend's house. He had sent a fax back to Fillip from the business center on the corner with a contract and a proposed fee. Everything came back this morning. Although Popov had proposed 3,000 rubles per hour, Fillip texted him back with a picture of a donkey's ass. Clearly, Fillip would not pass his proposal along. After fuming for twenty minutes, Popov had amended the contract to 1,950 rubles per hour *and not a kopeck less.* Of course, Fillip sent the contract back yet again with 1,650 rubles per hour and wrote in the margin, *Take it or leave it. $50 an hour in America is perfectly reasonable. Don't be greedy.*

Considering Popov hadn't had a client in many weeks, he calculated this little job would take approximately one hundred hours, plus expenses. He agreed. In the end, he figured 165,000 rubles would keep him in vodka and caviar for a long while. Fillip sent a retainer directly to Popov's bank. *The wonder of technology. But how much was Fillip taking off the top? Ah well.* The important thing was that Popov could get some gasoline for his car. He had parked it in a storage lot several months ago. Cars were still expensive to own in Mother Russia even in 2010.

So, once they finished the money negotiations, he needed to get to work. He read each document carefully. There wasn't much to go on, although the adoptive mother remembered the children's house number was eight. All the children's houses were numbered from small, for the babies and youngest children, to bigger numbers for the oldest girls and boys. If the little girl was three or four, number eight would make sense. After a few phone calls, he had the address and decided the children's house was a good place to start.

Upon arriving, Popov could see the years had not been kind to the big old building. However, as he walked up the steps to the front door, he noticed workmen power washing the yellow façade. Most renovations being done on city buildings since Medvedev came into power were part of a plan to attract tourists.

Popov rang the bell and a portly woman in a dull gray dress and matching hair answered the door.

"May I help you?"

"*Da*. My name is Rurik Nikolaevich Popov. I am a private investigator." He handed the woman his business card, the cleanest one he had
at the flat. Soon, he could afford to get new ones printed. The woman
looked down at the card and put it in her pocket.

"So?"

Usually, saying the word "investigator" would open any door, but this
doorkeeper appeared unfazed.

"I'm here to see your director, Ludmilla Demochevna."

"Do you have an appointment?"

"*Nyet*, but I only need a few minutes of her time, a small inquiry."

"Perhaps if it's such a small inquiry, you could call the office on the
telephone?"

"I prefer to work face-to-face."

This woman took her job far too seriously. What he wanted to do was
shove open the door, like in the old days, and demand to see who he
wanted to see. She continued to stare at him, and all he could do was
stare back. He smiled as disarmingly as possible. She rolled her eyes.

"One moment. I'll see if the director is available." She shut the door.
The damned woman shut the door on him and left him standing out in
the cold and snow. He gnashed his teeth.

After ten minutes, the doorkeeper returned, once again only opening
the door part of the way.

"The director wants to know what you want. She is very busy today
and is in a meeting."

"I don't mind waiting. I could come in and wait for the director until
she's free. I am inquiring about a child who was adopted out of this
house ten years ago." He pulled out his little notebook. "Anya Maximovna Antonova."

"*Nyet*. No more visitors today. Come back tomorrow." The door shut
once again.

This should have been the easiest part of the search. As he left, he
looked up and saw a lace curtain twitch. He waved, feigning friendli-
ness.

Back in the car, he looked at the list of three women Mrs. Spencer had given to Fillip. The coordinator who worked for the adoption agency would be an obvious interview, but he had nothing but her first name, Olga, a too-common name in Russia. The social worker, Talina Talerkavna Morozova, may or may not still be working at the government offices downtown, and last, the translator, Masha Vladislavna Utkin, might be difficult to find unless the adoption agency still had her on a list.

Well, nothing to be done. Like in the old days, one step at a time, one clue at a time.

When he looked up the address of the adoption agency, he found it closer than the social services offices downtown. He drove there next. With no warning, it began to snow. Since the car had been in storage, he hadn't bothered to switch out the tires or put on chains. Hopefully, this would be a light snow, but based on the size of the flakes, he could slide all over the place. Nor did he have his snow boots. Stupid not to check the weather forecast before he left the flat. He was rusty.

Finally, he found a parking spot four blocks from the address. When he pushed the button for the adoption agency office at the outer door, they greeted him politely and buzzed him in. He shook out his coat and hat and knocked the snow from his good shoes before going inside. His bad luck. The office was on the third floor and the building had no elevator, so he was quite winded by the time he reached the top. The receptionist took his name and when he said he needed to speak to the director; she asked if he would wait. She offered him a cup of coffee. Very nice indeed.

After thirty minutes, a beautiful and stylish woman in a dark blue suit and high boots came out to greet him personally. She introduced herself as Maya Petrivna Babyak, and they shook hands.

"Please come in," she said. "I'm so sorry you had to wait."

"*Spaciba*. Thank you. It's fine." From where he sat across from her desk, he had a wonderful view of the gold dome of the Cathedral. With the snow coming down, he saw a fairyland.

"I am working for an American woman who adopted a child from Children's House Number Eight ten years ago. The agency assigned her a coordinator by the name of Olga, but I don't have her last name.

Apparently, an Olga worked for your agency back then? I understand you partner with the American agencies. Correct?"

The woman picked up a pen from her desk and started running it through her fingers, flipping it, and then running it through her fingers the other way.

"Yes, and no. What do you know about the procedures for international adoption, Rurik Nikolaevich Popov?"

"Next to nothing, I'm sorry to say. But I would be delighted to learn."

"We are in a precarious situation right now, particularly with the Americans. The politics are complicated. Let me suggest you do some research on Sergei Magnitsky, who died last year in prison. His death started everything. The United States passed a law to impose sanctions, and now, our government's response will be to suspend the adoption of Russian children to America. When that happens, we will lose all partnerships with agencies there."

"But what does the current political situation have to do with ten years ago?"

"I'm saying the tensions are high at the present time, and your questions may not be welcomed in other quarters. We are trying to complete as many adoptions as possible in the next six to twelve months, and even then, we may be too late. Children will languish, and parents will grieve."

"But—"

"I know, I know. But if you want information from us, we simply can't give you anything right now. It's dangerous for us to open old records. We don't want to draw any attention."

"I merely want to speak to Olga for five minutes."

Babyak stood. "Thank you for your interest in our agency. I have your business card, and if I can help you in the future, someone in our office will contact you."

Very smooth, this woman. He got the message. She would not give out any information formally. She might pass the card to this Olga person, and if the woman was willing to speak to him, she would contact him. He didn't have high hopes, but it wasn't a totally shut door, not yet.

"Thank you. Let me write my post office letterbox number on the card, just in case."

"Very well. Nice to meet you."

"And you," Popov said, and he left the office to ponder what his next move would be.

He sat in the car waiting for it to warm up after sweeping off the worst of the snow, and reviewed the names. He could either work his way downtown and struggle to find another parking spot, or considering the snow and early evening shadows, he could go home and start again tomorrow. After all, it was only Tuesday. Yes. He would pay for some Internet minutes and search online. If he got lucky, he might find Masha, the translator. Perhaps she had started her own business. Besides, everything was out on the Internet now. And while surfing, he could check out a few of those new sex sites. He could use a little de-stressing.

Popov woke fresh the next day with a step-by-step plan. First, he would visit the social worker. Then, he would have coffee with Masha Vladislavna Utkin, the little entrepreneurial translator he found by searching on the Web. He convinced her to meet him in person. Then, after lunch, he would return to Children's House Number Eight and call at the door. If the doorkeeper turned him away, he would simply wait for the director to come out. His job was often a waiting game.

At the social services administration office, the guard at the door was more formidable. *Thank God I put my little Makarov PM pistol into the glove box of the car. It wouldn't do to have them confiscate my weapon.* The guard directed him to the office of social workers who handled child custody issues, orphanage placements, and adoptions. After another receptionist said the social worker, Talina Talerkavna, was in a meeting, he found an empty chair in the waiting room among many women and children. In one case, the mother looked like a child herself and kept weeping and talking loudly into her mobile. Most of the other women ignored her.

Finally, Talina Talerkavna came out to greet him and invited him into her cubicle, no doubt the result of slashing in government spending. They could hear each other well enough, but the murmurs of other phone conversations and crying mothers and children were very distracting. *Should I invite her out for coffee as well?*

"Mr. Popov, I'm afraid I don't have much time as I have a court hearing in an hour. Can you tell me how I can help you?"

She had a lovely smile, this social worker. Probably not wholly Russian, perhaps a little Irkutsk.

"Yes, of course, I will be brief. Here is my card." He tried to act like the little coffee stain on the back didn't exist. As soon as she read the card, her demeanor changed, and she became noticeably wary.

"I don't understand. What kind of investigating are you doing?"

"I'm verifying, you understand, a little verifying, that's all, from a long time ago, but I'm assuming you keep excellent records—"

"Yes, but those are confidential. You may be an investigator, but it would require a court order for me to copy or release any records."

"Oh, that's unnecessary, unless you need to refresh your memory." He paused, more for effect. "Do you remember, maybe ten years ago, at Children's House Number Eight, a terrible rash of whooping cough spread among the children and several of them died? At the same time, an American woman, a Susan Spencer, arrived to finalize her adoption."

Talina Talerkavna would never survive on the witness stand in a court of law. Every thought registered on her face. He could tell she remembered the name Susan Spencer.

"Do you remember her?" he asked.

Talina looked down, ostensibly to gather her thoughts, and said, "No, no, I don't think so. My goodness, such a long time ago, you understand?" She picked up a pencil and started doodling on a pad.

"You handle many American adoptions?" He opted for safer ground.

"Oh, we did. Then things dropped off because of the political issues, and now, there's like a flurry as the agencies try to squeeze in as many adoptions as they can."

"Yes, I spoke to Maya Petrivna at the adoption agency. She told me you are all facing many changes. But back to little Anya. Perhaps you could check your records for me. I have her full name, Anya Maximovna Antonova. Pretty little girl. I have a picture of her."

"No, that's all right. All those children look the same, you know? Blonde hair, blue eyes, you know the look."

"Not really."

She checked her watch. "Oh, look at the time. I must go. I must catch the metro."

"May I give you a lift? I have my car."

"No, no, please. No bother. Good luck." As she put on her coat, Popov threw in a few more arrows, just in case.

"I'll tell you truthfully, I'm looking for information about this girl because her mother in America is so concerned."

Despite the coat, hat, and gloves on, Popov had piqued the woman's curiosity. "Why?"

"Some kind of trauma, apparently. She's very sick, and the mother would like to know more, that's all, just a few bits of additional information."

He could tell the woman wanted to help, but then thought better of it.

"May I walk you out?" he asked, hoping to get a few extra minutes with her.

"I'm going to stop in the toilet. But thank you." As he left the cubicle toward the waiting room, she walked in the opposite direction. He lingered. He saw a colleague meet her along the way. "Talina, are you all right?"

He heard, "Oh, Valya, it's too complicated. Too awful. My worst nightmare—"

Then she stopped when she realized Popov stood within listening distance. She took her friend by the elbow, and they walked away from him, but not before he saw the other woman glance back at him with an uncanny look, like she knew something.

When he stepped out to the reception area, he took a chance.

"Excuse me, while I was speaking with Talina, she mentioned I might try making an appointment with her colleague, Valya. But I didn't write down her full name. Can you help me?"

"Certainly. Her name is Valentina Aleksandrovna Kovaleskaya."

"That's it. Yes. Thanks so much."

"Did you want to make the appointment now?"

"Unnecessary. I'll call. I must meet the mother of my client now. *Paka.* Bye." And he went out the door as quickly as he could.

Back in his car again, he wrote the other social worker's name. He wasn't sure how she fit into the picture yet, but he saw something in the way she looked at him. He had a little gut feeling she had information he could use. Yes, it felt good to do an honest job for a change. He had been feeling useless, a little depressed even, and had started drinking again. But today, he felt more like his old self, the detective who solved murders and mysteries.

It was coffee time. When he checked his map, he realized he could probably walk there faster than drive and hunt for parking, so he got out, pulled his ear-flap hat from the back seat, wrapped his scarf around his neck, and plodded through last night's snow, which had accumulated to nearly ten centimeters. Fortunately, most of the paths had been cleared.

When he reached Coffee 22, it wasn't crowded, and he easily found a table by the window and did some people watching. He wanted to test himself to see if he could guess which one would be Masha Vladislavna. When the shop clock read nearly half past ten, he expected her arrival. Sure enough, a woman, maybe a young fifty, in a long gray coat, fur hat, and boots, checked her watch as she approached the front door. He stood up and called to her.

"Masha Vladislavna? It's Popov, here."

She waved and walked over. "I hope I'm not late?"

"Not at all. What can I get for you? Anything. I'm having espresso and a few cookies. You?"

"Oh, just coffee. I'm watching my sweets."

Five minutes later, they had both taken off their outerwear and were enjoying their drinks. Popov's heart skipped a beat. *Would she consider going out to dinner with me? I hope my gray hair won't deter her.* She smiled over the rim of her coffee.

"How did you find me?" she asked.

The question confused him momentarily. *Had the social worker warned her?* "What do you mean?"

"I mean, did you see my ad somewhere? Or my business card on a bulletin board? I've been doing some advertising lately and I'm trying to track what works and what doesn't."

"I see." He laughed. "Yes. I did an Internet search."

"Ah, wonderful. That's good to know. So, now, show me what you have. I have reasonable rates for translation. I speak four languages: English, Russian, French, and Ukrainian. In a pinch, I can translate from Spanish to Russian, but don't ask me to speak it." She laughed.

"That's impressive. But I must apologize. I need some small bit of information from you instead." This was probably going to blow his chances for a date. *What was I thinking, anyway?*

"Oh? What kind of information?"

He handed her his business card. This one had been folded in half, but it was clean, at least, no coffee stains.

"Investigator? Should I be frightened? I promise I have broken no laws." And again, she laughed.

"Thank you for being so nice. Most people get nervous when I tell them I'm an investigator."

"Really? It's fascinating. How long have you been one?"

This woman is extraordinary. Perhaps I should delay my questions until after I try for a date. Her eyes, nearly violet in color. And those lips, so kissable.

"Mr. Popov?"

"Sorry. You are such a lovely woman."

"A flattering investigator, even better. You might be right out of a book. I love mysteries. Do you read?"

She's keeping me off track on purpose. "Not as much as I should, but let me go back to my question."

"Yes, you are the investigator, after all. Tell me, are those cookies very good? Perhaps I could have one?"

"Please." He handed over his plate, and she dipped one into her coffee before biting into it.

"Dipping sweets in coffee is very British, did you know that?" she said.

"I had no idea." He smiled. "Please. May I call you Masha?" He paused again, then plunged ahead. "Can you tell me what you know about Anya Maximovna Antonova? I'm hoping the answer is 'nothing' and then I can ask you out to dinner."

"Mr. Popov!"

"Call me Rurik."

"What did your family call you?"

He smiled. "Well, mostly Rikki, but you must keep my deep, dark secret. Does this mean you know nothing regarding this little girl? Of course, she's not a little girl anymore."

She thought for a moment. "I don't believe so. Who is she?"

"From a long time ago. Maybe ten years. An American woman, Susan Spencer, adopted her."

Masha's eyes froze on Popov's face. Her coffee cup paused in midair. His dinner date had left the room, he was sure of it.

"Masha? Are you alright?"

And just as suddenly, she snapped out of it. "Of course. Yes. So sorry. I was tripping down memory lane. I had so many adoptions back then. They blur into one another, don't they?"

"I have a picture of her back then, if it would help."

"*Nyet*, no, that's unnecessary. Wow! Look. I have to get going. So nice to meet you. I'm sorry I can't help you. I really am."

He got up as she did and gently blocked her way. "Listen, have dinner with me. We won't discuss little orphaned girls, I promise. We'll be like two younglings with a crush on each other. You like me a little, right? I know you do. And I like you. We have some chemistry. Please say yes."

Masha seemed more flustered than ever, but she didn't push him aside. "I don't know. I would think it would be hard to do, for neither one of us to include our work in conversation."

"A challenge, yes! But I'm telling you, I haven't met a woman like you in a long time. You are so vibrant and alive, and so lovely."

She hesitated and then flapped his card like a fan. "Let me think on it. Now, truly, I must go." She stepped around him and fled out the door in seconds.

Popov was almost ashamed of himself. *On the one hand, I like her, and I can imagine making love to her. But I can also tell she is not a woman of secrets. Eventually, she will tell all. And that's what I need.*

CHAPTER 13
TOWSON, MARYLAND
Saturday, Five Weeks After
the Fateful Mobile Party

Annie sat at the same table in the food court of the Towson Town Center and waited for Maks. This escape from home had been a little trickier since her mother had caught her in the research paper lie. Annie hadn't even started the paper. She had meant to, but forgot. *What an idiot.*

Fortunately, she pulled off the "it's my last chance to get you a Valentine's gift" line, and her mother caved. *So naïve.*

Dropping her off, Susan said, "I'll pick you up on my way home from grocery shopping."

"Okay. You know, if I had a phone—" Her mother rolled up the car window.

Annie did quick work of finding a necklace for her mother, but more importantly, she found a gift for Maks. Nothing big, a little something, a money clip with the initial "M" on it. After all, he had promised to bring her a gift, so she had to have something in return. Right now, it burned a hole in her hoodie pocket.

When she finally spotted Maks climbing up the stairs, she noticed several girls watching him. He carried a motorcycle helmet and wore leathers and dark sunglasses. Mesmerizing. He looked so much like Robert Pattinson in the *Twilight* movies, drop-dead hot. When he walked up to her, she could feel the watchers' envy. *Best feeling ever.* He kissed her on the cheek.

"And how is my lovely Anya today? Did you miss me?" he said in Russian.

"Of course. But isn't it too cold to ride a motorcycle?"

"Never. It's very fast, and I like to go fast," he said and winked. She tried to look away before the blush filled her cheeks. He chuckled.

"I have something for you," she said. She couldn't wait and pulled out the little box. She loved the way his face showed surprise.

"You are full of marvels, Anya. I thank you. But I have nothing to give you in return."

She tried not to look disappointed. She needed to remind herself that he barely knew her. But then he laughed.

"I'm kidding. Look! I have a cell phone for you. It's the kind you can add minutes to. I'll try to keep it full for you, but if I forget, you may need to add them yourself at Walmart. They sell AT&T prepaid phones."

"Really? Really? Thank you so much, Maks. I have wanted a phone forever. This is so great."

"You're welcome. And I have already entered my phone number, see? You can always call me. I am a good listener, yes?"

She teared up a little as she looked at the phone screen. "But, hey, open your gift."

"Of course."

He opened it slowly and smiled. "How did you know? This is perfect. I have always wanted a money clip. This will make me feel very rich."

She laughed.

"But I am sorry to say, I can't stay today and chat with you, Anya. Please forgive me. My mother is sick, and I must visit her. She is staying with my sister near Druid Park. But tonight, after ten o'clock, you can call me on the phone if you like. Then we can talk. Or I can just listen. We are friends, yes? And I want to get to know you."

"But will I get to know you?"

"No doubt." He stood and took her hand. "Come, walk me to the parking lot. I'll show you my beautiful bike. Would you like that?"

"Sure. I mean. Okay."

"Maybe next time we'll take a ride."

Annie wanted to say something nice in return, but truthfully, she didn't like motorcycles. She wasn't sure why, but the thought of it might have something to do with her childhood, like someone bad had one. Her skin crawled at the thought of getting on one. Lucky for her, Maks didn't notice her silence, and five minutes later, she watched as he caressed his bike, then quickly zipped up his jacket and put on his helmet. When he started up, she had to cover her ears. No, this would not be her preferred getaway, ever.

That night, and every night afterward, unless Maks said he wouldn't be available, they talked on the phone. And true to his word, he knew how to listen. She never felt judged, and he always commiserated with her. Bit by bit, he told her about his own life and how much he missed St. Petersburg where he grew up.

"I lived in St. Petersburg," she told him.

"Yes, you told me. "

"I can tell you something else, a secret few people know. And I mean, very few. When my mother adopted me, she convinced the orphanage people to switch the girl she was supposed to adopt, who died, with the living me."

"Wow," he said. "I've never heard of such a thing."

"I have family there—not my parents or anything. I know my birth mom died because I get little flashes of memory about her. But I'm pretty sure I have a brother and a sister. My mother here refuses to let me go back to St. Petersburg to find them."

"She doesn't want you to know?"

"I guess. She's being weird, like she'd get arrested or something."

There was silence on the other end of the line. She sat up.

"Maks, are you still there?"

"Yes, it makes me a little angry how American parents try to erase their adopted kids' cultures."

"She didn't exactly do that. I mean, she encouraged me to take Russian."

"Look, I'm not trying to bash your mother. I don't know her. But I've seen Americans hold their kids back. You deserve the right to go back to our beautiful country. I'm going back."

"What? You are? When?"

"I don't know exactly. I must make more money. It's why I do these jobs. I need the money. My mother is desperate to see her sister, but she is too sick to travel. Our family is poor. I shouldn't talk so much. I'm sure my family stories are boring you."

"Oh no, please."

"Well, anyway, I must raise the money to make the trip there and back again and, if possible, bring my aunt back with me, at least for a visit before my mother dies."

"Your mother is dying? Oh my God, Maks, how awful."

Again, silence on the line. Annie's mind ping-ponged between the sad story of Maks and his family and her own family trauma. She stood and paced her bedroom. Zelenka's head snapped up, eyes following her as she paced the floor. A seed of an idea blossomed in Annie's mind.

"Maks. Take me with you."

"What do you mean, Anechka?"

"Anechka?"

"Oh, I am sorry. I am being too familiar. This is how family members would speak to one another. They are like American nicknames, but sweeter."

"Is there one for Maks?"

"Of course, Maksik. But if you call me that, it can only be between the two of us, all right?"

"I promise, Maksik."

"But now, tell me, are you saying you want to travel to Russia with me? Do you have the money?"

"No, I would have to earn it somehow without my mother knowing. In fact, the whole trip would have to be a secret because she would stop me."

"You don't understand, Anechka, how much it costs, not only for the airplane, but you would need a passport and a visa. Your mother would have to provide that, unless—"

"Unless what?"

"Well, I have some friends who could make this happen. It would be tricky. But first, you would need to make a lot of money. I mean, babysitting or cutting someone's grass is not enough."

Annie breathed and pondered her situation. *It's not fair. My mother is the one who is blocking my plans. I'm not a child. I know there are risks, but it would be worth it. If only she wasn't so stubborn, so unwilling to travel with me, back to my real homeland.*

"Anya, are you still there?"

"Yes."

"I might have an idea. I want to be clear, most of the parties are not like the party you went to before. It's usually a lot of clean fun, with dancing and videos. Nothing terrible. They threw you a lot of tips that night, right?"

"Yes, but I lost it all when I ran away."

"Oh, I didn't know. But why did you run away?"

"I can't have people, strangers, touching me like that. Really, I become anxious and even throw up. It's hard to explain. It's embarrassing. I'm still in therapy for some of it. My shrink says it's childhood trauma."

"I'm so sorry. Look, our time is running out tonight. I'll be away for a few days, visiting old friends in New York. I'll ask around, all right? We will figure something out. Maybe you can be my scout. Help me find girls who like to dance."

"There would be money in that?"

"Lots of money. But now, I've got to go."

"Wait, one more question," she said. "This nickname thing, whatever you call it. What is it for Irina?"

"Irina? There are a few. The most popular one is Irishka."

"Irishka? Really? Oh, my God."

"What is it?"

The phone went dead. They had talked through the rest of her minutes. Perhaps it was fine anyway. She lay on her bed. Zelenka crawled up close to her and nuzzled her neck. Annie gazed at the dolls from her childhood sitting on her dresser now. Fedya and Elena. *Next time I talk to Maks, I need to ask him about those names, their nicknames. They are my family. My real family.*

She cried. When her mother opened the door, Annie pretended to be asleep. Susan turned out the light by Annie's bed, covered her up with a throw, since she lay on top of her blankets, and kissed her on the forehead. It was sweet, but it wasn't enough, not anymore.

CHAPTER 14
St. Petersburg, Russia
End of March and into April

Popov stood at the entrance of Children's House Number Eight once more. And much like the previous week, he rang the bell and waited. Eventually, the same dreary doorkeeper appeared.

"Oh, it's you again. She doesn't work here anymore."

"Who doesn't?"

"Ludmilla Demochevna."

"How odd," Popov said. "She worked here last week."

"I made a mistake." The doorkeeper tried to shut the door.

"One moment. What is your name?"

The woman stared at him a long while, trying to understand how giving her name might be dangerous to her. She couldn't find any. "Dominika Mikaelovna."

He smiled his most charming smile, although his colleagues in Moscow always said his smiles looked like he would be quick to kill the person and enjoy it. Hopefully, he had improved on it.

"Now, Dominika Mikaelovna, this is what I'm going to do. I'm going to leave you alone for the rest of the day. But after I leave here, I'm going to go back to the administration building and ask to speak to someone to review the names of the Children's House directors they gave me last week for all the houses from one to thirty. Between you and me, I'm guessing when they get to Children's House Number Eight, the name they will still have on record is Ludmilla Demochevna. And then, I'll have to tell them the *privratnik*, doorkeeper, here at Children's House Number Eight lied to me."

Popov watched Dominika follow his logic and quickly discerned she would suffer by maintaining a lie someone else told her to tell.

"Come in and sit in the lobby. I may have confused someone. Who is it you want to see again?"

"Ludmilla Demochevna. Ten minutes. That's all I need. Do you still have the business card I gave you the other day?"

"I gave it to her."

"Oh. Of course. I'll wait."

While poor Dominika waddled down the hallway, she reminded him of an old nun, or perhaps an elephant, from the rear. A few minutes later, she returned and gestured for him to follow her. She held open the office door, and he entered. An older woman, in a severe high-necked blouse, a beige sweater, and a brown tweed skirt, stood behind her desk and formally greeted him.

"Good morning. I am Ludmilla Demochevna Putina." They shook hands, and she gestured for him to sit in the visitor's chair opposite the desk. "I'm sorry for the confusion. Dominika Mikaelovna has become more muddled over the years."

Popov turned as he heard the office door slam shut. Apparently, Dominika had heard every word. As he turned to the director, he let sleeping dogs lie. The important thing now was to get the information he needed.

"Thank you for seeing me. I did not mean to cause a panic. An American woman has hired me to confirm or refute the existence of siblings of the girl she adopted from this house ten years ago."

"I understand. The records are right here." She opened a folder on her desk and scanned the information quickly. "Here we are. Anya Maximovna Antonova was a double orphan after the death of her parents in a train accident. She was the lone survivor. The social service agency could find no siblings or relatives. Anya came into the system at a very young age, approximately two and a half in 1999, and then came to our house a year later. And yes, an American woman adopted her. Is there anything else you need to know?"

Popov sat and stared at the woman in silence. It all sounded so normal. But then, if the entire proceeding was ordinary, why had there been the delay in meeting with him? Where did the abnormality come into the picture? Where was the threat? And the social worker's reaction, and the translator, Masha Vladislavna? All of them had behaved like more pieces fit into the story.

"That's wonderful. I'm sure my client will be relieved." He put on his coat. "Oh, one more thing. My client said there were several deaths that year because of a whooping cough outbreak."

"Yes. It can happen. It was not the first time we had such troubles. We try to keep the children who are sick isolated from the healthy ones."

"Who died that year?"

"I beg your pardon?"

"What were the names of the children who died?"

Ludmilla Demochevna took a deep breath. "Mr. Popov. Such information is not relevant to your inquiry. I believe I have given you the information you requested. Anything beyond your original request is snooping."

"Snooping. *Ai*. You're hitting me where it hurts. But alas, it's my job, Ludmilla Demochevna. And truthfully, your reluctance makes me even more curious."

She stood as a way of indicating their interview was over. He finished putting on his coat and hat and stopped at the door and said, "I assume the registry office will have the death certificates. You see, I'm curious."

"What difference does it make?" Ludmilla asked.

"That's the question I want answered. Goodbye, for now. And thank you for your time."

Several weeks later, time had become a dead weight around Popov's feet. Getting access to the death certificates was not so easy, after all. There were so many forms to fill out and submit, and then he had to wait for days and days. He tried calling Masha Vladislavna a few times, but she didn't pick up his calls or, when she did, she got off the line quickly. He tried the social workers' office, but, apparently, someone had instructed the receptionist to leave him hanging in the waiting room for hours. Eventually, he gave up the tactic and began waiting outside the building in his car.

Finally, he got a break and caught Valentina Kovaleskaya, the colleague, coming out of their building, so he followed her. His bad luck. She had no car and took public transportation. So, he jumped in and out of trams while trying to avoid being seen. And then, to make matters worse, most of her trips ended up being all business, visiting clients, schools, and other agencies. One day, he followed her to an apartment which he deduced belonged to her. At least he had a way to find her when the time came to confront her with what he knew.

When the registry office finally came through with the death records and one was for Irina Vladimirovna Lebedev—the same first name Mrs. Spencer had given him—he was gratified. But with so little detail, he had to reapply for her birth records along with the records for the Anya girl. After two more weeks passed, his phone rang, but instead of the registry office, it was his cousin's detective son, Fillip.

"Hallo, Fillip. How goes it?"

"I should ask you the same question. It's been weeks of silence, old man. And still, you keep sending bills to my poor distraught American mother. Tell me something worthy."

"You know how it goes, two or three steps forward, and then a great slide back. You don't know Russia, my son. The wheels of the bureaucracy move slowly. But I have the death certificate—which I assume is the false child—and I'm working on getting the birth records."

"But how will it help you find the siblings? They may not have been born in the same city. It's a waste of time."

"Maybe yes, maybe no. But the surname could be helpful. More importantly, I now have a social worker in sight who knows a great deal. Soon, I will set a trap."

"Popov, you need to move faster. The funds are running dry." And he hung up.

Rude little bastard, Rurik thought.

But the next day, he finally got the records he wanted for Irina Vladimirovna Lebedev, no father listed, but born January 8, 1996, in St. Petersburg. Died, supposedly, January 4, 2000. Mother Elizaveta Andreevna Ozola Lebedev, born in Rīga. The Latvian woman had married a Russian. But what other children of hers were born in St. Petersburg? He submitted one more request for any other children born to Elizaveta and for her death record. If his luck held, he might find confirmation of siblings that way. He also looked for school records, and last, he contacted the Latvian registry for births for the surname Lebedev. Her maiden name would have been a waste of time since it was quite ordinary in Latvia.

Of course, if there were older siblings, they could be living in Latvia. He would have no easy way of checking. Well, there was the long shot possibility that someone adopted the older ones over there. He would think it through. However, his gut told him the Kovaleskaya woman, the one he followed to her flat, knew something useful. He would take a chance and confront her. She might be the glue holding this story together.

CHAPTER 15
TOWSON, MARYLAND
Saturday, Mid-May

Annie pulled out her travel plans journal from under her pillow. She scanned her progress, including the number of girls she had recruited. *Thanks to Maks's training, I am a new person and rich.*

She kept track of the number of girls each week. Her total was up to thirty-one girls recruited for Maks. Many of the girls were repeats, which gave her a smaller percentage, but still worth it. These were the girls who wanted easy money. But for Annie, she had the best arrangement, getting a $200 share per girl per dance party and $50 for repeats. She had already earned nearly $4,500. Soon, she would reach her $5,000 goal. Annie discovered early on what an amazing motivator money could be. After every gig, Maks would send her a screenshot of her bankbook.

Her dream of going to Russia got closer and closer. Even the passport problem had turned out to be no problem at all. Back in February, on Valentine's Day, Susan had dragged Annie to what she and Aunt Kate called a "Galentines" dinner at Aunt Kate's house, just the three of them.

During the meal, Aunt Kate announced, "Here's my news. Number one, I'm getting a divorce. And number two, I'm going on a cruise to the Mediterranean next September."

"Oh, double wow," Susan said. "I guess my therapist didn't manage any magic with you and Sam?"

"No, she was great. Empathetic and thorough. She helped both of us realize we weren't good for each other. We'll do better as friends."

"And the cruise?"

"I'm ready to meet someone new. You could join me," Aunt Kate said.

"I wouldn't want to take Annie out of school. But it is tempting."

Annie rarely listened to the two friends talk, but when the subject turned to travel, she perked up. She asked, "Don't you need a passport to go on a cruise?"

"Sure," Aunt Kate said. "Do you still have your passport, Susan?"

"I do. We both do. I always make sure they are up-to-date, just in case."

"I have a passport?" Annie asked.

"Of course, sweetie. Ever since you were adopted. I just have to keep renewing them. Yours is updated every five years. I sent in your latest school picture with the renewal. I haven't gotten it back yet, but I'm not worried."

Annie shrank inside at the thought of her hideous school picture. Though she couldn't believe her luck. *Maybe God has hung around after all, despite my complaints.*

All the pieces were falling into place. Whether it was divine intervention or not, Annie believed her dream of reaching St. Petersburg and traveling with Maks was coming to pass.

One of the hardest parts had been figuring out an alibi for all those Saturday nights away from home. Once again, Maks came through with a solution. His friend Renee had a toddler, and she agreed to pretend she needed a babysitter on Saturday nights to keep her side job as a waitress. She came to Annie's house to meet Susan and to make the arrangements. Her mother would drop Annie off at Renee's apartment off Fairmont Drive while Renee would bring Annie back to the house after work. *Perfect.* Even better, on some of those Saturdays, Renee actually needed a babysitter, and Maks paid for it. *A win-win.*

The second hardest part became her clothes, hair, and makeup. Although Annie remembered some of the techniques LaShonda and Shelly used, Annie was a novice. This time, it was Renee and her roommate, Brittany, who guided Annie's hand, took her shopping, and created her "look." She ended up with four work outfits she rotated or mixed and matched. Acid-washed jeans, distressed jeans, a black skater skirt, three different leggings, a boat neck top with glitter, two crop tops, and awesome boots. No one could have guessed her age when she worked at the mall or park. And sometimes, if her mark was closer to her own age,

Annie learned how to change up her look with her own clothes to keep the girl more comfortable.

Of course, looking the part and acting the part were two different things. Once again, Renee helped her.

"I worked the parties for Maks about two years ago, before I had Benny."

"You did? Wow, I didn't know that. Was it good for you? Did you make a lot of money?"

"I did all right. But listen, kid, don't take Maks too seriously."

"What do you mean?"

"He's an entrepreneur. He works all the angles. Don't let your heart cloud your brain."

"But—"

"Never mind. Let's work out your schtick," Renee said.

"My what?"

"Your routine."

That's when the practices started up in earnest. They rehearsed routines and scripts over and over again until Annie sounded smooth and real. Annie started thinking of Renee as a friend.

Occasionally, Maks would show up, watch them, and give pointers. Maks often reminded her of the main point: get the girl talking and find out where her troubles lay, whether it was boys, parents, abuse, grades, whatever. All girls needed a sympathetic ear.

At first, Annie wasn't sure she could do it. After all, for years, she had been the broken one. Eventually, she got better. First, she had to learn what to look for in the girl's appearance. She had to figure out if the girl looked like she lived on the street, or just a regular kid hiding out from someone. Another hint was whether she carried a big backpack with all her stuff, or a small one. Did the girl seem nervous? And so on. If Annie determined—and this was only after several dry runs with Maks picking out the girls—she could approach the girl, it might go like this:

"Hi, anyone sitting here?" Annie might say.

"No. I don't know," the girl might say.

"Sorry, I'm not trying to get all up in your space."

"It's okay. It's fine."

"I'm feeling a little low and could use some girl talk," Annie might say.

If the girl answered favorably, then Annie would tell her a made-up story with a few triggers to see which one would hit. When it worked, Annie would invite the girl to a coffee or soda close by and then show more interest in the girl's story. And so on. Maks told her how, normally, Annie would need four "touches" before the girl would open up to her. But he kept telling her to trust her gut and stay quick on her feet. Be a real actress.

Back in January, Maks had already moved the operation away from the bowling alley after Annie told him how the police officers were planning to check for surveillance footage outside the alley. He kissed her on the cheek for the information. Now, the girls met at the Cineplex which was still walking distance from Renee's. Annie would meet the recruits in the lobby's ladies' room. She would explain the setup, they would dress, and then Annie would walk them out to the pickup point on Pennsylvania or York Road. Just to be safe, Maks changed the pickup spot every couple of weeks. Either Maks or Nick would be the driver. However, instead of getting an envelope full of cash handed to her out the window like Lincoln used to get, Maks put Annie's money directly into her bank account.

From the beginning, Annie told Maks she would never work with Lincoln after what he did to her that day at the bowling alley.

"He's a lowlife, Anya. No problem. He's gone."

Maks brought Nick onto the team because he never liked Lincoln, anyway. Unlike Maks's dark good looks, Nick was blonde and fair. Although he spoke Russian, it wasn't his first language. He came from one of the Baltic states, but she couldn't remember which one. Nick worked as an MMA fighter but had had a string of terrible fights and needed other work while he healed. The first time she met him, she saw the bruises and cuts all over his face. It gave her the creeps.

If someone had told her a year ago, or even six months ago, she would walk up to strangers at the mall or at the park, chat them up, and then invite them to a cool mobile party, she would have laughed. But with each success, her performance got easier. She was grateful for her beloved Maks.

He taught Annie everything: how to peg a target and what to say to gain her trust. He gave her expense money so she could take the girl out for food or coffee or even buy her something pretty. He even provided a burner phone for the client so she could communicate with Annie. Usually, as predicted, it took four meetings to get a girl's trust. So many times, they had terrible home situations and unloving parents. Annie didn't need to pretend she was sympathetic.

However, if a girl told Annie she was homeless from the start, Maks instructed Annie to call an Uber using a special account, and it would take the girl to a pleasant apartment she could share with other girls in the same situation. Annie didn't like this option, but Maks said those girls weren't part of her mission. Often, he said, "Girls like her don't stay in the area anyway, but move on."

The decision to steer clear of the hardcore homeless ones came after she messed up with a girl named Denise.

While walking home from school one day, Annie found Denise outside their local fast-food joint. The girl sat against the outside wall and was working her way through a few bags she had pulled from the trash can, obviously looking for food. Her clothes were dirty, and she looked dazed.

"Hey. You okay?" Annie had said.

The girl looked up and said, "What's it to you?"

"Come inside. It's cold out here. I'll buy you some food."

"What's the hitch?" the girl asked.

"Nothing. I'm trying to help."

So, they had gone inside to order at the counter, but after Annie paid for the food, the girl didn't want to sit inside. As soon as they hit the street, the girl knocked Annie down, kicked her several times, and then stole her purse. When Annie called Maks, he came right away and took her to Renee's. Luckily, Renee was home and helped clean her up.

"You've got to be careful with the homeless girls or the strung-out ones," Maks said.

"What do you mean? I didn't do anything. I bought her food."

"It's different with them," Renee offered, as her perfectly manicured hands wiped off the street dirt from Annie's face. Renee wore the greatest perfume, too. "I bet she was on the move. Traveling, and didn't trust you. If they decide your vibe is too squeaky clean, they figure you're a do-gooder looking to send them back home."

"They don't want to go home," Maks said. "That's where they got beat up regularly,"

Annie couldn't imagine such a thing. Maks explained how the organization had a different system for girls like Denise.

"Call me next time. Stick to the girls we described. The ones who need some cash to change things up. You're doing a good job."

And so, Annie became quite the actress and proud of her score. She learned to separate herself emotionally from the girls she approached as potential targets. This was a job. She provided them with an opportunity to make money and become independent. That's how she worked it out in her head. And so far, nothing like what had happened to her before occurred. The parties were simply dancing and money. Occasionally, she would ask Maks about the girls she didn't see anymore, the repeater girls who had liked the work, but disappeared.

"No worries. You're right. Most girls aren't allowed to do more than three or four in a row. I told you, the cops can shut us down at any moment," Maks said.

"Is it illegal, what I'm doing?"

"Look, it's like horse racing. The government wants to control everything. We make a good living and nobody gets hurt."

"And what happens to the girls after three or four visits?"

"You ask too many questions."

"Tell me."

"Look, everyone has a story. Sometimes, it turns out the police pick up the girl, and she has a record, so they send her home to Chicago or Washington, D.C. to stand trial or to juvenile detention. Who knows? You are helping them get a little cash, and maybe it's enough to get them set up in an apartment on their own."

One time, during a nightly phone call, Annie asked, "You know, you never told me whatever happened to LaShonda and River. Was it their third time?"

"Who?"

"You remember the girls who were with me my first night?"

"Hmm. Florida, I think."

"But River's cousin made it sound like River didn't go to Florida willingly."

"Her cousin? I didn't know she had a cousin in town. Who's that?"

For a second, Annie felt a twinge in her gut. She didn't know why, but a picture of Lacey shaking her head and slipping her a note gave Annie pause.

"I don't remember her name," Annie said, and then changed the subject. "Listen, I forgot to tell you. My passport arrived last week. Susan has kept both our passports up to date."

"That's great news. It means we can start making some real travel plans."

"Let's get together in person to celebrate, just you and me. It seems like all we do is talk business."

"I'm sorry. You know you are special to me, Anechka. I've tried to respect your boundaries. You yourself said you didn't like being touched. It's not like I don't want to."

His confession deeply moved Annie. She had said no touching; it was true, but that was before. Yes, before she fell in love with Maks. But did he love her?

"I think about touching you all the time," he said. "I'd like to run my hands through your beautiful blonde hair, to hold you close to me, and to feel your heart beating against mine."

Annie's breath caught, and she whispered into the phone, "I'd like that too."

"Can't you tell I love you?" Maks said.

And it happened, the words she had longed to hear. "I love you too," she said as tears welled up in her eyes. A silence lingered, and Maks broke it with a little chuckle.

"I have the best idea. Let me talk to Renee and maybe, this Saturday, after you send the girls off to the party, we can meet back up at Renee's and be alone. Would you like that? Would you be afraid?"

"Never," she said. "I trust you."

"And bring your passport. We are very close to flying away. Very close indeed."

CHAPTER 16
St. Petersburg, Russia
Same Saturday in May

Popov stood in the building's foyer on Shosee Lavriki street. It was one of the older buildings, but a renovated one, with new locks on the doors and new mailboxes. He studied the names and found Kovaleskaya, Valentina's last name, along with another name, apparently a roommate. It was Saturday, so a government worker like Valentina should be home. He buzzed it.

A man answered. "*Privet*, hello. Who is it, please?"

"Yes, well, hello," Popov said. "My name is Popov, Rurik. I'm a private investigator. I am here to see Valentina Aleksandrovna. I have a few questions."

"We're busy. Sorry. Call at the office." The voice disconnected.

Popov tried buzzing again, but no one answered. So, he pulled the old trick and buzzed a few other buzzers until someone answered. He identified himself as police, and immediately someone buzzed him in. But of course, such a building had no elevator. On the second floor, a rather old man with a cane, blue bathrobe, and unlit cigar waited for him.

"*Privet*," Popov said as he quickly flashed his identity card. "Is Valentina Aleksandrovna home?"

"Who? Who? Valentina? No. No. You have the wrong flat. The wrong flat. Fourth floor. Fourth floor. Keep climbing. Yes. We must all keep climbing."

"Oh, so sorry," Popov said. As he turned to go, he heard the old man mutter, "Stupid police. No wonder the country's going to hell, going to hell." The door slammed.

After puffing up the next two flights, Popov found Valentina's flat and heard piano music through the door. At first, he assumed it was a recording, but then, after a gaff in the playing, the piece started again. So, a musician and a social worker. Interesting combination. He knocked. The music stopped, and Popov prepared himself for an angry greeting.

He was not disappointed. The door flew open. A dark-haired, and slightly imposing man with traditional good looks and a solid build, filled the doorway. But the diaper over his shoulder ruined the effect.

"It's you, isn't it? The man who buzzed. I told you to go away. We don't want to buy anything. How'd you get in here? I should call the police."

"I have many friends there." *A big lie*, he thought. "Should I give you a name?"

"What? No. What?" he said. Obviously, the young man hadn't been listening. Popov heard a woman's voice and a toddler crying from another room.

"Kostya, why did you stop playing? Now Irishka is wide awake. She needs your music to sleep." The woman's voice grew louder as she walked into the room, but then she froze when she saw Popov.

"Hello, Valentina Aleksandrovna," Popov said as he stuck his head through the door opening. "Do you remember me from my meeting with your colleague, Talina Talerkavna? Please, I mean no harm. May I come in?"

"I can throw him out, Valya."

"Yes, Kostya, I know you can, but let me see what he wants first. Here, please take Irishka back to bed and sing her to sleep."

"But, this man, a perfect stranger—" Kostya said.

"*Nyet*, Mama. *Ya ne khochu spat,* I'm not sleepy," the little girl said.

Popov held up his hands in surrender. "Please, I am here for information only." He watched them look at each other cautiously.

"As long as Irishka is quiet, you may both stay," Valentina finally said and smiled. Kostya rolled his eyes. The little girl clapped her hands.

Popov stepped into the room and closed the door behind him. The main room was small but cleverly appointed with brightly colored throws on the small sofa and several chairs, prints of many famous paintings hung on the walls, an electronic piano stood against one wall, and a few vases with flowers bedecked the surfaces. *Quite cheery*, he thought. All this Popov saw in a flash, as he had learned to do back in his police days. Valentina directed him to sit.

He handed her a business card, the last one even marginally presentable.

"Yes," she said. "I remember seeing you at my office. But why are you contacting me? I wasn't on this case, nor is it my district."

"May I sit down?"

Valentina gestured to the stuffed chair while the family sat on the couch.

"I have good instincts. I saw the way you looked at me in your office. You know something. But you are not afraid. That's good," Popov said.

She interrupted, but he stopped her.

"Please, let me tell you what I know and why I am here. An American woman, a Susan Spencer, hired me. Do you remember her? I know it's been a long time, maybe ten years ago. She—"

"I never met the woman," Valentina said.

"But?" Popov paused, then plunged ahead. "But you know of the case, I'm sure of it. So, back in 2000, Susan Spencer came to St. Petersburg to adopt a little girl, Anya Maximovna Antonova, from Children's House Number Eight. Before she and Anya could get on the plane, the child died of whooping cough. The death devastated the Spencer woman until, a miracle, another little girl appeared in the waiting room, a mirror image of Anya. What did Susan Spencer do? She played the ugly American and bullied the director, Ludmilla Demochevna, into switching the identities of the children."

Popov noted Valentina's sudden intake of breath.

He went on, "Susan Spencer went home with a child, now called Anya, and they issued the other child," he checked his notebook, "Irina Vladimirovna Lebedev, a death certificate."

Valentina's hand still covered her mouth. She looked out the window and then at her man. Konstantin set his daughter down on the floor and handed the toddler a couple of toys, then sat with Valentina and put his arm around her. The room was quiet except for the child's little voice talking to her stuffed cat.

"She is well, then, this little girl?" Valentina finally said.

"As far as I know," Popov answered. "My job is to discover if there are siblings. Ludmilla Demochevna denied the possibility. But then, she gave me information for the girl, Anya. But the adopted girl, now fourteen, believes she has a brother and a sister."

"After all this time? How is it even possible?"

"You tell me," Popov said. "You're the professional."

Konstantin took Valentina's hand and said, "Is this safe? How do we know this man is telling the truth?"

Valentina stood and walked over to the front window. Finally, she turned and faced both men. Her daughter ran up to her and said, "Mama, look!" She held up her stuffed cat and said, "He's smiling." Valentina lifted her daughter and carried her back to the couch.

"I will tell you what I can, what I know from firsthand knowledge, and nothing more. Ten years ago, I befriended a girl in Children's House Number Twenty-four. Her name was Elena Ivanovna Lebedev. Her time at this house was difficult, and many of the girls bullied her, perhaps because she was the new girl. I don't know. She nearly died in a sledding accident. Over time, she trusted me and told me about her siblings, Fyodor Ivanovich Lebedev, her older brother, and a younger sister, Irina Vladimirovna Lebedev. The authorities separated them after their mother died of tuberculosis. For Elena, it was heartbreaking."

"You told this Elena her sister died?" Popov asked.

"Give me a moment." Valentina turned to Konstantin. "Please get Irishka a juice, Kostya." He walked toward another room, undoubtedly a small kitchen, and returned quickly. Valentina nestled the little girl in her arms and proffered the sippy cup, which the girl accepted hungrily. Popov predicted the child would be asleep soon.

He waited.

"When Elena and her brother finally reunited after an extraordinary series of events, they moved to Rīga with their uncle, a concert pianist and composer."

"And, to be clear, Irina is not dead, you understand me?" Popov asked.

Valentina looked at him carefully. She remained silent. He took in the silence, opened his phone, and scrolled to a photograph of "Anya Spencer." He handed it to the couple. Tears welled up immediately in Valentina's eyes. Konstantin gently shook his head, not in disagreement, but in amazement. Apparently, he knew this story as well.

His wife pointed to her cell phone on the small table beside the couch. Konstantin retrieved it. To Popov, she said, "What is your WhatsApp contact information?" Popov gave it to her, and moments later, he saw a phone number and address of one, Uldis Ozols, in Rīga, Latvia. "Does he speak Russian?"

"He does." Valentina stood and lay the sleeping child back on the couch and covered her with a quilt. Konstantin stood as well. This was all the information he would get from these people. He understood she protected her friends who had undoubtedly broken the law. The rest was up to him.

He turned to them at the door. "By the way, I had a lovely chat with Masha Vladislavna, the translator? Very discreet, she said nothing. But I liked her. Once I complete this contract, I thought I might ask her out for dinner. Maybe you could put in a good word for me?"

Valentina merely gave him an enigmatic smile.

In the hallway, he stood by their door, eavesdropping. He heard Valentina's laugh of joy and the words, "It's a miracle, it's Elena's miracle!"

CHAPTER 17
TOWSON, MARYLAND
Saturday Morning, One Week Later

Annie was supposed to be doing her homework this morning. Instead, she made lists of things she would need to pack for their trip to St. Petersburg. Last night on the phone, Maks said it might be as soon as two weeks. *My God, two weeks! To hell with school.* Also, on her "to do" list was to contact her new girls for tonight, Gabriella and Aiyesha. She was a little worried about Gabriella, who seemed spaced out and kept asking Annie lots of questions. Annie had promised to walk over to the coffee shop next to the Korean place in town around ten thirty. Annie would be furious if Gabriella bailed. Besides, tonight was special. *Tonight, I will have Maks all to myself for the evening.*

Susan's light tap on her bedroom door signaled Annie to put her journal under her covers. Zelenka, always near Annie now, looked up. No matter where Annie went around the house, the dog followed. Annie stroked her head and whispered, "good girl" in her ear.

"Come on in," she said. "I thought you left to go grocery shopping. Saturday morning routine and all that."

"I'll be going in a minute. Am I interrupting homework?"

"It's okay. It's math, and I'm doing better now."

"Better you than me," Susan said. "I was always terrible at math."

A silence descended, as it normally did after the first few "mom" questions.

"Annie, I need to talk to you."

"Anya. I told you. I want you to call me Anya now."

Her mother flinched. "Yes, yes, you did. Sorry."

Annie dreaded these times. Usually, Susan's special talks ended badly, with accusations on her part and defensiveness on Annie's part. *I need to keep my cool. The last thing I need is for Susan to get mad at me.*

"I'm listening," Annie said. "Wanna sit down?"

Susan sat at the end of the bed, and for several moments, said nothing. She pointed to the travel books on the bedside table.

"What are those for?"

"The books? Nothing really. I saw them at the bookstore and thought it would be fun to look at the pictures."

Susan nodded, then sighed.

"I might as well spit this out. After the travesty with Pastor Jake, I don't want to make the same mistake again and keep you in the dark. I've been going out with someone."

"Okay, wow. Already? Like on actual dates? Are you swiping?"

"What is that?"

"Online. Never mind. It's fine. I mean, it's none of my business."

Susan rubbed her ring finger, and for the first time, Annie noticed her mother had taken off her wedding band. Annie had paid little attention. In fact, her mother's social life was the last thing on her mind.

"I want it to be *our* business," Susan said.

Annie ignored this. "So, how did you meet?"

Susan stood up and walked over to Annie's bookshelf as though she were looking for a book.

And then Annie knew. "Omigod. It's Luke, isn't it? Lukyan Buzinsky."

Susan turned, her face ablaze. "How could you know that?"

"I don't know. I'm getting good at reading people. It's not a good idea."

"And why is that?"

What could she say? He's a cop. He could arrest me. Or Maks. Or worse, he might be on to me and using Susan. The last thing I need is a suspicious Luke nosing around. And at this point, I can't tell Maks. I am too close to getting what I want. No, not tonight, please God, not tonight.

"Annie? I mean, Anya. Did you hear me? Luke suggested we all go out together for a little fun. I could call Renee and ask her to give you a night off. We could eat dinner together and then go to a movie. There's a good one in town at the Cineplex."

"No. I mean, sorry, no. I can't tonight. Uh, another night, maybe." *I will not sacrifice my night with Maks. No way.*

Susan looked deflated, then said, "We'll have an early dinner then. We could drop you off at Renee's after dinner."

"I don't need to be part of your plans, mother."

"I know. But—" she paused.

"I need the money," Annie added.

"You keep saying that. What are you saving for?"

"Do you have to be all up in my business?"

Her mother reared back as though Annie had slapped her. She hadn't meant to be so harsh, but so much was happening all at once. She had to be strong. Determined. For Russia and for Maks.

"You can manage an early dinner," Susan said, and then took a big breath and blew it out through puffed cheeks. "I'll call Luke and let him know. Four-thirty, here at the house. No arguments. You're being difficult for no reason. If you insist on babysitting, we'll drop you off." Susan didn't wait for an answer and walked out the bedroom door.

Annie threw her pillow at the door.

*

Annie saw Gabriella hop out of a beat-up Honda Civic and wave to a much older driver. A car nearly hit her because she didn't bother to check the traffic. The first couple of times they had met, Gabriella had seemed different, more strung out, more hungover, even grungy. But this Gabriella seemed more like an upscale cheerleader. Until she walked through the door, that is, then Annie could see the dark circles under her eyes and patchy skin under the makeup. Gabriella was on something and running a mile a minute.

"Hi, hi, hi, give me a minute." Gabriella whisked by and up to the counter and asked for something fancy. Her hands kept moving as she

112

talked, first to the barista, then to anyone who stood near her. Finally, she walked back to Annie, coffee in hand.

"Hey there. How are you doing?" she said as she sat next to Annie at the window counter. Her hands shook a little as she added more sugar to her drink.

"Gabriella, are you okay?"

"Sure, yeah, sure. I just need a little pick-me-up today. Call me Gabi, by the way."

"Okay. But are we still on for tonight?"

"Tonight?"

"You know, the dance party? Remember?"

"Nope. I have a date. You know? Date, like with a boy? Well, he's a man. He'd be too old for you, though. How old are you, anyway?"

"Are you still in school? Notre Dame Prep? That's what you told me last time."

Gabi's gaze wandered out the window.

"Look at all those people walking. They're walking and walking, but who knows where they're going? Do they know where they're going? I don't know. I have no idea. I used to know. I'm gonna lose my job."

Tears sprang into her eyes. When she tried to pull out the little napkin from under her cup, the coffee spilled on the counter and onto her pants. Annie scrambled to right the cup and wipe up the coffee, but Gabi seemed oblivious.

"Gabi, stand up, you're drenched in coffee. Isn't it burning you?"

Gabi looked at Annie with vacant eyes. At that moment, Annie saw what drug use looked like up close. She didn't know what the girl had downed, but her looks, her voice, everything made Annie very uncomfortable.

She spoke slowly. "Gabi, look at me. Let's forget about tonight. Okay? We'll hook you up at another party some other weekend."

Annie put on her coat to get away from this crazed girl when Gabi grabbed her by the wrist, hard, and said, "Don't you dare cut me out of this party thing. I need this. I promised."

"But you said you had a date."

"I'm not allowed to date. I'm under a kind of house arrest. That was my mother's lover in that car. She doesn't know I know. She and Daddy dear are out of town on a business trip. Aunt Eloise lives with us. She's in charge. Poor Aunt Eloise. No, I need to show them I can pull it together." Gabi looked at Annie. "I mean, I need the cash. Didn't you say they pay cash?" She picked up her oversize bag and stood to go.

"Where are you going?"

"Shopping. Isn't that the mall? Isn't shopping what people do at the mall? It's a party. I don't have a thing to wear."

"Gabi, do you remember where we are meeting tonight? Tell me. Look me in the eye and tell me."

She laughed then. "Do you think I'm gay?" She laughed again. "Is that what people think?"

"What? No. But I'm afraid you won't remember where you are supposed to be tonight at eight-thirty."

Annie wrote the information down on a napkin and put it in Gabi's coat pocket. "Cineplex theater at eight-thirty. Around the corner. In the lobby's ladies' room. Dressed to party. Got it?"

"I love you, Anya. You are my best friend. Can I call you Annie?" Gabi said as she rushed out the door. She never drank even one sip of her coffee.

I should probably get a backup girl, but I'm not sure who to ask at the last minute. If Gabriella doesn't show up, there will be hell to pay, and it could ruin the whole night. What if Maks is so disappointed in me, he cancels our date? Maybe I should try another girl, that Katerina girl.

She pulled out her phone and dialed the number.

"Hey, Katerina, it's Anya. You up for something? I can guarantee you'll make at least a hundred dollars, and maybe two... No, I'm not kidding. It's one of those parties. I told you they happen on weekends. They're having one tonight... I know it's the last minute, but when I heard about it, I thought it would be perfect for you... take your mind off some of your troubles... Can you get away from your bruiser step-dad?... Great. Meet me at the Cineplex ladies' room off the lobby at eight-fifteen in Towson. And girl, dress hot!"

CHAPTER 18
TOWSON, MARYLAND
Same Saturday, Late Afternoon

Annie stood on the stairs in their foyer as Zelenka greeted Luke at the front door.

"She's not much of a watchdog," Annie said. "She didn't even bark when you came up the walk."

"That's because she recognizes me."

Susan asked, "Did she live with you? Was this your dog in K-9?"

"Naw. But her handler and I trained together. My dog was Jakob," Luke said as he stepped back out the door and dragged in a huge fluffy thing.

"What's that?" Annie asked.

"It's a dog bed. I forgot to bring it last time."

"She sleeps with me," Annie said.

"I know. Susan told me. And that's fine. She is a cuddler, but when you leave for the day, don't forget to put her in the crate."

"We do. But what other tricks can she do?" Annie asked. "I can get her to sit, stay, and down, but she's not every good with shaking hands."

"Her best trick is the evil eye," Luke said.

Susan gave him a look. Annie laughed.

"It's a joke," he said. "She can roll over and jump over things. I can show you later."

"Dinner will be ready in fifteen minutes, Annie. I mean, Anya."

"Come on, Zee, let's go back upstairs," Annie said.

"Put the dog bed in my room, please," Susan said.

Annie dragged the dog bed up the stairs as Luke and Susan walked back into the kitchen. He helped himself to a beer in the refrigerator as she went to the stove.

"I must admit, the dog has been great. But she eats like a horse," Susan said.

"Annie? Or the dog?"

"Anya. She wants to be called Anya, now."

"Oh, okay. Listen, while we're talking about the dog, I want you both to learn more of the basic protection commands."

"Are things heating up or something? Do you have concerns?" Susan said.

"I just want you to be prepared. For instance, if Anya or you say *útok,* that means attack in Czech and she will grab the assailant. I'll teach you more commands after dinner."

They were quiet for a moment. Susan put cherry tomatoes on the salad and tossed it with dressing.

"What happened to your dog, to Jakob?" Susan asked.

"It's called a line of duty death. We were giving chase, and the guy turned to shoot right as Jakob leaped for him. It was quick. Jakob didn't suffer. But I got pulled from the unit after that."

"Why?"

"I made a bad call. It could have been avoided, but I..." His voice trailed off.

She turned to him when he stopped talking. "I'm sorry."

He didn't look at her but fiddled with the bottle label.

"I'm sure it was hard for you," Susan finally said.

He took a long draw from his beer and said nothing. After a pause, they both spoke at once.

"What happened to us? Before," Susan said while Luke said, "About Annie. Anya. We need to talk." Luke chortled.

"You go," Susan said.

116

"So, to answer your question about our relationship, I wasn't ready. You weren't ready, and I wasn't even divorced yet."

"Don't remind me. Are you more sure this time?" she asked.

"Sure enough, to take a chance."

"Okay. Me too. But what were you going to say about Anya?"

He turned to make sure Annie wasn't nearby and said, "The incident in January is developing into something bigger than any of us imagined."

"What do you mean? After all this time?"

"There's definitely more than a local gang involved and it's undoubtedly trafficking. We could use more information, though. With Annie's and your cooperation, we could wire her up."

"You're out of your mind. I thought I made that clear. She's only fourteen."

"Do you know for certain she's not seeing someone? You said yourself she's changed in the last few months."

"Is this the real reason you're spending time with me? With us?"

Luke lifted his hands in surrender. "Come on, don't be that way. Of course not."

"What way?"

The kitchen door swung open, and both Annie and the dog rushed in. "Is dinner ready? I'll have to leave soon."

"Yes, yes, of course. You and Luke can set the table in the dining room."

Annie could sense something had happened between them, since Susan kept slamming cabinet doors and tossing utensils into the stainless steel sink.

Ten minutes later, they settled in for a dinner of shrimp scampi and salad. Fortunately for Susan, Annie and Luke chattered incessantly, which gave her time to think.

Susan had to admit the dog was good for her daughter. She watched as Annie kept putting her hand under the table to pet the dog's head. And the dog seemed to sense Annie needed the closeness. And she had to admit, the changes in Annie were quite dramatic. At first, Susan thought the trauma of her murdered friend would send Annie into a tailspin, and it did for a week or so. But then, overnight, she rallied and got focused and resolute. It made no sense. Possibly, Annie had secrets. It wouldn't be the first time. *But a boyfriend?*

By the time six rolled around, Annie excused herself to change clothes to go to her babysitting job. Zelenka followed Annie up the stairs as usual. What Susan didn't see was Annie slipping into the upstairs office and going through the desk drawers to retrieve her passport. Annie tucked it into the outside pocket of her backpack.

At six forty-five, they all climbed into Luke's car, including the dog, and took the brief trip to Renee's apartment building. The apartment was on the first floor and had sliders, where Annie usually went in. She hopped out of the car.

"I'll see you tomorrow," she said, then kissed Zelenka on the nose.

"I could walk you to the door," Luke offered.

Annie laughed. "I can handle it. I come here once a week. But let me take Zelenka up to meet Renee. She loves dogs."

"Put her on the lead, though," Luke said. "Just in case."

When Annie and Zelenka reached the sliders, Renee only opened them partway, and without warning, Zelenka pulled hard on her leash and growled. Renee slammed shut the doors but stood watching through the glass.

"Whoa. Zelenka. Stop. Sit!" Annie said. She looked back to Luke, who had stood by the open car door, but now came running. Annie pulled on the dog to retreat.

Luke yelled out, "Zelenka, *držet*. Hold." The dog obeyed.

Annie passed the lead to him. "Why did Zelenka get so hostile?"

Luke shrugged. "I don't know. Sometimes she reacts to certain smells."

"You mean, like drugs? Renee doesn't do drugs."

"Or fear, the smell of fear," he said. "You take care, okay?"

"I'm good," Annie said and walked through the sliders.

*

When Annie got inside, she turned and watched them drive away, then she saw Maks watching Luke out the window.

"Maks!" She ran to him and hugged him. "Did you see the dog? Isn't she amazing?"

"I don't like dogs. Looks like a police dog to me."

"She was, but she's retired. Did you see her, Renee?" Annie bent down to the toddler. "Hey Benny. How's my big boy?"

"Who's the man?" Maks said.

"What?"

"The man driving your mother with the dog."

"That's her new boyfriend. He's better than the last one." Benny waddled up to Annie to show her his new toy, and she sat on the floor to play with him. Renee sat in her TV chair and watched a game show she liked. This was their routine.

"What's his name?"

Annie turned to Maks again and saw the worry on his face. "Luke. Lukyan Buzinsky. Why?"

Maks didn't answer her, but stepped over to the sliders and started texting. Annie got up and walked over to him. "He's okay. We talked dog stuff and movies."

Again, no reply.

Annie turned to Renee. "Hey, Renee, are you, uh, still on for tonight? I mean, did Maks tell you we're coming back here for a while?"

Renee didn't look at her.

Annie turned back. "Maks, are we still coming back here?" He wasn't paying attention to her. "Hey, what's going on?" Annie's head swung from one to the other. Maks finally snapped out of it.

"Nothing baby." And then in Russian, "You'll always be my *malen'kaya kukla*, little doll. Go get dressed. I've got to get the car. Oh, did you remember your passport?"

"I did. Here it is. I left it in her drawer until the last minute so she wouldn't suspect."

Maks continued to speak to her in Russian. "Good job. That's my smart girl. Where's your old phone? I have a new one for you."

Annie rummaged in her bag. "Oh, dang. I must have left it on my bathroom sink. I'm sorry. Give me the new one now, and I'll give you the old one next week."

"What the hell is wrong with you? Can't you follow the simplest directions?" Maks said in English.

"I was so excited about the dog—"

"Give her a break, Maksi, she forgot," Renee said.

"Shut up, Renee, and mind your own business. Go get her another burner from my backpack and plug in my number."

Renee picked up Benny. "Come on, little man, let's change your diaper," and they went into the back bedroom, but not before she turned and gave him the finger.

Maks had never spoken to Renee like that, or to her. She felt herself back away from him a little. He noticed, took a deep breath, and exhaled slowly. "Okay, yeah, okay. I'll figure something out. But what if your mother finds it?"

"She never goes in my room when I'm not there. She promised," Annie said.

Maks stared at her for a long while and then ambled up to her to hold her. "I'm sorry, Anushka, I'm a little tense. You kind of threw me with the strange guy coming around with a police dog. Did he ask you any questions?"

"Like what?" Then she turned to console Maks. She took his face in her hands. "Please, Maks, tonight is special to me. Let's not ruin it now. Honestly, it was all about the dog tonight. The guy has it bad for my mother."

"Well, I can relate to that," and he kissed her on the forehead. "So, how many girls you got coming tonight?"

"Three, but I'm not sure Gabriella is going to work out. She's a loose cannon. I'll be surprised if she shows up. She was pretty high this afternoon."

"Come on, Anya, I told you to lose the junkies."

"I didn't know for sure. I told her it was okay to skip tonight, but then she acted like she needed the money. Probably to support her habit."

"Let's hope she doesn't bother. And the other two?"

"Aiyesha, a Black girl from my school, and Katerina. I think Nick brought her in."

"Yeah, yeah. Right. Okay. I gotta go." And then he surprised her and pulled her into his arms and kissed her long and lovingly. *Her first real kiss.*

"You've been great, kiddo. Really great. Thanks for everything."

Annie stood stunned and relished the amazing kiss for a long while. It wasn't until much later she would remember his kiss and his last words to her with their hint of finality.

CHAPTER 19
ST. PETERSBURG, RUSSIA
Previous Wednesday into Thursday, Mid-May

Popov held up his beer at the bar and yelled out, "The next round is on me." Since there were only six other men in the bar, it wasn't exactly the most generous of offers. He was in wonderful spirits. After all, he'd done it. He had the information the client wanted on his phone. His next call would be to the Lebedev siblings, and he would make his client a very happy woman.

And, surprise, surprise, he didn't have to break a single neck or violate any laws. It had been a long time since he had done a truly legitimate case. Maybe things were looking up. He called Masha Vladislavna.

It rang five times and then went to voice mail. He left a message.

"Now, Masha, I know you can hear me, so listen up. I have solved the case without involving you. Tomorrow, I am heading to Latvia to meet the siblings, and I will make a little girl and her mother very happy. I have done my good deed. Now, I'm wondering—"

She picked up the phone. "Rikki? Is that you?"

"Yes, Masha. I'm telling you. All is well. You are safe."

"But how did you do that?"

"Professional secrets, my dear. Now, when I return, will you see me?"

She stayed silent for a long while. Finally, she whispered, "All right."

"*Horosho*, wonderful! I should be back in a few days."

He drained his beer and asked for one more. What harm could one more beer do? He ignored the little voice in his head that reminded him of other nights when one drink led to another. He shook it off.

As he sat at the bar, he thought of Susan Spencer as his golden goose, and if he finished the job too quickly, the eggs would stop dropping. No, he could stretch out this time a little, at least for a day or two, and pad his invoice, just a little.

By the time he woke the next day, the sun blazed through his windows. His hangover caused him to stumble as he carried his toiletry bag to the shared bathroom down the hall. He was grateful his late start on a Sunday meant he would not have to wait for the toilet to be free. He took his time and shaved more carefully than usual. Eight years ago, when he moved to St. Petersburg, he had scoffed at the Stalin era flats. Soon enough, he discovered the Stalinka flats were less expensive and better built than the Khrushchyovkas buildings, built during Khruschev's time, so here he still lived. When he got back to his room, he downed a small shot of vodka, a little "hair of the dog," as they say, to take the edge off his headache. Eating, however, was out of the question. But he put some bread and cheese into a bag for a snack on the road. He looked at the beers in the refrigerator but closed the door against them. He'd better stick to water bottles.

No one considered Popov's Astra the best car on the road, but despite its hiccups, the last ten years had been fairly trouble-free. So, when she sputtered as he started her up, he held his breath.

"Not now, you little piece of shit." After several more attempts, the car started, and he slapped the dashboard. "That's my girl!" As the car idled, he studied the map. The drive to Rīga would take at least eight hours, which meant he should have gotten on the road earlier. So be it. If worse came to worst, he would pull over and catch an hour of sleep on the side of the road. He planned to stop for food in Pskov anyway, he guessed it was four hours away. Popov pulled out his old cassette case and pushed his favorite Eurovision cassette into the player, and with that, he left the city.

Everything was fine for the first three and a half hours, but then, close to Pskov, the car simply died and slowed to a stop. Cars whizzed past him as he did the best he could to steer the car over to the side of the road. He got out and pushed her the rest of the way.

"What kind of bad luck is this?" He hit the hood as he struggled to raise it up and began muttering to the car. "I thought you'd be happy to get a little exercise. And now, you treat me like this." He touched some of the wires and uncapped the oil reserve, but honestly, he knew nothing about cars. He looked up and down the rather desolate stretch of road, considering his options. *Karma,* he thought, *bad karma for planning to cheat the Spencer woman.*

Finally, a van pulled up behind him and a man in coveralls jumped from the driver's side. Mrs. Spencer's most recent payment was still in his wallet. *No time to pull my weapon from the glove box.*

As it turned out, Kuznetsov was his rescuer, a kind farmer on his way into Pskov to deliver his produce. He dropped Popov off at a car shop, only to find it would be at least two days before the car would be ready. Popov found a small hotel and telephoned cousin Fillip.

"So, Fillip, good news and bad news."

"This is always with you, old uncle."

"I am on my way to Rīga to meet the siblings, but my car must be repaired. I'm in Pskov, four hours from Rīga. It could be two days before I get there and complete our business."

"All right. Call me when you get there," Fillip said and hung up.

CHAPTER 20
TOWSON, MARYLAND
Same Saturday, Night

Annie usually got to the Cineplex early, but this time, she was nearly thirty minutes early and used the extra time to put on eyelashes and smoky eyes. *Tonight, I will meet Maks, and we will make love, and tomorrow, I will be a real woman.* She remembered the first time they met and how he walked her back into the row house to the old song "Sexy Back." *Yes. I will bring sexy back to our night alone.*

At eight-fifteen, both Aiyesha and Katerina slipped into the ladies' room. While they dressed, Annie complimented them and schooled them on their looks. "You need to be adventurous tonight. Here, I have some sparkles you can put on your eyelids."

Katerina said, "I thought there would be more girls tonight."

"Just one more. She's always late. Her name is Gabi. Don't worry. If she misses the ride, more money for you."

"How did you find out about this stuff?" Aiyesha asked as she slipped on her shimmery top.

"It's a long story, but basically, someone invited me like I invited you. We look out for each other, right?"

The door crashed open, and Gabi fell into the room. "Helloooo, my dearest friends. I am ready to dance the night away." She ran headlong into one of the stall doors and had to hold on to it to keep from falling to the floor.

"Whoa, Gabi," Annie said as she helped the girl to right herself. Aiyesha giggled.

"She's gonna call attention to us and get us kicked outta here," Katerina said.

Gabi pulled in close to Katerina. "You're not Anya. Where's Anya?"

"Right here, Gabi. I'm right behind you. Turn around, let me look at you. You're late, you know?"

Gabi turned and looked closely at Annie. "There you are. I don't have my contacts in, so I can't see a thing."

"Do you have your glasses?"

Gabi began foraging through her oversized bag. "I have all kinds of things in here. Look, I even have a gun."

"Holy crap," Aiyesha said. "Quit waving that thing around."

"It's a prop, relax. Goes with my James Bond outfit, don't you think?" She stood with legs apart and the gun pointing up to the ceiling.

"You're crazy. Put it away, for God's sake," Annie said and grabbed the bag away from her. Gabi put the gun on the sink while Annie pulled out Gabi's glasses. "Put these on so you don't fall all over yourself getting into the car. Katerina, turn up the music. Let me look at all of you."

One by one, even Gabi responded to Annie's commands and suggestions, although Katerina seemed unhappy. Annie picked up on Katerina's attitude right away, and her instant dislike for Gabi.

"It's all good, Katerina," Annie said to her in Russian. "There will be other Russians there. You'll have fun. Don't worry about the other girls. Dance your heart out and pick up the cash. The car will pick you back up again at midnight, like Cinderella."

"What are you saying?" Gabriella asked. "Did you say Cinderella? Will my 007 be there?"

Annie's phone pinged, and she checked the message. For a second, she looked confused. It wasn't Maks's number, and yet this new number gave them the five-minute warning.

"What is it?" Katerina said.

"Okay, girls. That's our five-minute warning. Collect all your things. Gabi, where's the gun? You can't take it with you."

"What gun?" she said.

126

"Help me with this shoe strap," Aiyesha said.

Katerina whispered to Annie, "I took it. Safer with me."

Annie looked up at her from the floor, where she was helping with Aiyesha's shoe. "What?"

But then Gabi started throwing up in the toilet. "Katerina, help Aiyesha with her shoe straps. Gabi, are you okay? You wanna stay home? It's okay if you don't feel well."

"No, I have to go," Gabi said.

"Why?"

"Because we're like in this together now. Right?" Gabi said as she came out, wiping her mouth and the front of her dress. "I gotta re-do my lips. I'm fine. Sometimes it's better to get the gross part over with, you know?"

"Unfortunately, I know more than you'll ever guess when it comes to being sick. Here, take a drink of water." Annie always carried an extra water bottle or two on party nights. "Anyone else need water?"

Annie's phone pinged again. "That's it, let's go. Remember to wave at the movie staff. They're used to us dressing for a party here."

And so, they waved as they filed out of the ladies' room and through the lobby. Gabi even blew kisses to the popcorn guy, but then ran over and gave him some money. He gave her a small bag of popcorn.

"Gabi, come on!" Annie wailed.

When they got outside, Annie sighed, grateful for the fresh air. But as they approached the curb, she saw a van instead of an SUV, and instead of Maks driving, it was Nick. And even worse, Lincoln stepped out from the front passenger seat.

"Hello, lovely ladies. Welcome." He slid open the side doors, and the three girls climbed in.

As usual, there were other girls in the back, at least four, which meant the van was going to be crowded.

"Annie, it's been a while. I've missed you," he said as he threw out his arms to hug her.

"Don't bother," Annie said and pulled back. "Where's Maks?"

"Who? Oh, you mean ole' Maximillian? He's moved on to greener pastures."

"What do you mean?"

"It's not your concern. Now, get in."

Annie took another step back from the vehicle. "I don't go to the parties, Lincoln. You should know that. Ask Nick."

Lincoln bent down and asked, "Is it true, Nick? Does little Annie get a pass on all the fun?"

"Not this time, Annie. We're all going," Nick said.

"What? I'm calling Maks."

"Just get in, bitch." He snarled into her ear and grabbed her arm and forcefully pushed her into the van and shut the door with a slam. The girls became quiet, unsure of what had happened.

"What's going on?" Katerina whispered.

"I don't know. But not to worry, I'll get it straightened out by the time we get to the party."

A girl in the back said, "Where's the weed you promised?"

Lincoln laughed and passed back two joints. Annie texted Maks several messages but got no replies. Then she tried calling him. Her heart started racing along with trembling, chill bumps, and lightheadedness. Even her chest began aching, and she was sweating despite the air conditioning. The tips of her fingers felt numb, which made her stumble over the phone keys when she tried texting again.

"Wait till you see what we have planned for you girls," Lincoln said as he turned to them from the front seat.

"Where are we going?" another girl asked.

Annie and her girls were all squished in the middle row, plus the van was filling with smoke. The space felt tighter by the second, like the walls were closing in.

She asked Katerina, who sat by the window, "Can we trade places? I need to open the window and get some air." It wasn't much help since the window only slid open, but she managed to press her mouth and nose through the gap. She kept checking her phone. Still no answer from Maks. While looking at the blank screen, Annie realized, outside of Maks and the three girls in the van with her, no other phone numbers were on this latest phone. Maks gave her a new burner every two weeks. The only other phone number she knew by heart was her mother.

In a flurry of unspecified angst, Annie texted her mother's number, "*Hi, it's me. I may be in trouble.*" She hit send. But before she could follow up with another message, Katerina nudged her.

"It's going to be okay, right?" Katerina said. Annie noticed Katerina did not smoke any of the joints. Aiyesha, on the other hand, enjoyed her high and Gabi, of all people, seemed to have passed out.

"I think so. It's different. Sometimes different is good, right?" Annie said.

"I hope so," Katerina said. "You still have a water bottle I can have?"

"Sure."

By the time she found the bottle in her bag and passed it to Katerina, Annie couldn't find her phone. *What an idiot.* It probably dropped on the floor and slid somewhere. She'd have to retrieve it when they got out. Another wave of nausea came over her, and Annie stuck her nose out the window again. And despite not smoking the weed, she was getting a buzz from inhaling it in the closed space.

Nick poked Lincoln, and Annie heard him say, "We've got company. Black cruiser, three cars back."

"Lose him," Lincoln said and looked back at Annie. "If this is your fault, you'll be sorry."

Annie turned back to him. "Why do you keep saying that?" The van sped up and careened around a few corners.

"Hang on, girls," Lincoln yelled back. "We're gonna show you how the fast lane works. Nick has a bet he can beat our other driver going to the party. You up for a wild ride?" Cheers answered him.

He turned to Nick and Annie heard him say, "Go to Iggie's garage. It's on Central Avenue. Here, turn here, and go through this shopping area." Annie looked out the back window but couldn't see anything. Lincoln texted while Nick drove, and within a few minutes, they were pulling into a commercial garage and the door slid down and closed behind them.

"What's going on?" Gabi said. Several girls followed suit.

Lincoln turned on the inside lights. "Girls, girls. You gotta trust me. This is our special stop, a secret hideout where I pick up the good stuff," he said, as he tapped his nose. "Who's thirsty?" He pulled out a vodka bottle from below his seat and passed it back.

"Hey, that's mine," Nick complained.

"Zip it. Wait here everybody. I gotta see what's up." He climbed out and disappeared through what appeared to be the door to an office.

A few minutes later, Lincoln came back and slid open the side door. "All righty, all righty. Did I mention how beautiful you all are? So, here's the scoop. In ten minutes, your surprise transportation will arrive. In the meantime, who's good with a mirror and a razor blade?"

Immediately, Gabi raised her hand. "Me! Me!" She sat right by the door, so Lincoln handed her the packet of coke, a shiny metal sheet, and a razor while two girls squeezed closer to her.

"I need to get out of here," Annie whispered to Katerina.

"Didn't you know this would happen?" she asked.

"What do you mean?"

"Nick said you know a cop or something," Katerina said.

"It's not like that. My mother is dating one, that's all."

But now she wasn't so sure. It was possible Luke knew something. He could have been watching her. And where was Maks? I have to find my phone.

While the girls busied themselves with inhaling their nose candy, Annie looked on the floor again for her phone. When she heard the familiar ping of an incoming message, she looked up to see Lincoln holding it.

"That's Maks. Let me talk to him," she said.

Instead, Lincoln texted an outgoing message. "*Just kidding, Mom. I'm fine. Going to a party with friends.*" Lincoln pushed send.

"What are you doing, Lincoln? That's not yours."

"Oh, really? It's a company phone, sweetie pie. We all have them. Oh, look," he said as the garage door opened. "They're here. Come on girls, hop out, we're ready to go in style on the best vacation you've ever had."

Annie looked out to see a huge bus parked along the street.

"It's a wild party inside already, girls, so Nick's going to collect your bags and put 'em in a locker for you in the back of the bus. You'll get them back on the return trip. We want to protect your valuables, of course."

"Not my phone? You don't want that, do you? I'm lost without my phone," Aiyesha laughed.

"Phones too. Because of all the electronics on the bus, you won't get a signal, anyway. Trust me. You'll see. Here we go."

And with that, the girls stepped away from the van and padded down the driveway toward the bus. Nick had a big blue bag to collect everything, and the girls walked over to the bus, eager to see what all the excitement was about. Annie held back and waited for all the girls to get on first.

"I'm on staff too, Lincoln. Give me back my phone."

"You'll do what you're told from now on." He got up close to her and said quietly but roughly, "Somebody's a snitch around here, and the Reisterstown operation is shutting down. I think it's you." He twisted her arm behind her back and marched her to the bus. Annie had never felt such pain before. She thought her arm would break any minute.

"Stop, please. You're hurting me."

The interior of the bus was like no bus Annie had ever seen. Inside, there were couches and a bar, a couple of gaming systems, and wall-to-wall people, not just the girls but guys too, very sexy guys. Plus, lights and music with a beat so loud, she could feel it in her bones. She looked around and found Katerina, who seemed to be off by herself. She headed toward her and sat down.

"What have you got me into?" Katerina asked over the music.

"What have I gotten myself into?" Annie answered, but she doubted anyone could hear her.

CHAPTER 21
TOWSON, MARYLAND
Same Saturday Night

"Luke, look at this." Susan held out her cell phone to him. They were sitting in the sunroom at the back of the house, the TV muted. Zelenka lay at their feet. Luke wore his signature UMBC T-shirt and khakis, while Susan was barefoot, in jeans and a cotton sweater.

He pulled his eyes from the cable guide and looked at her phone. A text message, "*Hi, it's me. I may be in trouble,*" displayed on her phone. "Who is that?" he asked.

"I don't know. I mean, I don't recognize the number. It's probably a mistake, right?"

"Ask who it is."

"But what if it's spam? If I answer it, they'll have my number."

"They already have your number."

Susan gave him a look. "I mean, they'll know it's a working number." She texted back anyway. A part of her had a queasy feeling, and she thought, *What if it's Annie?*

Who is this? She texted.

"Hey, here's a good movie," Luke said. "Did you ever see *Hurt Locker*?"

"That movie is super sad. Can we watch something happier like *Up*? That's a nice movie."

He rolled his eyes. For the next several minutes, Luke continued to click through all the movies on Netflix and they discussed their merits and preferences. They finally settled on *He's Just Not That into You.*

132

Luke labeled it a chick flick, but Susan won him over when she told him they filmed it in Baltimore.

Susan's phone pinged again and this time, she read the message aloud: *"Just kidding, Mom. I'm fine. Going to a party with friends."*

Susan sat up. "That's not Annie. She doesn't call me Mom. Besides, she's supposed to be at Renee's, working. I'm calling Renee."

While Susan looked up the number, but before she could click on it, she saw Luke stand up abruptly while reading his phone.

"Shit," he said. "Susan, I gotta go." Luke grabbed his parka from the back of the sofa where he had tossed it earlier.

"Why? What's going on? Luke?" She followed him through the house. The dog padded after them. "Wait a minute. Stop. You're scaring me."

When he turned to look at her, his face showed something terrible had happened.

"Listen," he said. "I should have told you sooner, but you were so adamant and didn't want Annie to help us with these local traffickers, and I didn't want to break my promise to you...." His explanation petered out, and he kept looking around as though he would find the words floating in the air.

"You're leaving now because something has happened to Annie? I'm going with you."

"No, it's not like that. Well, it is, and it isn't. I've got to go. I'll call you when I know something concrete."

"The hell you will." Susan grabbed his arm and shoved him as hard as she could. Angry tears were already gathering, but she would not cry, not yet. The dog growled.

Luke commanded, "Zelenka, *sedět, pobyt*, sit, stay." Immediately, the dog sat.

Susan stood as close to his face as she dared, her anger like a cudgel. "Is Annie a puzzle piece to this operation of yours? Is she a pawn in your little chess game?"

"No. Please, Susan. I care about you and Annie so much. I want this relationship to work, I promise. But you don't understand. This is my big chance. And yes, I'm part of a team. But, if I screw this part up, I could be transferred. There are people's lives at risk. And in some ways, Annie is involved, yes. But she's involved in a different way than the other girls because she is working with the gang. She's a player."

"You're a liar. That's impossible. My God, she's only fourteen. What are you saying?" Susan's heart pounded in her chest. She felt as though a great wind blew through her head. "Stop it. This is crazy talk. You're grabbing at straws."

"Sit down. Here, right here on the steps and listen." He took a breath as he sat her down and kneeled beside her. "We believe Annie has been groomed by a Russian American man called Maksim Bobenka. Originally, back in January, she was a victim when she went to a mobile party. They use the dance parties to appraise girls they want to keep, to transport, and to sell."

"What, oh my God. Annie?"

"So, yes, Annie attended one of those parties and found herself in harm's way, but somehow, she escaped. Her other three friends were not so lucky. In fact, that's when they killed one of them. But somehow, instead of scaring Annie off altogether, the guy has wooed her. Men like him pretend to be a boyfriend or even a lover. In any case, instead of attending the parties, Annie became a recruiter herself."

Susan shook her head and kept whispering, "No, no, no." Her mind raced as she kept asking herself, *how can this be happening? My little girl. My beautiful little girl.*

"Let me get you a drink."

"No. Tell me the rest. What is happening right now? You want to rush off somewhere because of something. What?"

"Look, I don't know exactly. My team leader is calling me in. Something has gone wrong. I'm going to text Kate and ask her to come and sit with you."

Susan made a guttural sound that erupted into a wail. "But Annie. Where is Annie? Is she dead? Is Annie dead?" The dog began barking and Susan rose in one motion and started pounding on Luke's chest. "Is she dead? Did those people kill her?"

Luke grabbed her wrists and then wrapped his arms around Susan as she sobbed. He tried to calm her and repeated, "No, it's not like that.

Please, listen, Susan." Finally, she quieted. He led her to the sofa in the living room and Zelenka jumped up and lay her head in Susan's lap. Luke continued to hold her as he tried again to explain.

"We have been watching and following Annie, yes."

Susan moaned.

"We know she goes to Renee's every Saturday, but then she leaves and meets a small group of girls at the Cineplex. At nine o'clock, a car picks them up while Annie returns to Renee's. At midnight, Annie walks back to the movie theater, meets the girls, and then Renee gives her a ride home."

"It's all my fault. I let her take that babysitting job," Susan said, and began crying again in earnest. Luke held her, but then his phone pinged again.

"I will do my best to protect her," Luke said.

"But, her part, it doesn't sound like trafficking."

"Often, one or more of the girls doesn't return with the others. When the return vehicle is short someone, this Maksim goes into the meeting place to explain away their absence. He keeps the scouts in the dark when it comes to the actual operation. We've watched, and most of the time, they drive the girls who don't come back to Annie to a hotel. We've been monitoring the various row houses they use for the parties for a while now. We haven't fully raided one yet because we want the architect behind the operation. Maksim and, to be honest, Annie too, they are small parts of a much bigger setup."

"How could you let Annie, my daughter, continue in this dangerous setup and not tell me? You and your people let those men take girls and they disappear? And now, it's Annie."

"Sometimes we manage to separate the girl from her handler without it appearing too obvious. But not always. I know it sounds harsh, but we are so close to getting the big fish."

They sat quietly for a minute. Luke's phone rang. He looked down. "I've got to take this. Please trust me. Please. I will do everything I can to protect Annie."

He stepped into the foyer and closed the French doors. Susan sat in a stupor, listening a little to his conversation while petting the dog, but most of what she heard wouldn't compute. She looked down and found her phone still in her hand. She had gripped it so hard it left marks on her palm. Susan looked at the messages again. The first one was from Annie. She was in trouble. Something went wrong tonight. Annie would never have messaged otherwise.

Susan stood and walked to the French doors that separated the two rooms and opened them. She heard Luke say, "You put some kind of rookie on the tail? Yeah, well, that's great. How many girls are there? Okay. Okay. Let's put out an APB. Maybe the van will turn up again. Okay. Yeah, out. I'll be there in thirty minutes."

As he got off the phone, Susan said, "Something has gone very wrong. Not just for you, but for Annie. She would have never texted me, not in a million years. You know that. Tell me everything."

Luke took in a breath and blew it out slowly. "An officer saw one man grab Annie and push her into the van. The van is new. Usually, they use a Suburban or other big SUV. Maksim, her mentor, was nowhere to be seen tonight. This Maksim guy saw me at Renee's when we dropped Annie off. I don't know why that mattered. Regardless, Annie is in the van with the other girls. They are not going to a row house. The officer following the van lost them."

"You don't know where she is?"

Luke could barely look at Susan, but finally, he brushed his hand gently across her tears. "No, we don't. But there is still hope. We have someone undercover. We hope she'll be able to get us a message."

Susan collapsed in on herself, and Luke picked her up and carried her back to the sofa. Pulling out his phone, he texted Susan's best friend, Kate, telling her of the emergency and to come to Susan's house right away. He knew she would come. He didn't have the heart to tell either of them that Annie's odds for survival were not good. The longer she remained in their control, the lower her chances became.

CHAPTER 22
RĪGA, LATVIA
Sunday

Ausma sat in Uldis's flat at the kitchen table in her brown robe while he scurried around in pajamas, packing for his upcoming tour in the Balkans. She had tried to help him pack earlier, but he kept taking things out of the suitcase to see what she had put in and what was still missing. Having a cup of coffee and listening to him seemed to be the better plan. Before they went to bed, she would review everything again, anyway.

"I wish you could go with me," he said as he covered his tuxedo with a garment bag. They both spoke in Latvian, as was their custom.

"Darling, you know Karel is determined I play Mahler's Fifth with the orchestra during the last concert of the season."

"Yes, yes."

"And this is your first solo tour in several years. I am proud of you," she said.

He stopped what he was doing and came to her, pulled her on to her feet and held her close to him. "I owe so much to you. And now, with the children leaving the nest, what would I do without your sturdy presence?"

"Oh, the Rock of Gibraltar, am I?"

"And more. I love you. Marry me, Ausma." She looked away. "Why won't you marry me?" He turned her face to his and spoke directly. "Or let's live together. It's a modern world. No one would blink an eye, certainly no one in the symphony would care."

"But the piano—"

"I have a plan. I spoke to Martin at the conservatory. He has agreed to put my piano into one of the larger practice rooms and will give me exclusive use of the room for a much smaller fee, which we can offset when other students pay to use it. Perfect."

She opened her mouth to speak, and he silenced her words with a kiss. "You have until my return to make a final decision. Until then—" Before he could say more, his cell phone rang. It took him nearly six rings before he could find the thing hiding under his underwear on the bed.

"Hallo. Elena?"

"Uncle Uldis," she sounded like she had been running. "You won't believe it. My God, my God. Is Ausma there? Put me on speaker. Do you remember how to do it?"

He had no clue. He handed the phone to Ausma.

"Hello?" she said.

"Ausma, put the phone on speaker. I have the best news."

"Don't tell me you're marrying the Australian boy?" Uldis said, as though through a megaphone.

"You don't have to yell, Uncle. Speak normally. And no, nothing like that. It's Irina. We have found Irina!"

Uldis's eyes widened, and his mouth dropped open. Ausma spoke first. "How is it possible?"

"It's a long story, but basically Irina's adopted mother hired a detective. He will be in Rīga tonight. He had car trouble or something and I heard from Valentina in St. Petersburg, and she gave me his phone number. Fedya doesn't even know yet. We must meet tonight."

"But I'm leaving early tomorrow morning for Zagreb, for Croatia tomorrow morning."

"You'll be fine. The four of us can meet at the Skyline Bar tonight and watch Fedya and Daina perform. The detective is staying at the Radisson Blu but doesn't expect to arrive until nine-thirty or ten. It will be perfect."

"But Fedya doesn't want—" Uldis said.

"We won't tell him, that's all. And once you hear them, you will be amazed," Elena said. "Okay, I've got to run. Danny is flying in tonight for a recruitment interview with the Latvian League on Monday. I'm meeting him at the airport." And with that, she hung up.

Uldis looked at Ausma, who smiled. "We should go. It's time to heal."

*

The Skyline Bar was a popular tourist destination, with its beautiful views of the city. Uldis and Ausma waited at the entrance until Elena arrived, Danny in tow. Danny paid the entrance fee for all four of them.

"I reserved a table near the windows because this is a special occasion. We'll have a good view of the stage, but not right in their faces," Elena said.

"Probably wise," Ausma said and pulled Uldis closer to her. She picked up on his anxiety about facing Fedya. Ausma had made him promise not to bring up their fight or Fedya's leave of absence from the conservatory. It had been a hard three months of change, not only Fedya's big move into commercial music, but Elena's transition to jazz dancing. In both cases, the children were making grown-up decisions, whether or not Uldis liked it.

Ausma smiled as she remembered her own big decision to file for divorce from Jānis Ķeizars only to discover he had died without explanation weeks ago, undoubtedly assassinated. She had never told Uldis or anyone else that Jānis had been a member of the KGB of the LSSR, nor had she told anyone how the government secretly tried and convicted him fifteen years earlier. Ausma had pretended to be a widow all along to protect herself, but now it was true. Soon, she would accept Uldis's offer of marriage, especially now as she saw his adopted niece and nephew finding their own way. *Oh, how God worked*, she thought.

They ordered drinks, and the lights dimmed as the couple entered the small stage, Fedya, elegant in his black satin shirt and dress pants, while Daina wore a stunning sequined top and long black skirt. They hit the right note in this classic setting, a familiar melody transformed by Fedya's unique embellishments. Originally, she thought he had gone into some kind of progressive rock, but she found his work reminiscent of Miles Davis or Thelonious Monk. But then, Fedya would switch it up even more and give Daina a place in the music vocally.

When Ausma turned to Uldis, she saw him sitting back with his eyes closed, his mouth in a small toothless smile. He was traveling along with

Fedya's performance. The two of them had shared music this way, back in the beginning, when Uldis discovered Fedya's love for music.

After the set, many in the crowd spontaneously rose in applause and appreciation. Elena started screaming Fedya's name. When Fedya found her in the crowd, she pointed to her uncle, also standing, who had clasped his hands and waved them like the winner of a boxing match. Uldis was proud, even exultant.

During the break, Uldis turned to Ausma and said, "I should have trusted him. He has melded what he learned at the conservatory into his own unique sound. An artist, a genuine artist."

"Aren't they great?" Elena nearly squealed. Danny laughed at her. She explained, "They're only playing one set tonight since they are sharing the time with another trio. They'll be regulars after this, don't you think?" she asked her uncle.

"Indeed. Indeed. Thank you, Elena. Thank you for making this happen. I am grateful."

And then they were there, Fedya and Daina, coming toward the table. Uldis stood and bowed to Fedya, who nearly ran around the table to encase his uncle in a bear hug.

When they pulled apart, Uldis held Fedya's face in his hands and said, "My son, my beloved son. You were right, and I was wrong. I am proud of you."

Ausma thought Fedya might weep, but then Elena's phone chirped a Broadway tune, maybe something from *West Side Story*.

"It's him. Quiet, everyone," Elena said, then into the phone, "Hello?… Yes, this is Elena Lebedev. I'll meet you at the entrance to the Skyline Blu club on the top floor." She clicked off and all six of them looked at each other in total silence for several seconds.

Danny finally broke the hush. "What are we waiting for? Let's go get the bloke." He grabbed Elena's hand, and they weaved through the crowd.

"Daina," Elena called back. "Order champagne."

"What's going on?" Fedya asked.

"It's another surprise," Ausma said. "A bigger surprise than finding your uncle here."

"I can't see how anything could top that," Daina said as she called to a waiter to bring champagne.

"Uldis, pull up a chair for our guest," Ausma said.

"What guest?" Fedya said. "What's going on?"

Elena's voice answered him as she dragged a rather frumpy looking man through the tables with Danny following behind. When they reached the table, Danny grinned like a cat who swallowed a canary.

Uncle Uldis stood, and Fedya copied him from habit.

Elena now spoke in Russian, "Uncle Uldis, Ausma, Fedya, and Daina, this is Popov, Rurik. He only speaks Russian, so please oblige him." In Latvian, she said, "I'm sorry, Ausma, but he only speaks Russian." To Danny, she said, "Sorry, old mate." He waved her off.

Daina chirped in, "I can help translate the essentials into English."

Ausma smiled and quietly said, "And it's all right, I speak Russian fine."

"What? But—" Uldis said, she interrupted him with a finger to her lips. Fedya grinned. He remembered Ausma's confession to him many years ago when he was still a boy and Uldis was in recovery from a terrible alcoholic binge, one that almost killed him.

"Rurik, call me Rurik," the man said to everyone. "And please sit down, sit down."

The champagne arrived. The waiter distributed the glasses and poured the bubbling liquid all around.

"First, a toast," Elena said. "A toast to reunions, truth, and the power of love and family forever."

The sounds of "*Prost*" and "*Na Zdarovie*," along with the clinking of glasses, resounded.

"Now, tell them, Rurik. Tell my family your story. Our story," Elena said. She squeezed Fedya's hand as he looked at his sister.

Rurik began, "I was hired to find you, Fedya and Elena, by the adopted mother of your sister, Irina Vladimirovna Lebedev." Fedya leaned back suddenly as though someone had shoved him in his chair. Elena literally cried out in sheer joy, "Yes! Finally!"

"Please let me tell you everything I know. I'm sure you'll still have many questions. Most of what I had to work with came directly from the American mother, Susan Spencer. However, there are a few facts I filled in on my own in St. Petersburg."

And with that, he gave them the steps of his journey from Cousin Fillip's phone call in America to Valentina Alexandrovna Kovalevskaya, the social worker who befriended Elena in Children's House Number Twenty-four in St. Petersburg.

"Tomorrow, Monday yes, I have made arrangements with Fillip to call the Spencer home. You will be able to speak to your sister, Irina. I understand the American mother encouraged the girl to continue her studies in Russian, so it will not be necessary to hire a translator. Let's meet here at the hotel for the phone call. The Internet is good here."

"But I have to leave," Uldis said, clearly disappointed to miss this big moment. Ausma patted his arm. "It will work out, Uldis. This is their sister, Fedya and Elena's. We will meet her another time, another day. This is the beginning of a whole new time in all our lives."

Fedya sat stunned while Elena bounced in her chair. She acted like a little girl the night before her birthday or the night before New Year's. "Fantastic! Yes, Uncle, we can go to America together!"

Uldis shook his head and smiled. "You and your dream."

"Absolutely," Fedya grinned. "Dreams are made to be lived." He called the waiter over and ordered another bottle of champagne.

CHAPTER 23
Saturday Night into Sunday on the Bus

The movement of the bus and the marijuana smoke had finally lulled Annie to sleep. But when the bus jerked to a stop because of a highway accident, she jolted upright. It was still dark outside, and the driver had dimmed the interior. The emergency vehicle lights gave off an eerie glow that flickered throughout the bus.

She searched for her phone, as she habitually did, to check the time, until she remembered Lincoln took it. No telling what else he had texted her mother. One thing, since Annie wasn't supposed to have a phone, any text pretending to be from her would send warning bells, for sure. Not that her mother could do much, except call Luke. *Better than nothing.*

She twisted in her seat to see what damage the night's blowout had caused to the back of the bus. Most of the girls were asleep and oblivious to any danger. But then, who was she to talk? She had been equally blind while working for Maks. She noticed the sexy party guys from last night were gone and all that remained were a dozen girls and a few guards. One stood near the front, murmuring to the driver. Annie saw what looked like a gun tucked into his jeans. *Oh my God*, she thought. *I should do something, but what?*

When she looked outside, the flashing lights were close by. *Maybe I can flag someone.* She tried to open her window, but a hand stopped her.

"Don't even think about it," a man said in Russian.

"But this is a terrible mistake. I shouldn't be here. I'm not one of them," she said. Then she shrank at her own words.

"Shut up," he said, and returned to his post at the front of the bus.

Katerina awoke. "What time is it? Where are we?"

"I don't know. I'm sorry. I'm very sorry, Katerina."

"Yeah, thanks for nothing. You screwed this up."

"I didn't know," Annie said. "I—" but the girl turned away, raised her hand, and asked the guard if she could use the toilet. The man gestured her to the back. Annie dropped her head into her hands. Everything had gone so wrong and so quickly. And where was Maks? *He told me he loved me. He kissed me like a lover.*

But then, she remembered him saying, "You've been great." She hadn't heard the finality of those words while standing there in Renee's apartment. Now it seemed obvious. *He was saying goodbye to me and abandoning me to this nightmare. Maks knew this would happen. He must have. And he took my money. All of it was a hoax. The whole thing was a charade, a circus, and I was the clown.*

She heard a groan from the seats in front of her. When she peeked over, she saw Gabi pull herself up into a seated position and begin rummaging around in her pockets. Eventually she pulled out a mangled cigarette.

"Hey, lover boy," Gabi called to the guard. "You got a light?" Her hand shook as she held the cig to her lips.

"No smoking on the bus," the guard said.

"You've got to be kidding. People were smoking all night long. Where were you?" Gabi turned and saw Annie watching her.

"Hello, Anya. You got a light?" Annie shook her head and pointed at the guard watching them. Gabi looked at him and smiled, then swung back to Annie. "You're such a rule follower, aren't you?" She sat up on her knees and draped her arms over the back of her seat.

"Do you have a pillow, Annie?"

"No. How can you sleep anyway? Aren't you worried? Do you know what is happening here? How can you be so—"

"Nonchalant? Nothing I can do about things at the moment," Gabi said, and shrugged.

"Look, I'm sorry, I know it's my fault, but—"

Kristina was back. "That's for sure. I heard them talking in the back. They say there's a snitch on board. Is it you?" Katerina said as she sat next to Annie.

"Me? That's Lincoln causing trouble. He hates me. I'm not even supposed to be here," Annie said.

The guard stepped in close to them and said, "No talking," this time in English.

Gabi flipped him off. The guard yanked her hair and shoved her against the window, causing her to hit her head hard. She yowled.

He looked toward the back of the bus and then said in a loud whisper, "You do what you're told. All three of you. And if you don't, a few of our guys know how to change your attitudes real quick." He grabbed his junk to make the point.

Annie looked away. She bent over to whisper through the seats, "Gabi, are you okay?" All she heard was a whimper. Annie looked at Katerina, but the girl shook her head, put her finger to her lips, and closed her eyes.

Annie looked out the window as she wiped away tears. The bus was moving again. So much darkness. Until the last hour or so, Annie had held some small hope that someone in the organization would realize the misunderstanding. Maks would call in and tell them she was on his team. She was one of his scouts. Instead, her extraordinary folly was dawning. The bosses were regrouping. They shut down the mobile parties and must be taking the last set of girls to Florida. And where was Maks?

Oh my God. Florida. How will anyone find me? I am no different from the rest of these girls. Not a scout anymore, not on staff, but a product to be sold and traded. What was I thinking? I'm a kid.

A single sob exploded from her. She covered her mouth. Her thoughts jumbled.

When Luke told her mother that a gang was trafficking girls, Annie couldn't see how the mobile dance parties were any part of that. But now she remembered the videos, and the numbers, and the fat man who attacked her waving hundred-dollar bills. He was ready to buy her. Annie shook. She needed air. She stood up awkwardly and hit her head on the overhead bin.

"Ow," she cried out.

"Sit down," the guard said to Annie.

She sat and did her best to breathe through the brewing panic attack. This is what trafficking looks like. Drugs, alcohol, music, and dancing to keep the girls in a fog.

Where were the good guys? She knew Luke and his team were working to catch the gang. Their goal, he had said, was to protect vulnerable young women and girls from the evil men abducting them. Could Luke save her? Save them? Probably not now. Her mother had called traffickers dangerous men. But Susan didn't know the half of it. This was pure evil. The bad guys were winning.

Oh God, help me. Please.

So many girls were lost already. Girls like River and LaShonda, not to mention all the other girls Annie had recruited in the last three months. Sure, some of them went to the parties for the money and nothing more happened, but now she understood what happened to the girls who never returned. Guys put them on a bus like this one. While other girls, like Shelly, said "no" and died for it.

I was part of this. And when River and LaShonda vanished, I hardly asked any questions. I believed everything Maks told me—every lie. I didn't just let it happen—I'm an accessory to murder. Annie wept now in earnest, but silently. No one else could or should bear her guilt. This was God's punishment.

Oh, Mama. I'm sorry. I have hurt you so much. You got damaged goods. They warned you. The orphanage people told you not to take me. But you did anyway, and it got you nothing but pain. More and more pain, more loss. I am worthless. Oh God, help me. If there is a way to help me, please help us all.

In this way, Annie suffered through the next several hours. As the sun finally rose above the horizon, she watched the landscape fly by and saw signs announcing various cities, like Fredericksburg and Richmond, and then a "Welcome to North Carolina" sign. How many hours had it been? They were heading south for sure. She assumed they were heading for Miami. Finally, they pulled off the highway and into a small town that had a McDonald's. Apparently, the gopher guard chose random meals and then handed them out to the girls as he walked through the bus. No one complained. Except for Gabi, of course.

"Dude. Hey, I'm raising my hand, see? Nice and polite," she said. One of the other guards stopped at her seat but did not speak to her. "Listen, I'm not feeling so good. So, I need a little help. Got any of that blow from last night? I bet there's some left over."

The man answered her in Russian and walked away.

Gabi peered over the seat. "What did he say, Anya?"

"It wasn't nice. Just forget it."

"What else is new?" Gabi looked through the seats. "You gonna eat that sandwich?" she asked Annie.

"I'm hungry, but the idea of eating fast food nauseates me. I've got a weird stomach. You can have it." Annie draped the bag over the top of the seat and Gabi snatched it.

Katerina whispered into Annie's ear in Russian, "It's the drugs. She'll go through a bunch of stages, but food is a big one."

Annie looked at her. "You speak Russian really well."

"My father was American, but my mother was Ukrainian. A match made in hell—I told you before. My mother tried to leave him once and got the shit beat out of her. She's all strung out now, probably homeless. I stayed home with my father, and for my devotion, got to meet his needs."

"You cooked for him?" Annie said.

"Are you as stupid as you sound?" Katerina said.

Annie pulled back as though the girl had punched her, but then she realized what Katerina meant. Here was another girl wise to a dark world in a way that Annie never had been. Like River.

And what about Maks? She had wanted to give herself to him. She had wanted that rite of passage with him. But now, would it be someone else like that awful fat man from last January?

Her heart pounded like it was trying to break free, too fast, too loud. She couldn't get a full breath, like she was drowning. Her hands tingled. *Stop*, Annie thought. *Not now. You can't panic now. No one will care.* She concentrated on her breathing, like Dr. Madlyn had taught her. Slowly, it got better.

By the time they crossed into South Carolina, it was dark again. Her stomach rumbled. She had had nothing to eat since dinner on Saturday with her mother and Luke. She stood up to go to the restroom.

Katerina stopped her. "You'd better ask for permission."

Annie looked up in time to see the guard heading for her. She pointed down the bus aisle, and he gestured his agreement. Walking back, she noticed that many of the girls had found companionship with one another. One or two stared out the window. Three or four of the girls she recognized from previous parties, which surprised her. Annie must have been one of several scouts. She wondered if any of the scouts were on the bus, also betrayed, like her. But then, hadn't she betrayed all her girls? Everything had been about her dream to go to Russia, at any cost. The girls were a means to an end.

Three rows back, she found a kind of living room area where two lounger chairs opened into beds. She wondered, *what price did the girls pay to get one of those beds to sleep in?* Some kind of movie played on the big screen TV, but everyone who watched had a headset. Further back, she found a kitchenette and, of all things, a bowl of fruit and granola bars. These were probably something she could eat without making herself sick. She slipped a couple into her jean jacket pockets. Inside the small refrigerator, there were bottles of water. Who knew?

When she stepped into the bathroom, she used the toilet quickly and thanked God she hadn't started her period yet. Her mother had told her to keep track, but she never seemed to manage it. Besides, she was so irregular, she couldn't see the point. When she came out, another girl was waiting to use it.

"Hi," the girl said. "Isn't this the coolest thing ever?"

"You mean the bus?" Annie said.

"Yeah," she said, elongating the vowels like Annie was the dumbest girl in the room.

"But aren't you afraid?" Annie asked.

"Of what? Lincoln said the place we're going is like a resort. I can't wait."

"Lincoln? He's the biggest liar ever," Annie said.

The girl's eyes widened as she looked past Annie and then scurried into the bathroom.

"Annie, Annie, Annie." Lincoln said. "You are such a little pain in the ass. I shoulda thrown you in the dumpster." He grabbed her by the throat and pressed her up against the closed bathroom door. Annie struggled to catch her breath and flailed her arms at him. He only released her when one of the other guards came up and said the boss wanted him in the back studio. She dropped to the floor, gasping for air. She coughed and heaved, but with nothing in her stomach, she only gagged.

"If I find out you're the little rat, you're dead for sure," Lincoln said. He kicked her as he walked past her.

"You okay?" a guy asked in her ear.

When she looked up, she saw Nick. He pulled her up from the floor as though she were a feather. She hadn't seen him since he drove them away from the movie theater. He opened the bottle of water she had dropped on the floor. Up close, he smelled like he could use a shower.

"Do you even care?" she asked.

"You shouldn't have told the cops," Nick said, nearly under his breath, as he escorted her back to her seat.

"I didn't tell the cops anything."

"Keep it down. Nobody believes you. Maks told me he saw you with him. He texted me that a cop dropped you off at Renee's."

"That's my mother's new boyfriend. I told him that. Where is Maks, Nick?"

They stopped by her seat row. Katerina no longer sat there. Instead, it was Gabriella.

"Hi, Nicky. Remember me? I remember you and those big powerful hands," Gabi said. She stood up and put her own hand on one of his pants pockets. "You got anything in there that would help a girl with a little hangover."

"You mean a major crash, don't you?" Katerina said over the seatback.

"Maybe a joint or a little vodka to take the edge off?" Gabi said, her eyes fixed on Nick.

"Back off, Gabi," he said.

The other guard from the front of the bus stepped in between them. "Got to break this up, Nick," the man said.

"Nick, I'm feeling bad. Help me out, uh?" Gabi said as she tried to grab his sleeve.

Annie's eyes bounced from one to another like a ping-pong match. Gabi sounded so pathetically desperate.

"Come on, Gabi," Annie said. "Let's both sit down before someone hurts you."

Gabi looked at her blankly and then with recognition. "Oh, hi, Anya. How have you been?"

Annie pulled her into the seat row while Nick and the other guard parted ways. She never got an answer to her question about Maks.

Gabi touched Annie's neck. "What happened to you?"

"Nothing. I had a run-in with a guy named Lincoln."

"I told you," Katerina said between the seats, "they believe you're the rat fink. You know, bad things happen to informants."

"Why me? Why not you, or even Gabi?"

Gabi laughed then.

"You know, my daddy once told me the story of a *Twilight Zone* episode he loved. Let me see, it was called something like the 'Monsters are Due on Maple Street.' It's about a neighborhood where a few strange incidents cause them all to mistrust and blame each other. In the end, they become the monsters they feared."

"And your point is," Katerina asked.

"She passed out," Annie said.

"Well, what was her point?"

"I don't know," Annie said. "Maybe that we should stick together?"

CHAPTER 24
MIAMI, FLORIDA
Early Monday Morning

"You know, Detective Buzinsky, this is not our first rodeo," the older detective said, who sat across from Luke in a small, frigid air conditioned office. The man looked close to retirement, but someone had told Luke that Abrams had an excellent reputation. The captain sported a small gray mustache and was balding. He kept taking his readers on and off, whether to read the report on his computer, or to look up at Luke.

"I'm aware. My apologies," Luke said. "We got caught with our pants down and lost the vehicle that has our undercover on it. No signal."

"So, what makes you so sure they're headed here?"

"Bits and pieces. We think they're on a bus. There are half a dozen buses that have crossed two state lines, so we're monitoring them. We picked up a bidding war a couple of weeks back and identified at least three of the bidders with Miami area homes, and when we cross-checked the names with large yachts registered here, two could transport the girls pretty far out of the country."

"And what makes you think it's a registered ship?"

"Gut, I guess."

"And you're known for good gut?"

Luke looked down at his feet. He heard the echo of his supervisor in that question. But it was more like, "Quit following your gut, and start building a case on facts." He blushed at the memory.

Abrams fiddled with a mechanical pencil, tossed it onto his desk, then took a swig of his Diet Dr. Pepper. Why so many paunchy cops drank diet soda, he would never understand.

"I don't know what kind of manpower you imagine we have down here, but we certainly don't have enough to scout all the marinas for all your maybes."

Luke wanted to jump across the desk and strangle the man. Their team had been working on this operation for over a year. That they may have screwed up now ate at him. Not to mention his stupid idea of getting closer to Susan and Annie. He had assumed Annie was safe since she never went to the mobile parties anymore. His partner swore her routine never changed. But then, he had to admit, dropping Annie off at the babysitter's was a stupid move. He probably spooked Annie's key contact. If he lost Annie in all of this, Susan would never forgive him. He would never forgive himself. He still suffered shame for losing his K-9, Jakob. If only Jakob hadn't given chase. If only. Luke shook his head to clear his thoughts. He had to convince Abrams to help.

"Look, help me check out the few yachts we know are here. I told you, we have someone inside. If she can, she will signal us. We have two or three scenarios."

"And if she is blown?"

"Then she'll be dead, and the rest of the girls will be on their own to escape when and if they can or want to."

"All right, Buzinsky. We'll investigate those owners and yachts and anything else that looks suspicious the next day or so. One thing in your favor, there's a storm coming. It may slow the whole thing down. But let me say this: you may be climbing up the wrong mast. If these folks are super rich, they'll be in Palm Beach, not here. You might try going up to Palm Harbor or Cannonsport Marina. Those are new ports, and if you ask the right questions, you might learn something. Most of the folks there won't talk about their own, but if there are Russkies hanging around, then they'll stick out like a sore thumb."

Luke stood. "Thanks. Here's my contact information." He left Abrams's office and headed for the lobby where he had left his partner, Rodriguez. Thank God he had someone with him who could speak Spanish. The guy had already navigated them into a decent rental car.

"Rodriguez," he called out, "let's go. We may be in the wrong damn city."

"What?"

"I'll tell you in the car."

Once they were on their way, Rodriguez punched in Palm Beach Marina.

"Jesus, Luke. It's an hour and a half away. I thought we were concentrating on Miami?"

"So did I, but I'm trusting this guy Abrams's intuition. Let's ask some questions. I get the impression this is where the super-rich park their fancy boats."

"Dock, bro, dock. This isn't a parking lot."

"You know what I mean."

"You'd better get this right."

"Don't remind me," Luke said.

While Rodriguez drove, Luke texted Susan, *Have arrived in Miami. Long story. Nice weather for now, but a storm is coming. That's good news for us. Have a few leads. Don't despair, not yet.* He contemplated an emoji or two, but then reconsidered. Unlike his cop pals who broke up anxiety with humor, Susan was a civilian and undoubtedly walking the floor.

*

Susan hadn't left home since Luke drove away. She stood at her sunroom window and stared at the swing that still hung from the sycamore in her backyard. She doubted Annie had been on that swing even once in the last five years, but Susan couldn't bear to take it down. Tom had put it up on the day they received Anya's picture and they knew they would be parents. Two weeks later, the doctor diagnosed Tom with esophageal cancer. She had tried so hard to believe Tom would make it, that God wouldn't bring them to the brink of their dreams and then snatch him away. If only Tom hadn't waited so long but gone to the doctor right away. Such a stubborn man. And so, instead of a five-year survival rate, he had months. Months! She had been so angry.

But now, here I am, ten years later. No Tom, and if God doesn't in-
tervene, I might lose Annie too. Maybe this is my fault. Maybe I should
have waited and adopted later. Or maybe I should have told Annie soon-
er about the circumstances of her adoption. Maybe Annie would have
heard how desperate I was to have a child. Stupid! Even at fourteen,
Annie can't understand. Why should she?

All along, I've focused on getting what I want and what I want Annie
to be. I tried to mold this damaged child into my picture of a little tow-
head girl who would laugh and twirl her way through life. I never really
considered what Annie wanted. What does Annie want now? I need to
face the reality of her losses and hopes.

Madelyn said from the beginning, "Susan, accept this. Annie is not like other little girls. She suffers from a type of PTSD we call 'developmental trauma disorder.'"

Annie had only just begun acting out when Susan brought her to the therapist. "But Madelyn, Annie was only four when she left Russia. She has had everything a little girl could want."

"Yes," Madelyn had said. "But you don't know what she left behind. It's called unprocessed trauma. There are therapies we can try, but Annie must cooperate with them. She's not there yet."

And that's where they were still. Susan had held on, hoping Annie would reach a point when they could try some therapies like EMDR or Cognitive Brain Therapy. But the time never seemed right, and now it was too late. All of it was too late.

The doorbell chimed, her phone rang, and then the dog started barking. She turned in place, unable to process which to address first. The vibration of the phone got her immediate attention, so she answered it.

"Hello. Luke?" And to the dog, "Shush, Zelenka."

"No, sorry, this is Fillip. Fillip Popov. I am a friend of Luke's. I'm calling about the Russian detective you hired. We tried to schedule a phone call yesterday, but no one answered my email."

"Oh. Oh yes. My God, I'm so scattered. Please forgive me. And no, I haven't checked email at all."

The doorbell rang a second time. Zelenka ran to the door and barked.

"Please hold on one moment. Someone is at my door. Zelenka, stop."

Susan ran to the door, forgot to look through the peephole like Luke had insisted she use, and opened it.

"Katie, since when do you use the doorbell?" Susan said.

"Since you started locking the door. God, Suse, are you okay?"

"Down, Zelenka!" Susan yelled. "Sorry, sorry. Did Luke call you?"

"Yes, I couldn't get here sooner. Amanda and I were at the beach house." Kate flounced in wearing the perfect sundress. Susan hadn't changed clothes since the night before and hadn't noticed how warm it was outside.

Looking down at Zelenka, Kate said, "This is some dog. When did you get it?"

"Oh, honey, there is so much you don't know."

Vaguely, Susan heard her name being called in the distance, and she realized it was the man on the phone.

"Oh God, Mr. Popov. I'm so sorry. Kate, come in. Make yourself a drink. What time is it? Make me one too. A stiff one."

"A stiff iced tea?" Kate said.

"What?" Susan said.

"Never mind, honey. I got you. I know you don't drink during the day. Go talk on your phone." Kate walked off to the kitchen.

Susan nodded and went back to the sunroom. "Mr. Popov, my apologies."

"No problem. I've been trying to contact Luke, but he's not picking up my calls either."

"Yes, well, I'm afraid we've had some unpleasant developments."

"Oh?" Fillip said on the other end.

"Yes, I'm sure Luke can fill you in better than I can. I'm the mother of the missing girl."

"What are you saying?" Fillip's voice took on an odd tone.

"I'm saying that Annie is missing. She got herself involved in some kind of gang. Some kind of trafficking or something. They threw her into a van, and no one knows where she is. And there's this undercover person in the van or whatever, but no one has heard from her. And now

Luke is in Miami because he figures that's where they are headed. I don't know why he assumes that because there are lots of waterways between here and there. And, and—" And like before, Susan collapsed onto the floor as she sobbed.

Kate came running and enfolded Susan into her arms on the floor. She pulled the phone from Susan's hand.

"I'm sorry. This is Kate."

"It's Fillip, Kate. I'm a friend of Luke's."

"Yes, I remember you. Listen, it sounds like this is a bad time."

"Of course, but if she settles down at all, have her call me. The detective she hired, the one in St. Petersburg, found Annie's siblings. Not in Russia after all, but in Latvia. It's a long story. But it's all true. Annie has a biological brother and sister, older, but eager to see her. Please have Susan call me when she's ready."

"Omigod. All right. I will. I will." Kate disconnected the call and then simply rocked her best friend and let her cry nonstop.

CHAPTER 25
ON THE BUS
Monday

The bus pulled up to a truck stop again. Annie wasn't sure where they were now. Maybe South Carolina still. Her geography felt sketchy at best. Some girls asked to go inside the building to use a real restroom, but the guys laughed.

Lincoln kept saying, "Trust me, ladies. Where you're headed is paradise."

Annie thought, *these girls are so pitiful and high all the time, they don't realize they're prisoners. I am a prisoner, too.*

Annie's whole body felt stiff from sitting so long. She rubbed her thighs and found a tear in her black leggings. She wondered when that had happened. At least she still had her blue jean jacket that covered her skimpy hot pink top, as though any of this mattered.

One guy came through with more fast food and followed up with cans of soda. Annie was hungry but didn't trust her stomach to hamburger and fries. She asked for a bottle of water, but none ever came. She thought the bus would take off again once the guys picked up the trash. Instead, the bus sat there and idled.

Gabi still sat beside her, but slept a lot. Whenever she woke, she groaned. She still wore her short shiny gold dress and long flowered scarf, which she had wrapped around her head like a turban. Her feet and legs were bare.

"Gabi, are you going to be okay?" Annie finally asked.

"Headache," she said. "Really bad headache." Gabi gazed at Annie, then leaned in close and said, "Tell me about you, Annie. Tell me the story of the real you."

Annie whispered back, "What do you mean?"

"Look, I know why I'm here, but why are you here?"

Katerina interrupted from the seat row ahead. "She's a snitch, that's why."

"I'm not. Why do you keep saying that?" Annie said.

"Mind your own business, Katrina," Gabi said.

"Katerina. My name is Katerina. My mother is from Ukraine."

"Mail-order bride, probably."

"You shut up. You know nothing," Katerina said, and then huffed out of her seat to join some of the other girls watching TV in the back.

Gabi turned to Annie, "You were saying?"

"I wasn't saying. I don't know what to say."

"So, how did you fall into trouble with Lincoln?"

"Oh God. Him. That's another story altogether."

Slowly, Annie told Gabi about her first friend, River, and River's friends and how they hung out together. "I still miss River so much. She never treated me like a weirdo. She even said I was pretty and told me I shouldn't listen to the cheese bags at school."

Gabi laid her head on Annie's shoulder.

"Keep talking," Gabi said.

"Lincoln started asking River out in the fall. She thought he was cool—even though he'd dropped out of school, he was making bank. She even said he was sexy. But I had my own experience with him the week after the girls disappeared. He told me to mind my own business and then he pushed me up against a wall and kissed me. It wasn't a nice kiss at all. I hated it. Plus, he smacked me."

"I'm sorry, kiddo," Gabi said.

Annie teared up, so she looked out the window. A limousine pulled up. Two men in suits got out and walked toward the bus. It was raining by then, but neither man acted like he felt a thing, reminding her of the old movie, *Men in Black*. The front door of the bus opened, and they walked in, bringing their heavy cologne with them. The second man stopped when he saw Annie. Gabi sat up. The man tapped his friend on the shoulder.

"Edik!"

The other man turned, saw Annie, then nodded and kept walking.

"Mr. Bok?" the driver said, "Okay to leave now?"

Both men stopped. Mr. Bok hissed at the driver, "Shut up and drive," then complained, in Russian, all the way down the aisle. "Everyone here is an idiot. Did you hear him say my name out loud? No wonder the operation is falling apart."

"Golubov would have pulled a gun and shot the guy. If we aren't careful, we'll be blamed for this mess," Edik said.

They went through a door in the back, and Annie missed the rest of the conversation.

She heard the bus go into gear and watched it slowly pull out of the parking lot and onto a secondary road. *That's odd*, she thought.

"When did we get off the big road?" Annie asked Gabi.

"A while ago, just after the turnoff to Jacksonville. Something spooked them, like extra cops maybe."

That might be a good sign, Annie thought.

They were quiet for a bit. Gabi bit her nails.

Annie asked, "Have you been all the way in the back of the bus? Do you know what's behind the door?"

"I don't know. It's a big bus. Probably a bedroom that converts into a meeting room. Tell me more about you. Who is Maks?"

Annie sighed. "I thought he was my boyfriend. He said he would take me back to Russia to find my brother and sister." Then she explained how she found her mother's travel diary and how Susan had tricked the authorities and how Annie's Russian name was Irina Vladimirovna Lebedev and how, because of her American mother, she had lost her identity. "I mean, my real last name means swan in Russian."

"That's pretty. Now, you're like a swan out of water," Gabi said.

"Yeah. What's your last name, Gabi? We're not supposed to ask, I know, but I don't see how it matters much anymore."

"True enough. Gattini. Gabriella Gattini. It's Italian. But what makes you so sure you have a brother and sister in Russia?"

"You have a lot of questions," Annie said.

"I'm bored. Unless you have any smokes on you?"

"No, sorry."

They were silent again. Then Annie said, "I have two dolls, a boy and a girl, and I've had them since I came here. When I arrived in this country, at four years old, I was already a mess. My mother told me I didn't speak for the first two years except at night. At bedtime, I would say good night to my two dolls, Fedya and Elena. As I got older, I would sometimes remember little things from the orphanage. I had an imaginary friend back then, too, a big blue cat. And he's the one who told me to say these names, Fedya and Elena, every night before I went to sleep. 'And someday,' he said, 'you'll see them again.'"

"That's amazing," Gabi said.

"Yeah, well, that little story has gotten me here, which is sheer stupidity."

Before Gabi could say anything back, Lincoln came to their row and pulled Annie up from her seat.

"Come on," he said. "Boss wants to see you."

"Owww, you're hurting me."

"Lighten up, dirtbag," Gabi said to Lincoln.

But he back slapped her as he yanked Annie to her feet and pushed her down the aisle to the back of the bus.

When they got through the back door, Annie marveled at the sense of space despite its compactness. The men, Bok and Edik, names she would never forget, sat on two easy chairs. Lincoln shoved her onto the edge of the bed, facing them. He stood next to her as though she might run away.

"Take off your jacket. We want to see a little skin," Lincoln said.

She pulled off her jean jacket. Her bare shoulders and midriff made her feel quite naked.

The taller one, Bok, lit a cigarette and rocked back in his chair. In Russian, he said, "You speak Russian, yes? So, let's keep this simple. I will

160

ask you questions, and you will answer them. If you answer correctly, nothing happens. If not, you will get hurt. A shame for such a pretty girl."

Lincoln lit a cigarette then, too. To make the point, he grabbed her left wrist and burned her with the cigarette.

"Oh my God. Stop. Stop." Annie cried. She had never known so much pain from such a small thing. Her heart raced.

If they keep this up, my body will shut down or something. I'll start vomiting or pass out.

"Please don't do this," Annie said.

Bok spoke. "So sorry. You need to understand how serious we are. So, tell me, Little Orphan Annie, what exactly did you share with your policeman friend? Whose names did you give him?"

Annie couldn't stop crying. "Nothing. I didn't tell anyone anything. I swear."

She kept holding her wrist, but then Lincoln pulled her good hand away.

Lincoln took a drag from his cigarette and then touched the burning end to her wrist again. Annie screamed. Mr. Bok snapped his fingers at Lincoln to turn up the music out in the main cabin at the console. Annie could feel the beat. She panted. Lincoln took another drag.

Annie cried, "No, please no. No one. Not Lincoln, not Maks. Just Renee, because I had to. She was my cover story."

The other man, Edic, looked at Lincoln and said, in English. "Who is this, Renee?"

"Nobody. Not really," Lincoln said. "She's Maks's woman. They have a kid. He keeps her in line."

Annie fell backwards onto the bed, her mouth open, and tears flowed down her face. Lincoln jerked her back up so hard, she fell forward onto the floor and coiled into a fetal position.

Lincoln swore. "Sit up, damn it. Do you want me to tie her to a chair?"

"It will take too long," Bok said.

Edic asked Lincoln, "Where is Maksim? He did not report in? Was he caught?"

"I dunno. Renee was pissed off. She said he grabbed a duffel and left before the van even got the girls."

"*Trus*, coward," Edic said.

"We'll find him," Bok answered.

Throughout this brief exchange, Annie's thoughts raced around in her head like a spinning puppy dog. *Renee and Maks? All this time? Not me at all? Never? And the little boy, Benny? I see it now, the resemblance. I am so stupid.*

Lincoln pulled on her hair to yank her head up to face the men, her back against the bed. The pain in her arm reminded her of the time she had burned herself with an iron. Suddenly, Lincoln poked her again.

"Please stop."

Lincoln held onto her hair.

As she sobbed, the snot dripped down her face. It was disgusting. *I am disgusting.*

Lincoln got in close to her face. "Maybe you'd like a little razor blade instead? I could draw my initials into your skin so that you'd always remember me."

Bok said, again in Russian to her, "Listen, you have cost us a lot of money. We had to change the time schedule because of you. We told Maks to bring you in last night. Are you telling me Maksim is the traitor?"

"No," Annie screamed. "I don't know."

"What do the police know?" Edic asked.

"I don't know," Annie cried, and then screamed when she looked down and saw two lines of blood form on her other wrist.

She didn't know she had collapsed and lost consciousness until she woke up next to Gabriella at the front of the bus again. She found her jacket draped over her like a blanket. Gabi was wrapping something around her wrists.

"What happened?" Katerina popped up in the next row along with another girl, Misty, she thought.

"What did they do to you?" the girl asked.

"You might as well tell them what they want to know. Nick said they'll start on your face next," Katerina said.

Gabi looked up sharply. "Shut up."

"Who put you in charge?" Katerina said. She and the other girl turned back around and clinked glasses.

"What are you drinking?" Gabi asked.

"We talked Bobby into sharing his bottle of vodka. It's raspberry. Very yummy," Katerina said. Annie saw Gabi lick her lips, then look over her shoulder toward the back.

"Bobby keeps the bottle, so you have to pay him for the shots, if you know what I mean," the other girl said.

Annie leaned her head back. "I don't know what you mean."

"Doesn't matter. You don't need to know," Gabi said.

"She's even stupider than she looks," Katerina said.

"Why are you being so mean?" Annie asked.

"Nick and I had a long talk. He's gonna take me with him. Misty, listen. I love that song. Let's go to the back." The girls left their seats and headed toward the music.

Annie glanced at Gabi and saw her hands shaking.

"Are you okay?"

"I'll be all right. I made a mistake, that's all. A big mistake. It's time I made things right. Here, try to hold your hands up a little, especially the one with the cuts. Are they throbbing?"

"Yeah. Thanks for the wrappings. You tore up your scarf?"

"Better than nothing. Try to sleep. We'll get there in a few hours."

"Where?"

"I don't know. Near the water. Now, close your eyes."

"You seem different," Annie said.

"I'm different all right. I'm an idiot."

This time, Annie leaned over and rested her head on Gabi's shoulder. Gabi pulled the jacket up to Annie's chin. They were both silent for some time.

"Annie?" she whispered. But Annie didn't have the energy to answer and allowed herself to drift off, despite the throbbing in her wrists.

*

When Annie woke, it was full dark and raining hard. The wind lashed at the bus as it stood in some kind of parking lot near a marina. The area must have lost electricity in the storm. Annie could hear clanging bells and, somewhere, a siren. The bus swayed slightly. When she looked next to her, Gabi had disappeared. She sat up to look around and saw Gabi in the back with the other girls and men, laughing loudly and hanging on to one guard like he was her best friend. It felt like another betrayal, seeing Gabi like that. She thought they were sort of friends, but clearly, wrong again. Gabi was much older anyway. Truthfully, Annie envied her confidence and fast talking. Gabi was everything Annie could never be.

River had been another one who oozed self-confidence. Annie always knew she was out of her element, and yet River had embraced her anyway, teaching her how to talk and walk and dress. River changed Annie's life in three short months. So what if River thought of her as a fixer upper? She had done for Annie what no psychiatrist or counselor or doctor could ever do. River loved her and never judged her.

She imagined River sitting on one of these buses. Had she been afraid or brave when they transferred her to a yacht one dark night and sailed out of the country? I'll never know.

Tears sprang up again. So much crying. So much loss. *I've tossed everything away. My mother tried to be my family, but I threw it back at her.*

Standing at the head of the bus, Lincoln's sandpaper voice interrupted her reverie.

"All right, ladies. As you can tell, there's a storm outside and our little boat ride to paradise has been delayed." Some girls groaned in the back. "But I promise you, tomorrow, or Wednesday at the latest, we will be drinking champagne and lying on some of the most beautiful sandy beaches in the world." Several of the girls cheered. "We selected you for this experience, and my bosses will not disappoint you. But, unfortunately, because it's the last minute, we will have to stay in a nearby apartment building. Please be patient with me. All right?"

"We love you, Linc," a girl yelled from the back. Annie turned to see who yelled, and saw Aiyesha, of all people. Two or three of the girls started chanting his name as though he were a celebrity. They already forgot about those lousy hamburgers and sodas. What had he given them to make them so loyal? Apparently, drugs and alcohol were enough.

But then, how had he fooled River? Annie had considered her totally street smart, and yet Lincoln had conned her big time. She turned to look toward Lincoln, and this time, she saw Gabi sidle up to him as he grinned his way down the aisle. Annie also saw Gabi give Katerina the finger; those two were in some kind of rivalry. Annie leaned back. Her head started spinning. She accidentally leaned on her wrist with the burns and it jolted her with a sudden stab of pain. *God*, she thought, *don't let them hurt me again.*

The bus roared back to life, and soon they were meandering through silent city streets. She couldn't imagine what time it was. The rain made everything look like a blurry dreamscape punctuated by the streetlights that barely illuminated their way. Shortly, the bus pulled into a neighborhood with small houses and an occasional two-story building. It reminded her of old Ocean City, with its small apartment buildings and tiny rooms for beachgoers to rent. Old school.

When they stopped, she saw the building she assumed would be their digs. Annie put on her jean jacket while the other girls giddily trounced by. They were still in their party clothes, which were none too attractive after their long bus ride. She considered peeling away from the group, but then Gabi ran up to her and said, "Let's stick together," and secured Annie by the elbow to help her out of her seat. Katerina shoved past them and down the bus steps, disappearing into the dark. When Annie looked up, she saw Nick standing nearby, waiting for them to get moving.

"Where's Maks?" Annie asked Nick.

"You ask too many questions. I told you, he bolted. No one knows."

Gabi spoke up then, "Maybe he was the snitch all along. I mean, it sure looks suspicious."

"You don't know Maks. He'll go where the money is."

"But his mother is dying?" Annie said.

"His mother?" Nick laughed. "You fell for that? She died in Brighton Beach some ten years ago. He may still have a sister there, I don't know. Either way, he's dead if they find him," Nick said.

"Who's they?" Gabi asked.

From outside the bus, Annie heard Lincoln calling, "Nick, get those skanks out here. Put them on the end, number six on the second floor."

"Let's go," Nick said.

CHAPTER 26
TOWSON, MARYLAND
Monday Night into Tuesday Morning

For the longest time, Susan paced her living room but eventually dragged herself upstairs and lay on her bed. Kate said she would stay in the guest room after making a few phone calls. Susan didn't bother to undress or get under the covers. She lay there with Zelenka at the foot of her bed and kneaded the dog's fur with her bare feet. She wasn't sure who enjoyed the practice more. Sleep eluded her.

Kate knocked on her door before coming in with a cup of tea and milk.

"You're not sleeping yet, are you?" Kate said.

"No, not yet."

"I called Fillip back. He's arranging for a family liaison officer to come to the house tomorrow. They're trained to help people in grief and trauma. Plus, she'll be our contact with the department and keep us updated."

"I don't know. Do I need that? I'm sure Luke will call when he can." But then she remembered her little breakdown on the living room floor earlier. "Maybe I do. I can't seem to process anything properly." She rubbed her face with her hands and Zelenka crept up closer to her side.

"I know. None of us can. But listen, Suse, there's more. Fillip wanted you to know that he heard from the detective."

"No more bad news, please."

"It's not bad news. Not at all, in fact. He said he'll drop by as soon as he can tomorrow and share the details. But he found them, Susan. The detective found Annie's brother and sister."

Susan pushed herself up from the pillow. "That's wonderful. My God, that's wonderful." She pulled Kate into a hug. But then quickly pulled back, realization setting in. "What if it's too late? What if Annie is lost to us? And lost to them, again?"

"I know. It's too horrible to even consider."

They held each other again, and Susan wept.

"Come on," Kate said. "Here. Drink this concoction. It's good and will help you sleep." Kate puffed up Susan's pillows and then crawled in next to her. "Give me the remote. Let's watch something pointless and silly."

Eventually, Susan fell asleep, and Kate turned off the television and the lights, and stepped across the hall to the guest room.

But Susan hadn't slept deeply. She heard her friend tiptoe out. She rolled to her side and watched the numbers flip on her old clock radio, one minute to the next. At three o'clock, Susan considered getting up again when Zelenka lifted her head suddenly, sniffed the air, and then jumped off the bed and whined by the closed door. Susan thought guard dogs started barking like crazy if someone came into the house. Was this part of the dog's military training, her stealthiness? Or maybe the dog just needed to go outside and pee. *Get a grip.*

Susan pushed her feet into her favorite sneakers, the heels long ago squished flat, and followed Zelenka out her bedroom door and down the hall. Honestly, Susan hadn't heard a thing. But, at the foot of the stairs, the dog paused, then slowly stepped toward the French doors of the living room. Susan followed. She heard a kind of scraping sound, she thought. Zelenka stood motionless, waiting. Then Susan saw a small beam of light dancing across her living room floor.

All at once, he appeared. A man dressed in black stepped into the doorway, his phone light in hand. *The command, what was the damn command for the dog to attack? Butok? TikTock?* Fortunately for Susan, the dog didn't seem to need a voice command to sense danger and act. Immediately, Zelenka leaped for the hand that held the phone. Susan screamed.

The lights came on upstairs and Kate came running down. "Omigod," she yelled. Susan screamed, "Call 911. Call 911," while the man tried to hit the dog in the head to get her to let him go.

"Stop hurting my dog," Susan yelled and then grabbed a vase and hit him over the head.

"Shit," he screamed.

"Isn't that supposed to knock them out?" Kate said.

"You've watched too many movies," the man said in accented English as blood poured from a gash in his head. "Get this damn dog off me."

"I don't know the command for that," Susan said.

When a Baltimore County Sheriff arrived, he had K9 training and knew how to release the dog. It sounded like the officer said "boost it" but Susan knew that couldn't be right.

"An ambulance is on the way," the sheriff said. His partner came in with a first aid kit and pulled out gauze to put pressure on the head wound.

Susan and Kate sat on the stairs and watched the action, still stunned by what had happened. Zelenka sat alert at Susan's feet.

"I'm Sheriff Wakefield, by the way. John Wakefield. Are you ladies all right?" Wakefield asked. "Which of you is the owner?"

"I am," Susan said. "Susan Spencer and this is my friend Kate Isaacs.

"Either of you know this man?"

"No," Susan said. Kate merely shook her head.

Wakefield turned to the man, now sitting upright, but leaning against the door frame. "You want to tell me who you are and what you're doing here? What's your name?"

"Maksim Bobenka. This is all a mistake. A misunderstanding."

"No. This is breaking and entering. You here legally, son? You got any ID?" the sheriff asked.

"What the hell. You think anybody with an accent is illegal? I have dual citizenship. I've been here the last ten years, Smokey." Maks leaned over to pull out his wallet with his good hand.

The officer went for his weapon immediately. The women yelped and stood up. Zelenka barked. At that moment, Susan understood how terrible things could happen in an instant and how traffic stops escalated so quickly. Maks stopped and held up his hands.

"My wallet. My ID is in my wallet in my pants pocket," Maks said.

"Stand up and take it out slowly and toss it over." And then to his partner, "Cover him." Wakefield caught the tossed wallet, opened it, and studied the driver's license.

"You gonna let me explain?" Maks asked. "I didn't know anyone was home. A friend of mine lives here. We had a beef, and I wanted my stuff back."

"What friend?" Susan interjected. "My daughter? You're calling my fourteen-year-old daughter a friend of yours? Where is she? Do you know? Are you the asshole who took her to that party?"

And before Wakefield or Kate could stop her, Susan lunged at Maks, her fury unrestrainable. Again, Zelenka was there too, standing on her hind legs, front legs on Maks's chest, barking.

"Mrs. Spencer, hold your dog, please." Wakefield and his partner separated them, and Susan pulled on Zelenka's collar but stood close by.

"Tell me, you piece of shit, where is my daughter?"

The storm door opened, and an EMT came in with a jump bag. Wakefield pointed to Maks, and the guy took Maks by the arm and sat him in a chair in the foyer and began working on him.

"Mrs. Spencer," Wakefield said. "Please remove the dog for now."

"I'll take her to the kitchen. She has a crate there," Kate said and pulled Zelenka away.

For several moments, no one spoke as they watched. Wakefield turned to Susan. "Can you help me understand what I'm missing here?"

"I don't know why this man broke into our house, but he's probably part of some gang that abducted my daughter. You can call the department. Luke Buzinsky is a detective on the operation. He's hoping to track her down."

"He'll never find them. They are probably on a yacht by now. She should never have told you about us," Maks said.

"You're wrong. She never told me anything, or Luke."

Maks looked muddled for a moment, then said, "They assume she did. I'm sorry."

"I don't understand. What are you saying?"

"Mrs. Spencer, please sit down. On the steps here is fine and let me do the talking," Wakefield said.

"But—"

Wakefield held up his hand and directed her to sit. The other officer came over to Susan and sat with her. Wakefield asked the EMT, "Does he need to go to the hospital?"

"Probably should. He got hit pretty hard."

"Fine," Wakefield said and then turned to Maks, "You're under arrest for breaking and entering and it looks like we may have other questions." To his partner, he said, "Benfield, go with them in the ambulance and monitor him. I'll meet you there." To Susan he said, "I'm assuming he came through your back door and in through the living room. Please stay out of there for now and touch nothing. A crime tech will be here in the next hour."

Susan stood. "All right. But Annie—." Kate came back in from the kitchen and held Susan's hand.

"Ma'am, we'll keep you informed," Wakefield said as he closed his notepad and returned it to his jacket pocket.

"A family liaison officer is coming in later today," Kate said. "And Fillip Popov can fill you in on what is happening in the department."

As the deputy escorted Maks out the door, Susan ran after them. "If something happens to my daughter, I'll be sure you rot in hell," she yelled.

Wakefield gently stopped her. "Mrs. Spencer, I know you are upset, but hear me out. If this guy is part of an illegal enterprise, and his people find out we've arrested him, his life is over. He'll talk and hope for our protection." He tipped his hat and strolled down the front sidewalk.

When Susan turned back into the house and closed the door, she leaned heavily against it. Kate came to her, and they embraced.

"What time is it?" Susan asked.

"I don't know, maybe three or four. Too late for a stiff drink and too early for coffee," Kate said.

"Maybe ice cream."

"That works."

CHAPTER 27
RĪGA AIRPORT
Tuesday Morning

Popov stood with Fedya and Elena outside the security gates. All three were sullen as the news that Irina had gone missing tempered their plans for a glorious trip.

"Maybe we should have waited until we know more," Fedya said.

"I understand your reluctance," Popov said. "But my cousin, Fillip, thinks otherwise. He knows these people, and he believes it will be good for everyone to be together."

"She is so rich to pay for our tickets?" Fedya asked.

Popov shrugged. "America is America. They weigh value differently. But the main thing is the potential for a reunion. I did not speak to this Mrs. Spencer personally, so I must trust that Fillip knows what is best for her. For you, he will help by translating whatever is necessary."

"My English is good," Elena said.

Popov patted her arm. "You believe that now, but I have friends who have traveled to some of these English-speaking countries and once those people are speaking at full speed, it doesn't sound like English at all."

Fedya laughed. "You are probably right. How can we thank you, Rurik?"

"Here is my card. Brand new, you see? Very fancy. I have plans for a new start when I get back to St. Petersburg. I even have a nice lady to take to dinner. So, send me an email now and then."

Elena hugged the man, who blushed. "We will. We certainly will."

"You'd better go now. Let me help you with your bag." He lifted it to put on her shoulders. "My God. It's so heavy. I'm surprised you got past the ticket agent."

"Books. My journals. I've been writing to Irina ever since we started living in Rīga. I want her to know about our lives. I always believed we would find each other again. I believed God would make that happen."

"Faith is a potent thing. Your story gives me pause," Popov said.

"Come on, Elena," Fedya said. "The lines are getting longer as we stand here."

Fedya shook Popov's hand and Elena hugged him again. They stepped into line. He watched them until he couldn't see past the final security gate. As he walked back through the terminal, and to the shuttle that would take him to the garage, he considered how much this job had changed him. So many assignments over the years had been nothing more than chasing down a criminal or outing a cheating husband. They held no heart. But this one had reached inside to a place he had guarded for many years. Perhaps, yes, perhaps, the time had come to try his own reunion. He would have to call his ex-wife to ask for Georgiy's phone number. Possibly, the boy—well, he wasn't a boy any longer, but a man—would hang up on him. But maybe, just maybe, if he tried, something good would come of it. He had failed his family. All true. But the only way to find out if he had any chance for reconciliation was to make the call. First, he would take Masha to dinner. She would be his lodestar.

*

Fedya let Elena have the window seat since it was her first airplane flight. Not that he could claim expertise. His experience was a regional flight for a piano competition in Poland. Once they were seated, he pulled out the flight information and read everything. He checked for the exits even before the flight attendants started talking. Both he and Elena listened carefully and even felt for the life jackets under their seats. The businessman next to them had already tucked into his neck pillow and closed his eyes.

Both kept their eyes out the window until the plane topped the clouds with nothing more to see. Elena pulled a magazine out of her tote bag. While she read, he reminisced about their early life before his mother died, before she invited Vlad, Irina's father, into their lives, whose drinking and violence destroyed their family. He cast back even further, before the war in Chechnya that took their papa, Ivan. He cherished the laughter most of all. His mother had been a musician, too, like her brother, their Uncle Uldis. Fedya found out later that his mother could have had a career if she hadn't fallen in love with Ivan, who took them to St. Petersburg. *How different their lives would have been if they had stayed in Latvia.*

Elena interrupted his thoughts. "What are you thinking?"

"The old days, when we were little. You don't remember living in Rīga as children, do you?"

"No. It's a blur. Our terrible years, the ones after Mama died, have shrouded my early life."

"You're probably right."

"It's one reason I wanted to write about our daily lives for Irishka. I never showed them to you. Would you like to read them now?"

Fedya said nothing.

Elena continued, "The journals start out simply. I mean, we were so young, but then the entries become more detailed in high school. By then, I called the diary Irishka, like Anne Frank called her diary, Kitty.

"And now?"

"You mean, do I still write in the diary, or to Irishka? Good question. A little of both. You can skip the parts when I am angry with you."

"All right. Let's see how it goes."

And so she pulled out an old notebook. On the front, Elena had written, "Letters to my Sister." He opened it to the first page.

1 March 2000. Wednesday.

Dear Irishka.

You won't believe it, but we don't live in St. Petersburg anymore. All kinds of terrible things happened to us before we found our mother's brother, Uldis. I lived in a terrible place called Children's House Number Twenty-four. You were in one too, but with a different number. Some girls were so mean. One girl even tried to kill me in a sledding accident, but ended up killing one of the other girls instead. Anyway, I finally got out of there because a friend of Mama's (Vasiliy) came looking for me.

Fedya had bad luck at first. Some terrible people hurt him. A very rich man found him and saved him. There is lots of chasing in Fedya's story. One day, when we see each other again, he can tell you everything.

Fedya put down the notebook. He wasn't sure he could keep reading after all. *Elena was only eleven when she wrote those words and I was fourteen.* He worked out the dates and realized Irina was the same age now as he had been when the worst of his life had happened. Yes, he was grateful. He laid his hand flat against his chest and felt gratitude without guilt for the first time.

If the Americans found their sister and they reunited, then he would have to admit there was a God, and Elena's candles and prayers had been worthwhile. And perhaps he needed to reconsider the power of faith. Despite the news of Irina's disappearance, he knew Elena's faith remained unshaken.

"She will be found," Elena had said to him that morning.

"How can you be so sure?"

"Because God is good, and He wouldn't have us come this far, only to be disappointed."

Fedya smiled as he remembered how she looked, truly defiant. He turned the page to read her second entry, "5 March 2000."

CHAPTER 28
AN APARTMENT IN PALM BEACH, FLORIDA
Tuesday around Noon

There wasn't much to the so-called apartments. Annie assumed they were all identical, where the door opened into a living room/kitchen with a counter between, and two barstools, a couch, a coffee table, a TV on the wall, two bedrooms down a short hallway to the right and a bathroom. The kitchen had a coffee maker and a few plates, mugs, and silverware, but the refrigerator stood empty. All the windows had blinds, firmly closed in all the rooms. Both bedrooms had one queen-sized bed, and according to Nick, the couch opened into a bed. Sheets and pillowcases were in the dressers. Everything seemed clean enough, but worn out.

By the time Nick escorted Gabi and Annie into their assigned place, the other two girls had chosen the bedrooms for privacy, they said. But then, Katerina talked Aiyesha and Misty into sleeping on the pullout couch in the living room so they could watch as much TV as they wanted. As a result, Katerina got the front bedroom that faced the parking lot and side street for herself. Gabi and Annie got the smallest bedroom that looked onto a tall privacy fence with a few houses on the other side of it. All was dark and quiet.

The girls found men's T-shirts tossed onto the beds to sleep in after taking showers. Annie wanted to take off her smeared makeup, even though she knew she would go back to looking her age. Would anyone even notice? She didn't know or care anymore. She couldn't bother to wait for a shower, assumed she could do it in the morning, and crawled under the covers. When Gabi climbed in next to her, she could have sworn she heard Gabi whisper, "I'm gonna get you home, kiddo. I'm gonna get you home."

176

The next morning, a man flung open the apartment door and pushed a hanging rack covered in a plastic tarp into the living room. No change in the weather, still raining. When he pulled the tarp off, it revealed an assortment of colorful dresses, accessories, and sandals. A second man followed with a stack of pizza boxes and several 2-liter bottles of cola. Behind the delivery guys trounced in more girls, almost all of them in an array of T-shirts. Most of the girls were from the bus, but a few Annie had never seen before. There were now fifteen or more girls crowded into their apartment, pawing through the dresses like they were on some game show or something. Moments later, they demolished the pizzas. Apparently, all of them believed they were on their way to some tropical paradise. For them, these were all gifts, a cornucopia of toiletries, food, alcohol, and now, dresses.

Annie sat with Gabi in a corner out of the melee. Gabi seemed to tremble again, which Annie now understood was withdrawal from drugs.

"What do you guess is going on?" Annie asked her.

"I'm going through withdrawal."

"I know that. I don't mean with you. I mean the wardrobe thing."

"They want to impress the goons on the yacht."

"What yacht?"

"I'm assuming we will climb aboard a yacht or something similar and sail away."

"Are you going to be okay?" Annie asked.

"I don't know. I've screwed things up, I know that. But I've got to get it together."

"What do you mean?"

"I'll tell you later. Go pick out something for us to wear. If you can, pick out a couple of extra things without them noticing."

"What do you mean?"

"Like scarves or jackets or sweaters. Anything extra, if they have it."

"Why?"

"Just do it. Please. I wear a medium size. I need to get myself something to drink that has lots of caffeine in it to help stop the shakes." Gabi got up and ambled over to the kitchen where the coffeemaker sat on the counter.

The last person to saunter in was Lincoln, with an armful of totes and handbags. These were their belongings, and everyone hailed him like a hero. Until they realized someone had rifled through the bags.

"Hey, where's my phone? I miss my phone." Several girls yelled. This was the biggest complaint from nearly everyone. Gabi said nothing.

"Ladies. Please listen to me," Lincoln said. "You are ruining all the surprises. Look at all this. These clothes are from our hosts on the yacht, *Tatiana the Beautiful*. Everything on this yacht is beautiful and you must also be beautiful. So, for this reason, we have given you your makeup and hair products. Use them well. There will be a fashion show on the boat, first thing. Show your stuff, ladies."

"But," Aiyesha said again, "my phone?"

"Not yet, because—no, no, I can't tell you. See, you almost made me tell you another secret." He put his finger to his lips and then grabbed the closest girl and gave her a big kiss.

Annie heard someone say, "I bet we're getting new phones." It sounded a lot like Katerina.

Eventually, the other girls found what they wanted to wear and went back to their apartments further down the balcony. From what Annie could tell, five or six girls were in each of the three apartments on the second floor. The men must be on the ground floor.

Annie brought over the clothes to Gabi and after the other girls had left, they went into their own little room to change. Annie had hoped for something with long sleeves to protect her injuries, but no luck. She found a couple of beach wraps, a straw hat, two sun dresses that were plain since the other girls cleared out the fancy ones, and two pairs of flip-flops. They both looked through their carryall bags and, sure enough, Annie found everything there except for the phone and her wallet. Her wallet held little value, her school ID and maybe twenty dollars. She nearly cried when she found the little picture she had taken from her mother's memory box. She had tucked it deep inside a side pocket of the tote. In the picture, she still lived at the orphanage: Irina Vladimirovna Lebedev.

"What's that?" Gabi asked.

In normal times, Annie would have said "it's private" and secreted it back into place. But nothing was normal about this day or whatever days lay ahead. She showed the picture to Gabi.

"This is you?" Gabi asked.

"Yeah, at the orphanage."

"And here I thought you were a bottle blonde. You were quite the towhead."

"Very funny," Annie took the picture back.

"What happened to your arm there?"

Annie looked at the picture more carefully. She hadn't noticed before. Her arm lay quite off kilter. Two memories flashed in her mind, falling out of a window and crying while a boy carried her inside, and a second memory of a woman from the orphanage yanking her up from the floor by her bad arm. That was the day she met her imaginary friend, Lezunchik. He had been her best friend. Could she conjure him up again? She held the photograph to her heart and cried.

Gabi crawled over the top of the bed to hold her.

"Hey, kiddo, I'm sorry. I meant nothing by it. I mean, you're okay now. Your arm looks normal."

"Yeah. My mother took me to so many doctors back then. One of them had to re-break my arm to repair it. I was scared all the time. One reason I didn't talk to anyone. I must have been in a cast for weeks, but I don't remember that part."

A tap on the door and Katerina came in. "What's going on in here?"

"Nothing, Kat Girl. So, where have you been? I'm guessing you must be tight with that good-looking Nick. What's his last name?" Gabi said.

"Smirnov, like the vodka," Katerina laughed, and then sobered quickly. "Why do you want to know?"

"Just curious."

Katerina had already dressed in a beautiful white strapless dress with a huge pink hibiscus that wrapped around her midsection. She had the figure for it. Her auburn hair draped her shoulders.

"You need to get dressed too," she said. "Those two men who've been staying in the back of the bus, they're gonna take a look at us soon to make sure we are ready for the boat."

"When are we getting on the boat?"

"Why would I know?" Katerina said. But then she shrugged. "Whatever, no sense playing games anymore. After dark, around nine or ten, maybe later." Then she looked at Annie more closely. "How old are you anyway, Annie? My God, you look like a ten-year-old girl. You'd better up your game. Although, I hear there are guys who like them young."

"You're disgusting," Gabi said.

"You don't seem to realize what is happening here." Annie said. She jumped off the bed and pushed past Katerina into the living area. Aiyesha and Misty were watching a soap opera. "Hey, guys. We are prisoners. We are being trafficked. God only knows where we will end up."

"Shut up, Annie," Katerina said behind her.

"Didn't you notice all the Russian accents? They are like mafia or something," Annie said.

"But you said it was all good stuff. You said we'd make a lot of money and be on our own. And you told me you've been working with them for months. You're still here. And look at this stuff. Best prison I've ever known," Aiyesha said and laughed.

"I'm tryin' to watch TV here," Misty said and turned up the volume. "This is my favorite show."

Katerina pulled Annie back through the hallway and into her and Gabi's room. Gabi stepped back from both, her hands up in what appeared to be surrender.

"Katerina," Annie tried to reason with her. "I'm sorry. These are dangerous people. I shouldn't have invited you to the party. It all went wrong."

"You didn't invite me. Nick did. I was already going before you called me. This made it easier to spy on you."

"On me?"

"You think we're not on to you? Quit denying it," Katerina said. "They're trying to decide what to do with you. Throw you overboard or into a cathouse in Cuba."

"Cuba? We're heading to Cuba?" Gabi asked.

Katerina looked sharply at Gabi and backed away. "You ask a lot of questions, Gabriella. I'm wondering who you are. Maybe I need to tell Nick and Lincoln to take a closer look at you."

Gabi walked toward Katerina as she spoke. "I'm a junkie. You saw me yourself. Lighten up Kat Girl. I feel sorry for the kid. She's out of her league. Not like you. Not like me. We've been around."

Katerina tried to pull the door shut, but Gabi was quicker and blocked it. Katerina let go and bolted into the living room for the apartment door. Gabi gave chase, Annie behind. The two girls on the couch started yelling, "Cat Fight." Gabi had Katerina on the floor. They rolled around, both stronger than they appeared. Finally, Gabi turned Katerina face down and pressed a knee to her back and pulled her arms around hard. Katerina screamed.

Gabi yelled at Annie, "Get into my bag. At the bottom, there's a hidden zipper, open it and bring me a couple of zip ties. Bring me a pillowcase too while you're at it." Annie obeyed.

"Hey, are you a cop?" Aiyesha said.

"Once upon a time. No more. But I remember the moves," Gabi said and chuckled.

"You're gonna die, bitch," Katerina said.

"No news there. We're all gonna die if we get on that boat. And if you are relying on little Nick to protect you, forget it," Gabi said.

Annie brought the pillowcase and zip ties. Gabi put part of the pillowcase in Katerina's mouth to shut her up and then secured the girl's arms with the ties. Gabi pulled Katerina up by them. Katerina tried to scream through the cloth. Gabi pushed her into their room and onto the bed. Then she zip-tied her ankles.

Misty and Aiyesha had stood up now and were creeping toward the apartment door. Annie saw them and used her most commanding voice. "Sit down. You're not going anywhere. You can either sit here and keep watching TV, or we can tie you up."

Misty said, "Is there any pizza left?" Aiyesha looked at the girl as though she were crazy. Misty shrugged. "I always eat when I'm scared."

Gabi came in. "Help yourself." She turned to Annie. "Now, I need you to wrap something like T-shirts or maybe a pillowcase around the sprinkler heads up in our room. Can you figure out a way to do that?"

"Why?"

"I'm working on an idea, and I don't want the sprinklers to go off too soon."

Annie left.

Aiyesha said, "You gonna burn us alive?"

"I'm gonna send a signal. What time is it?" They both shrugged. Gabi opened one blind toward the back of the building. The rain had stopped, but it was still overcast and hard to tell the time. She guessed four o'clock, give or take an hour.

Suddenly, they heard Annie scream in the bedroom. Gabi went running and found Annie on the floor and Katerina, half on and half off the bed, stomping on Annie with her bound feet. Gabi pulled her off and flung her once more onto the bed. "You try that again and I'll dump you in the closet. You okay, Annie? Come on, I need you to brush it off. We have things to do. Watch her while I get this sprinkler head. Here, use this stick from the blinds and hit her hard if she moves." Gabi got up on the bed and quickly wrapped the sprinkler head, then jumped down and tossed another shirt to Annie. "Go do the other bedroom. I'll do the living room."

Misty and Aiyesha were both in the kitchen now, going through the boxes and looking for leftover cold pizza. Gabi came in and turned on one burner. Slowly, an electric glow appeared. She turned it off. She took one of the pizza boxes and tore it into strips of cardboard and laid them next to the stove.

Then she grabbed one of the bar stools, found one scarf Annie had picked out from the wardrobe fiesta, and wrapped it around the sprinkler head closest to the kitchen. She dragged the stool to the smoke detector and pulled out the batteries. The girls watched.

Gabi walked back into their bedroom and sat on the bed. Annie followed. Without a doubt, their roles had reversed. Annie didn't mind.

When Gabi said these people were out of her league, that was an understatement. Her wrists still ached from the burns and cuts.

Katerina looked miserable on the bed, but when Gabi sat near her, Katerina scooted to the other side.

"Now, Kat Girl, I'm going to pull off your gag so we can have a little chat. If you scream, I'll put it back in. That simple. All right?"

Katerina nodded her head slowly. Gabi removed the pillowcase, and while talking, used a knife from the kitchen to cut it into smaller strips.

"What is the timetable for today? Tell me what you know," Gabi said.

"They'll catch you. And what they did to Annie will be child's play compared to what they'll do to you."

"I've got that part," Gabi said. "I need information. This place is going to be a zoo soon and I may lose track of you." She held up the wads of cotton again to show she would insert them if necessary. "Annie, get her a glass of water, please." Annie left. "Now it's just the two of us. Go."

"I don't know that much. I told you, Nick said the plan was to leave by nightfall. We're going to Cuba, but that's not the last stop. It depends on the clients. The boat goes to them, and we drop girls off along the way. We may have a quick stop in the Bahamas."

"How did you get involved?"

"Nick got me out of a jam with my stepfather and gave me a place to stay. I met him at a Russian bar in Pikesville."

Gabi said, "He won't be able to protect you." Katerina rolled her eyes. "Okay, whatever," Gabi said. "I am not here to hurt you or kill you. But you are now officially one of them, and therefore, I have to treat you that way. I will sequester you during this operation until the last minute, and then you can make a run for it like everyone else."

"What operation?"

"Need to know basis."

Annie came in with the water and offered to hold the glass while Katerina sipped it. Katerina said to Annie, "She's going to get us all killed." Annie looked at Gabi, who shrugged.

"One last thing," Gabi said. "Where's my little prop gun?"

"That's not a prop. It's loaded, I looked."

"With blanks. Sorry to disappoint you."

"Nick has it."

"Okay, now you have a choice. Stay quiet in here or I gag you again."

"No gag."

Gabi signaled to Annie, and they went back out to the living room. The girls sat on the couch again as if nothing had happened. Gabi said quietly, "Gummies with cannabis, it's a new thing." Annie looked at them quizzically but could tell they were out of it. "All right, we need to put together some flammable supplies, but hide them until the last minute. You look in both bedrooms and bathroom for anything that will burn. Toilet paper is a good start and bring it in here and put it on the counter. I'll find a place for everything. I may have to break up one of the folding closet doors."

"You strong enough to do that?"

"Never tried before, but necessity is the mother of invention, as they say."

For the next twenty minutes, Annie gathered, and Gabi sorted. Eventually, everything would go on the couch, a base for the fire.

"If the guys visit again, everything has to be out of sight. Our biggest problem will be Katerina. If Nick comes looking for her, that will have to be the trigger for Operation Smoke and Fire."

Gabi used the lower cabinets to store their flammables and put all the pots and pans and dishes in the refrigerator. She visited the bedrooms one last time and did her best to break down a closet door, but all she did was take it off its hinges. But the real bonanza turned out to be a couple of wooden shelves inside the closet, which she could get out easily. Those would only come into play once a fire was going good and by that time, they'd better be out of there.

Annie and Gabi sat at the counter for a few minutes. The other two girls had passed out.

"What happens now?" Annie asked.

"We wait," Gabi said.

CHAPTER 29
PALM HARBOR MARINA
Tuesday Morning

L uke, Rodriguez, two local officers from Palm Beach PD, and finally, two special agents were sitting at a coffee shop on Rose-
mary Avenue. Luke had been asking for agents to join their team
for the past two weeks, first in Baltimore and now here in Florida. The
two feds were out of Miami, and Luke suspected that Captain Abrams
had something to do with their appearance today. Abrams appeared im-
pressed when Luke reported he found the names of two yachts that were
expected to arrive any day, both with Russian names and big as hell. In
fact, *Tatiana the Beautiful* was a 200 footer that had thirteen crew, and
with special permission, could carry up to twenty guests. The second
one, smaller at a hundred and sixty-seven feet, the *Anastasia II*, was a
possibility as well. Or, for all he knew, they might work together.

"There are a couple of different scenarios. They'll have to use a tender
to ferry people from shore to ship. We have an opportunity to achieve a
two-pronged apprehension. The girls being taken by tender and the girls
who are staying somewhere on land," Luke said.

"But you can't arrest the girls for being guests on a boat. The girls
would have to say they were being taken against their will. You know
that rarely happens," Agent Matthews said.

Agent Timons chimed in. "I agree. Usually, they treat these yacht girls
to anything and everything they want until they reach their destination.
That's when the shit hits the fan, and they're out of our jurisdiction."

"Your best bet," Matthews said, "is to grab them at the holding place
because most of them are going to be underage and they have crossed
state lines. Now, some girls will prefer to be with these men, but we can

take them in and try to work with them, bring in social workers and so forth, and give them some kind of reality check."

One of the local officers, Diggs, asked, "But where are they? You don't even know."

"Not exactly," Luke said and covered his discomfort with more coffee. His hope of hearing from Gattini was iffy, at best. When he found out she ditched her tracker at the movie theater, he had a gut feeling she was committing some kind of suicide by a cop or, in this case, suicide by gangsters. He hated to imagine it that way. Then again, she had been an amazing officer at one time until the smack got her. Some of her survival instincts may come back. She had insisted that the last recovery program had worked. But on the surface, her conversations with him before she went undercover were sketchy at best. Too upbeat, like she was on uppers instead of heroin.

"What does that mean?" Diggs asked and took Luke out of his thoughts.

"Here's what I need to confirm about their location. I'm sure they're near the marina, most likely in West Palm Beach. If you guys have a drone, we could do a circular sweep, say, a three-mile radius in concentric circles. That fancy bus will be an eyesore wherever it's parked. Second, our asset said one of the easiest ways to cause some chaos and alert the authorities is to start a fire wherever they're holed up. We need to work with local fire stations. How many are there?"

"Quite a few," Officer Sumner said. "Two are close to the island, one in West Palm off the Dixie Highway, and the other off Route 1. There're quite a few stations downtown, but I'm guessing these jokers won't go down that way. The other two are on the island and specialized for the water."

"Okay, so is there a way for us to monitor their calls today and into the night? The weather is clearing, so I assume the transfer will happen in the next twelve hours."

The two feds looked at each other and back to Luke with a lot of skepticism.

"You have little to go on, Buzinsky. This could be a huge waste of our time and resources."

Luke wanted to get in their faces, but he knew they were right. He had made progress, and felt he had a pretty good chance of something going his way. Unfortunately, their hope of getting to the top of this food chain wouldn't happen. If they were lucky, they'd get a couple of mid-range tough guys along with most of the low-level jerks.

"Look, I know all that. But there's a fourteen-year-old girl in there who I know personally, and our department has an asset in there. Give me twelve hours and if nothing gels, I'll call it off."

Matthews blew out a long breath and finally pulled out his cell phone. "Let me see if we can wrangle a drone."

"Thanks. Really. Thanks," Luke said. The other Fed kept playing some game on this phone. Luke looked at the two local officers and waited for them to chip in with whatever they could do.

Finally, Sumner said, "I'll call Nathan over at the emergency operations center and tell him what we need. If we're lucky, it will be a slow day. Are you thinking they're in a house or something bigger?"

Luke scratched his neck. He had no idea. If they were in a McMansion then things could get more difficult, but since the move to a holding place probably happened at the last minute, maybe it was more low level, like a motel or beach apartment building. "Well, we don't believe it's going to be in a busy downtown area, so it's either a mansion or a cheap beach rental. But it won't be too far from their destination, the marina."

"Here's the thing," Diggs said. "The only way we, the cavalry, can show up in a big way is if we have something corroborating the fire, like the drone report. We will not send our black and whites to every fire."

"Got it. Makes sense," Luke said but gave Rodriguez an eye roll as he drained his coffee cup. That would be his fourth cup already.

Diggs said, "Let's call Banyan Street station our base of operations. It's close to all the major highways and we should be less than ten minutes from anything major going down,"

Rodriguez finally spoke, "We shouldn't give up on the yacht people. Isn't there some kind of inspection someone could drum up?"

"Jesus, man. Now you want us to get the Coast Guard Auxiliary involved? This thing is all jacked up and you guys are running on next to no real intel," Diggs said.

Luke could tell that this guy hated extra work. "So, give me their number. I'll call and ask."

"You have the authority of a horse's ass," Diggs said.

"We could ask for a favor," Sumner said. "Let me call Ned Blake. He's an old buddy of mine. It won't hurt to ask." He turned to Luke and said, "My kid is fourteen. I get it. I'll do my best."

Luke nodded his head but said nothing. This kindness sparked hope in him.

Diggs grunted and said, "I'm outta here. I'll go set up the conference room. Meet me there in thirty minutes."

Agent Matthews came in and said the drone would start its search in twenty minutes. His partner, Agent Timons, got up, and they left together to meet up at the station.

Luke and Rodriguez sat at the table quietly. They both knew the plan to save the girls, including Annie, had become quite a long shot. The operation in Baltimore was a lost cause. To make matters worse, most of those girls wouldn't want to be saved.

Last year, Luke had been part of an operation in Middle River, much smaller than this one, but they had successfully pulled out seven girls. He remembered their stories now. Three of the girls had fled from abusive fathers and uncles, and the last thing they wanted was to go home. Two of the girls were living in foster homes that were trashed by too many kids in too small a space. And the last two, although they went home willingly, a follow-up visit revealed they had run away again. Disheartening. The chances of it happening again were high. He tried to send these memories to the back of his mind. He had to keep Annie in the forefront, and even Gattini.

"You okay, Luke?" Rodriguez asked.

Luke shrugged. "Let's go."

*

Susan picked up the phone on the first ring. Everyone in the room watched her as she covered the phone and she mouthed to them, "Luke." They went back to their business, and she walked into the sunroom. Her living room had become a maelstrom of activity. Kate was still around, but joined by her ex-husband, Sam, and their college-aged daughter, Amanda, at home on summer break. Three ladies from the church had brought food, and they were setting up a smorgasbord for anyone who walked in the door. The family liaison officer, Jasmine Esposito, was on her phone now, and honestly, most of the time. And at one point, even Susan's pastor had dropped by for prayer. He didn't stay long. Zelenka, of course, the hero of the hour for the previous night's escapade with the intruder, was ever vigilant and followed Susan's every step.

Into the phone, she said, "Any news?"

"Yes, and no. Lots going down. Today is the day. If anything good comes out of this, it will be today. We have the cooperation of four different agencies, including the Coast Guard Auxiliary, the FBI, the local police, and the fire department. I'm hopeful."

Susan tried to steady her breathing. "Okay. I'll try to be hopeful too. But you'll call me as soon as you know something definitive?"

"I'll do my best. While I was at a meeting today, I realized how connected I am to this daughter of yours. I want this to work out. But Susan, I have to say, even if she makes it out, this experience will add another layer of trauma. You know that, right?"

"I do, but I also have one silver lining. The detective in St. Petersburg found her siblings."

"No kidding. That's great. I mean, I hope that's great."

"Exactly," she took another slow breath. "They called twenty minutes ago from Dulles. Your friend Fillip is picking them up and bringing them here. I mean, I don't know where else they should go. I spoke with them both on the phone. The sister and the brother speak beautiful English."

"Well, if anyone can handle all this, you can. Look, I gotta go." A slight pause, and then, "Love you. Just have to say it."

"Bye." But after she disconnected, she said to herself, *Do you?*

CHAPTER 30
THE APARTMENT BUILDING, WEST PALM BEACH
Tuesday Afternoon

As luck would have it, the bigwigs from the bus visited only one apartment, the middle one, and everyone else went in and out. Annie went in separately so Gabi could monitor Katerina, who earned a return of the gag, while Misty and Aiyesha went with Gabi when it was her turn to go. No one seemed to notice that Katerina didn't appear for the fashion show. They walked into the room, stood in front of Bok and Edic, who either approved or disapproved. In her case, Bok smiled bitingly and asked how she felt.

She answered insincerely, "Yes, much better, thanks. Looking forward to the tropical breezes. I'm glad I know how to swim."

Edic looked at her with slit eyes, but she smiled with gritted teeth. Before she could leave, however, she heard Bok say, "Give her something to cover those arms." And before she could even turn around, a woman who looked vaguely familiar handed her a white sweater. As she walked back to their place next door, Annie recognized the woman from the row house on her first night. The gatekeeper. A chill went through her.

When Gabi came back with the other two, she encouraged them to have another gummy to kill time because they wouldn't be able to sit in the living room anymore.

"Why not?" Aiyesha asked.

"Operation Smoke and Fire will start soon," Gabi said and, once again, put her fingers to her lips. "It's our big secret. But I want you both to be safe. You stay in the other bedroom and as soon as it's safe, we'll call you out."

"That's crazy. There's nothing to do in there," Misty said.

"You could try some lesbian love moves," Gabi said. Annie's eyes bulged, and she stepped behind the kitchen counter to hide her embarrassment. *Who said things like that?*

Misty took Aiyesha by the hand and led her into the bedroom.

"I was only kidding, guys," Gabi said to their backs, but neither turned around.

Annie stood up, stared at Gabi, and said, "Weird."

"Well, this is a pretty weird situation. Okay. Let's get our stuff out. Put everything we collected on the couch. I see nothing else soft that would burn. I don't even know if the couch will burn. It might melt if it's as synthetic as it feels."

Annie got to work, piling flammables on the couch while Gabi turned on all three burners, but only one worked. "Shit," she said. She got out the cardboard strips and lay them next to the stove. "This will take too long," she muttered to herself. She went to the door to check on the activity next door, but a guard stopped her.

"Hey lover, I'm checking to see if the bigwigs were still around or did they go back to the bus."

"I dunno."

"Could you check for me, please?"

"None of my business. I'm s'posed to keep you inside. So, go back inside."

"Right, sure. Hey, you wouldn't have a smoke, would you? A regular cigarette? I'm dying for one. I could do a little trade for one. You'll see, I've got great hands."

His eyes widened, and he looked around to see if anyone was watching.

Gabi looked down at the end of the balcony. And sure enough, she saw a little dark corner covered by an ice machine. She pointed him toward it.

"Nah, I'd better not."

"Well, before I talk you into it, I wanna make sure you've got the goods. Cigarettes, yes? Matches?"

191

"I've got a lighter."

"Perfect, so let me give you a preview." And before he knew what happened, Gabi slipped her hand to his pants, pulled down the zipper and got a good grip on his lunch box. "Oh, you've got the best goods of all."

And with that, she scampered behind the ice machine, and lover boy followed. Less than eight minutes later, Gabi had three cigarettes and a lighter. After blowing him a kiss, she opened the apartment door. Before she closed the door behind her, she heard talking outside and deduced the big shots were leaving the apartment next door. She distinctly heard one of them, the younger one, say that he'd be seeing them again in an hour. Time to start the fire. She locked their door from the inside.

"Okay, let's go. Put Misty and Aiyesha in the bathroom along with all their stuff. Tell them it's life or death. Here's the lighter. You can use that to light the bed in there if the cardboard doesn't work out. Get our stuff out of the other bedroom and put it by the front door. We do Katerina last. I don't trust her. I'll start on the couch flammables." She said this as she lay strips of cardboard on the bright red electric burner. As soon as they flamed, she tossed them into the nests of toilet paper and paper towels she had made on the couch and pushed it up against the back wall. Gabi tried to open the window a crack to get some oxygen moving in the room to fan the flames, but they wouldn't budge. She grabbed a pan from the refrigerator where she had stashed them and broke a window.

She heard pounding on the door, "Hey what's going on in there?"

"Nothing, lover boy. I broke a glass in the kitchen. Can we come out soon?" she asked

"Not yet. But keep it down in there," he said.

Annie came back in, breathless. "There's a smoke alarm in the hall. Did you disable it?"

"Crap. I forgot." She dragged over a kitchen stool as quickly as she could and climbed up to pull out the batteries. Smoke began accumulating around them. "Wet a scarf and wrap it around your nose and mouth. I'll be putting the batteries in the kitchen detector in a minute. Take a knife and cut Katerina's zip ties." The girls in the bathroom opened the door, smelled smoke and closed it again.

192

Annie slipped past Gabi standing on the stool and opened the door. Katerina's face was ashen with fear and her eyes grew even wider when she saw the knife. Annie pulled out the gag.

"Are you out of your minds?"

"We're leaving now. I'm cutting your zip ties, and then we run." Of course, the dull bread knife wasn't effective. But after intense sawing, she finally freed Katerina's feet. The girl rolled off the bed and presented her bound hands to Annie, who started the same process there. The whole time, Annie heard Katerina muttering all the things she would do to them.

Just as Annie had almost cut through the tie, she heard Gabi yell from the other room, "I'm engaging the smoke detector. As soon as it goes off, we run and yell fire."

The smoke drifted into the bedroom from across the hall. She could hear Gabi coughing. Annie kept sawing and finally the plastic gave way. But, instead of running, Katerina turned and grabbed the knife from Annie, twisted her around, and put the knife to her throat.

"You little bitch. You and your friend have ruined everything."

The alarm went off. A sprinkler went off, crazily, because of the scarf wrapped around it. Gabi ran into the hall and opened the bathroom door.

"Run! Ayiesha. Misty, run out the apartment door. It's a fire. Call it what it is. It's a fire. Do not get on the bus, I promise you. Run away. Anywhere. We'll find you later." The girls did as they were told, pressing Gabi up against the wall, but then they got stuck at the locked front door. Gabi glanced in the bedroom and saw Katerina ready to slice Annie's throat. She stepped in quickly and kicked her hard in the side and pulled Annie out of harm's way. Annie and Gabi ran to the door and Gabi unlocked it. As the air hit the room, the flames mushroomed. The two girls went out first. Annie stooped to grab their bags when she heard Katerina.

"Stop now. Slowly step onto the balcony backwards. I swear I'll shoot."

As they backed up, Gabi said, "I told you those are blanks."

"And I say you are a liar, or you wouldn't obey me now."

When they were out of the inferno, Katerina gestured for them to turn right, not left, toward the stairs. Mayhem had erupted on the balcony as the girls in the other apartments ran out. The men down below had evacuated as well, but they were directing everyone to the bus.

"Don't get on the bus. It's a death trap," Gabi yelled. The girls slowed their pace, confused. Then Gabi heard a buzzing underneath the clamor. She looked up and smiled. A blessed drone. Katerina saw it too and shot at it. Gabi used that moment to throw Annie to the ground. Katerina turned back and fired and hit Gabi in the chest. Annie screamed, but the sirens, both fire trucks and police cars drowned out her scream. The vehicles pulled up along the street, blocking the exit.

Katerina looked over the balcony and saw Nick sprint for the bus. "Nick, wait for me." He didn't even turn. The mayhem exploded as Lincoln came out of his room carrying an automatic weapon and started shooting at the police cars. Everyone took cover, but the police returned fire.

Katerina screamed and waved her hand, holding the gun. "Nick, help!"

A cop heard her, saw the gun, and shot her immediately. She collapsed. As Nick turned to look, the same cop shot him as well.

No one noticed Annie sitting on the cement up against the hot wall, holding her friend in a yellow dress that sported a bright red splotch oozing from her chest wound.

Lincoln's carnage lasted less than a minute before they shot him and silenced his weapon. Annie thought she heard the bus start up and gun its engines. It sounded like they were going to ram their way out. She could see through the metal bars of the balcony railing as the bus jerked forward. When it rammed the first police car, shots blasted at the wheels and dozens of holes dotted the windshield when they fired at the driver. Unlike the windshield, several of the side windows shattered when bullets hit them. Silence lasted for a single breath and then voices broke the moment the police swarmed the bus, calling for everyone to file out.

When she scanned the parking lot, there were bodies everywhere, both girls and men. When the shouting started, those who could, rose slowly. But others, several of the guys, lay still. Everything in her wanted to shrink inside or, better still, vomit. Her body shook. She looked down at Gabi, her eyes still open, but they held no life. *That bullet was meant for*

194

me. Only then did she look down along the balcony and saw Katerina slumped against the railing. Her legs folded oddly underneath her. She held the gun limply in her hand; her face crushed against the metal bars. Annie had never seen death up close. She never wanted to see it again. Her body froze in place. Firefighters raced up the stairs of the balcony, aware, as only they could be, that the fire was dangerously spreading. One called for an EMT through his radio on his shoulder before entering the apartment. Another one followed.

"Are you ok?" he asked before entering the apartment.

"I'm alive. That's all. But she's not."

"Someone's coming to help you. Can you move?"

"I don't know." The tears came unbidden.

"What's your name?"

"Annie. Anya. No. Irina. My name is Irina Vladimirovna Lebedev. My brother's name is Fedya and my sister's name is Elena. Born in St. Petersburg, Russia, I am fourteen. Susan Spencer adopted me at four years old."

The firefighter looked into the swarm of bodies in the parking lot. One man called a girl's name.

"There's a girl up here, alive," he said. "She's in shock." A man raced up the stairs. The firefighter went into the apartment.

When Luke got there, he found Annie repeating her details, her identity, as though she were a prisoner of war. He listened to her litany for a moment and then ran his hand over her hair and face, arms and back. She seemed whole. He looked down and saw Gabi Gattini dead in Annie's arms. He crossed himself three times in the way of the Russian Orthodox, then pulled Annie away from the dead girl's body. The EMTs arrived. One took Annie from his arms and laid her on a stretcher to carry her down to an ambulance. The second one checked the other girls for vital signs. Finding none, he shook his head at Luke, who nodded and followed the stretcher.

The first EMT informed Luke that Annie would need to go to the emergency room to treat her shock and to stabilize her. He nodded. "I'll be there later."

Rodriguez walked up to let him know they had snagged at least two lieutenants in the trafficking ring, as Luke had hoped, but they lost the yacht. "One of those guys must have called them as soon as we arrived. The Coast Guard Auxiliary was on the way when they saw the yacht blow out of the marina and into open water. They didn't bother to give chase."

Luke looked around and sighed. "I didn't expect firepower," Luke said. "How many?"

"Not sure of the last count," Rodriguez said. "Stray bullets wounded most of them or they injured themselves from running and falling. A couple got hit inside the bus. The guy with the automatic rifle is dead, along with another guy in the middle of the parking lot. We're bringing in more transport vehicles."

"There are two more on the balcony. Gattini got it," Luke said.

"Yeah, I heard. Sorry, man. I saw the feds, Matthews and Timon. They headed back to their offices and said they'll add to your report when you were ready. Diggs and Sumner are still checking out the bus and the apartments. They're securing the area. They called in the evidence techs. You want to look around?"

"Yeah, I'll walk it so I can get everything into my head. Pretty good fire that Gattini started."

"She got what she wanted, to go out in a blaze of glory," Rodriguez said.

Luke looked at his partner and wanted to reprimand him, but then thought better of it. Everyone had their way of dealing with tragedy. "All right, clown, let's walk the scene and then head back to the Banyan Street station to do a brief report. Then I'm going to the hospital to check on Annie and call her mom. I'll have to find out how long they want to keep Annie down here for questioning."

"We can always come back," Rodriguez said.

"Yeah, that's my strategy."

CHAPTER 31
TOWSON, MARYLAND
Friday, Late Morning

S usan stood by the front window, waiting anxiously for Luke and Annie to arrive. Zelenka, still watchful since the night Maksim broke in, lay at her feet. Luke had called Susan from the airport and said to expect them around noon, and they would be hungry. No problem there. Her church friends and neighbors had generously supplied a refrigerator full of casseroles, lunch meat for sandwiches, and a variety of desserts and drinks. Her Bible study group made a sign for the front door that said, "Welcome Home, Annie," and the children's church kids decorated the front porch with colorful balloons.

From the outside, Annie might have been gone for months, when it was only a week. But this would be a week of sorrow Susan would never forget. She had always cherished Annie and the wonder of having her in her life. But this week had shown her how she had also tried to mold Annie into the daughter she thought Annie should be. It was time to allow Annie to blossom. Susan knew, despite how difficult it would be, but important to Annie, that Susan call her daughter Irina.

Irina's troubles were not over. Her PTSD would still play a major part in her daily life, along with her erratic behaviors and idiosyncrasies would not disappear overnight. But under all that, Susan believed in her daughter's fortitude because Irina was a survivor. Luke told her about the shoot-out and how close her daughter had been to a life of slavery by evil men, or worse, death.

Kate interrupted Susan's thoughts and offered her a cup of tea.

"It's going to be all right, Susan. There are many people who are here and will be here, to support you both, to help in the transitions to come."

"Did I do the right thing to send everyone else home? I thought it might be overwhelming."

"Not everyone would go. Sam is here. He told me he had let you down the last few years and wants to make it up."

"That's silly. Your ex is a busy man."

"Yeah, well, I wouldn't say no to an on-call handyman because I have news for you. Luke is all thumbs when it comes to fixing things around the house," Kate said. "And Amanda is keeping your new step kids occupied, particularly the male one."

Susan swiveled to watch Elena, Fedya, and Amanda sitting on the couch, hunched over one of many photo albums of their sister's growing-up years in Maryland. They laughed. Little did they know how so many of those pictures came with a battle which accounted for all the grumpy poses.

Through the sunroom doors, Susan saw Sam chatting with Fillip, who had been the wonderful go-between for her and his detective cousin in St. Petersburg. Without them, the miracle of discovery would have been impossible. Over breakfast, although both young people had excellent English, Fillip helped them tell the story of their losses, the deaths of their parents, and the cruelty of the system that had separated them. They had had their own miracles over there and ended up with an uncle who loved them deeply.

The next few days would be a wonder. There would be so many plans to make. How would Irina, her brother, and sister rebuild their lives? Susan didn't know what her place would be. And what of their uncle and his partner—whose name she could not remember now, what would their expectations be?

A honk outside stopped everyone. Susan handed her teacup to Kate and went to open the front door and run out, but then changed her mind and simply stood in the foyer, unconsciously wiping her hands on her gray trousers. She commanded Zelenka to sit and stay. She didn't know who would walk through that door, this teenager who had been through so much. Finally, the door opened and Annie/Irina burst into the space and froze. They both stood, fixed on one another, unsure what to do next. Susan slowly opened her arms, and it was a young Annie who rushed into them.

Words tripped out from Annie as she held her mother closely. "I'm so sorry, Mama, I'm so sorry. How can you ever forgive me? It was terrible. Everything was terrible. I made so many mistakes. And people died. I was so scared."

Susan took it all in and murmured back to her as quickly as she could, "I did too. I wasn't paying attention. We'll do better. I'll do better. There is nothing to forgive."

Finally, they pulled apart and looked at each other.

"You look beautiful to me, Irina. Would you like that? Would you like me to call you Irina?"

"I would," Annie/Irina said. "And you, would you like to be Mama again?"

And then they hugged and cried joyful tears. Amanda went to her own mother at the window and wrapped an arm around her waist. Luke closed the front door and stepped into the living room. Kate met him with a hug and the two young people stood up. Without speaking, Luke shook their hands and then met Fillip and Sam with man hugs as they came into the room.

"Too early for a beer?" Sam asked.

"Never," Luke said. He walked over to the couch and spoke to Fedya and Elena. "Your turn comes soon. I told her nothing on the way here. She has no clue."

They smiled and held hands as they stood to the side of the couch, facing the open French doors as they watched the reunion between mother and daughter. Irina kneeled then to greet the dog, who relished the attention. Susan also kneeled.

"Honey, we have more big news, unexpected in some ways, but miraculous." Irina looked up into her mother's face as Susan merely pointed toward the living room.

Irina stood transfixed and confused. She looked again at Susan, her eyebrows scrunching as they often did when she didn't understand something.

Fedya said, "*Privet sestra*, hi sister."

Elena simply waved slowly, tears flowing down her face.

And then Irina gasped. "Omigod, Omigod, you're here. You're real." She ran to them and as three in one, they hugged and swayed and eventually collapsed onto the couch in a tangle of arms and legs. The mix of languages and laughter filled the room. They didn't know whether to speak English or Russian, and it all came out in a jumble. Fillip came up behind the couch in case they needed translation, but in the end, they sorted it out and slowed down.

"How did you get here?" Irina said in Russian.

Fedya said, "My God, listen, Elena, she speaks Russian like an American."

Elena laughed and poked him, "And you speak English like a Russian."

Fillip interrupted. "We will tell you everything over lunch. Is that correct, Susan?"

"What? Yes, yes." She beckoned to Kate and Amanda. "Let's go, ladies. It's so beautiful outside. Let's sit on the patio."

"Everything's ready. We have to carry the stuff out," Kate said.

Happy to have something to do, they left quickly. The guys followed, leaving the three siblings alone. For a long moment, the three looked at each other, taking in the differences, trying to find something they could remember.

"Your hair is still very blonde," Elena said as she put her hands through the spikey tresses. "You like it so short?"

"Yeah, well," she said in English, "I thought I was being cool that way. And look at you, your hair is the opposite, so long. I don't remember it having red in it."

"We have hairdressers in Rīga. It's cosmopolitan. So, I too, am trying to be stylish," Elena said in Russian and smiled.

They were quiet for a moment.

"How did you find me?" Irina asked.

"We didn't. Your mother hired a detective in St. Petersburg. He found my friend, Valya, a social worker, who helped me in the orphanage. She and I have kept in touch by email. The detective came to Rīga where we live now and told us everything. You can visit us there. No fear of broken laws."

"Not in Russia. You don't live in Russia?"

Fedya answered this time, "No, not for many years. We are international now."

Irina shook her head and thought of the fool's errand she had intended to make to St. Petersburg, a city where no one lived who knew her.

"These terrible things happened to me because I wanted to find you. When I left the orphanage, which I don't remember very well, someone put two dolls in my pink backpack. My friend, Lezunchik, said their names were Elena and Fedya Lebedev, and I must say those names every night: to say good night to you."

Elena put her hand to her mouth, holding back tears. "My God," she said, "a miracle. And I have something for you. I wrote many letters to you and kept them in a journal. They tell our story. They are yours to keep and read."

"Funny," Irina said. "My mother, my adopted mother, she kept a journal too. She wrote every day while she was in Russia for my adoption. I found it accidentally and learned about the funny business that led me here. That's how I got the idea to look for you."

"Elena never gave up," Fedya said.

"And you?" Irina asked.

"I thought I was the realist. But it may be time to try faith in something besides myself."

"How long will you stay?" Irina asked.

Fedya and Elena looked at each other and both laughed. "We didn't know what to expect. Before we left, we heard of your kidnapping. Funny, an evil man kidnapped both Elena and I before we found each other again. I hope we are done with that tradition."

"I will talk with Fillip Popov. He'll know what we should do with our tickets. Maybe we can change the date for going back later," Elena said.

"That would be wonderful. Where are you staying?"

"Here, here, of course. Your mother has been very kind," Elena said.

Irina cried again. Elena reached out to hold her.

"Who am I? Am I Irina or am I Anya? And is it wrong to call Susan my mother? She can't be your mother, you and Fedya."

Elena stroked Irina's head as she did when they were little. "You are all and both, a Russian born, but an American too. You are special. And we will embrace your mother like an aunt, and when you come to visit us, you will embrace Uncle Uldis and Ausma with joy. We have proven that family is a rock upon which we can build a life."

"Children," Susan called. "We're ready to eat."

"Children?" Fedya said.

"Why not?" Elena answered. "For today, let them spoil us. We deserve it."

The End

www.ingramcontent.com/pod-product-compliance
Lightning Source LLC
Chambersburg PA
CBHW030521020726
47494CB00004B/1181